Seco

Second Chances
© 2019 Mark A. Roeder

Cover Photo Credit: Simone Van Den Berg on Dreamstime.com.

Cover Design: Ken Clark

ISBN: 9781083033802

Acknowledgments

No book is without error, but there are a number of individuals who help me remove as many as possible before publication. Ken Clark, David Tedesco, Jim Perez-Hertwig and Jim Adkinson have all put a lot of time and effort into proofreading this novel. Ken is also responsible for the great cover, in fact nearly all the covers of my books and audio books.

A Special Thanks to My Patrons

Books do not make authors rich. Often, they don't even pay the bills. This book was made possible in part by my patrons on Patreon.com: Russell Harkins, Albert McCann, Robert Beemer, Victor Freeman, Mark Andrews, Robert Powell, Jaime Vidal, John F Callow, John McGrath, John Smeallie, Paul Covert, John McGrath, Ken Clark, Jon Lukas, Martin Jaragosky, John Gagliardi, Jeff Hall, John Webb, and Ken Chambliss.

Patrons get the inside track on my novels, sneak peaks, serial novels and other perks. They even get to read my novels before they are purchased. Even if you can't become a patron, check out my page because some posts are public.

Check it out:
https://www.patreon.com/user/posts?u=8324548 or go to patreon.com and search for "gay youth novelist".

Other Novels by Mark A. Roeder

Also look for audiobook versions on Amazon.com and Audible.com

Blackford Gay Youth Chronicles:

Outfield Menace

Snow Angel

The Nudo Twins

Phantom World

Second Star to the Right

The Perfect Boy

Verona Gay Youth Chronicles:

Ugly

Beautiful

The Soccer Field Is Empty

Someone Is Watching

A Better Place

The Summer of My Discontent

Disastrous Dates & Dream Boys

Just Making Out

*Temptation University**

Marshall Mulgrew's Supernatural Mysteries

Christmas in Graymoor Mansion

The Fat Kid

Brendan & Casper: Older & Better

Light in the Darkness

Transitions

Second Chances*

Bloomington Gay Youth Chronicles

A Triumph of Will

Temptation University*

The Picture of Dorian Gray

Yesterday's Tomorrow

Boy Trouble

The New Bad Ass in Town

Bloomington Boys—Brandon & Dorian*

Bloomington Boys—Nathan & Devon*

Bloomington Boys—Scotty & Casper*

Bloomington Boys—Tim & Marc*

Bloomington Boys—Elijah & Haakon*

Phantom Begins

Peralta's Bike Shop

Hate at First Sight

Colin University

A Boy Toy for Christmas

Hoosier Boys

*Second Chances**

*Crossover novels that fit into two series

Other Novels:

Benji & Clyde

Cadets of Culver

Fierce Competition

The Vampire's Heart

Homo for the Holidays

For more information on current and upcoming novels go to markroeder.com.

Chapter One
Casper
Verona, Indiana
June 2026

The red checked tablecloths fluttered in the breeze and the scent of steak wafted from the grills. Clint and his wife sat at one of the tables, while their twins, Dax and Drew, played volleyball with Ethan and Nathan. I couldn't believe the twins were fifteen. They should be in grade school, not high school.

"Need help carrying anything else out, Dad?" Cameron asked.

"No, I think we're set. As soon as Brendan finishes the steaks we can eat."

Leaving Verona was going to be difficult. My family was here and Brendan and I had lived on our farm for years. We wouldn't have even considered the notion, but when Brendan was offered the position of head football coach at Indiana University, we couldn't pass it up. Brendan lived for football. He has as long as I've known him and *that* is a long time.

Brendan would have passed up the position if I'd asked. We discussed it when he received the offer. He asked me what I thought and if I had told him I didn't want to leave Verona he would have turned down the offer and never looked back. I know that's what he would have done because I know Brendan. We have been together since we were teens and he loves me that much.

Truthfully, I didn't want to leave, neither of us did, but we were ready to start a new chapter in our lives. At the time when most were considering retirement, we were starting out on a new adventure. Besides, Cameron and Spencer needed to get on with their lives. I don't think they minded living in the farmhouse with Brendan and me, but I think they would come to appreciate having it to themselves, just as Brendan and I did in the beginning. It was time to let the next generation take over.

The entire family was here: my brother Jason, his sons Clint, Cameron, and Conner (whom Brendan and I thought of as our own), Spencer (Cameron's boyfriend), Brendan's mom, Ethan and Nathan, and Shawn and Tristan. Some of our friends, such as Brandon, Jon, and Marc lived in Bloomington so we'd see them soon. Others were spread out here and there. Jack and Ardelene were the only family who should have been here but

11

weren't. Jack died three years ago, only two days after his 100th birthday. Ardelene died less than a year ago, shortly after her own 100th birthday. We all missed them and yet a century was a good long time to live. Jack had threatened us to shed no tears for him when he died or he'd come back and give us what for. Thinking of that always made me smile and knowing Jack, he would have found a way to do it. We did shed tears for both Jack and Ardelene and yet we were relieved that they died before they experienced any serious health problems. I hoped Brendan and I would be as lucky.

"The steaks are ready!" Brendan called out.

The twins immediately abandoned their game and were the first in line. Everyone else followed at a more leisurely pace. I smiled at Cameron and Spencer, his significant other. It had taken Cameron a long time to find someone, but I was convinced he had found someone special.

In addition to the ribeye steaks there were baked beans, potato salad, baked sweet potatoes, and slaw. There were galvanized tubs of soft drinks and pitchers of iced tea, both sweetened and unsweetened. For dessert there were brownies, chocolate chip cookies, and also a large sheet cake that Brendan and I had not been allowed to see.

We talked and laughed while we ate. Get-togethers like this were not unusual and I had no doubt Brendan and I would travel north from time to time to attend some of them.

Brendan and I had lived on the farm for years, ever since we bought it at auction back in 1987. It was hard to believe nearly forty years had passed. During that time, Brendan had coached football at Verona High School and had become Verona's winningest high school football coach ever. Together, we had created Brewer-Westwood Farm. We grew and sold Christmas Trees and had become a destination for farm tours and our special autumn and Christmas events. Cameron had a big hand in everything concerning the farm. He and Spencer had been effectively running the farm for a few years now. It was hard to believe Cameron was the same troubled kid who had been dropped in our laps along with his brothers all those years ago.

I looked across the table at Brendan. He was sixty-three now and it was exceedingly hard to believe. He was still extremely fit after all these years and if he got around a little more slowly than he did when we were young, it was only because he did so very much.

I completely enjoyed myself at our farewell cookout. I absolutely loved our cake when Cameron brought it out. On one side were the barn and Christmas trees and on the other was the IU Football stadium. Icing spelled out, "Good Luck on the Second Half of Your Life."

"I think we already started the second half some time ago," I said.

"You're just getting started," Conner said.

It was a shame to cut the cake, but we did and it was delicious with homemade vanilla ice cream.

I wondered how many get-togethers had taken place on the farm—birthdays, graduations, Thanksgivings, and Christmases. Brendan and I had spent a big chunk of our lives here, but we had lived in other places; hundreds of miles away in Kentucky where we had grown up, the Selby Farm less than a mile away, and Bloomington where we had lived during our college years. All of these places would always be home, so moving to Bloomington didn't feel like leaving. Instead, it felt like returning home. I would miss this old farm and the life we'd built here, but it was time for a change. I was far more excited than sad.

Everyone lingered after we more or less all finished eating. Later, we built a bonfire and roasted marshmallows. We sat around the fire talking, laughing, and reminiscing until late. When the party broke up, everyone helped carry everything inside and then all those who wouldn't see us in the morning before we departed hugged us and wished us good luck.

Brendan and I offered to help put everything away, but Cameron and Spencer insisted they would take care of it. We bid them goodnight and then headed upstairs to our bedroom.

I gazed at Brendan's muscled torso as he undressed for bed. He was still hot after all these years and put much younger guys to shame. I loved Brendan for reasons other than his body, but it was a nice bonus.

"There's still time to back out," Brendan said as he slipped under the sheet beside me.

"I have no intention of backing out and I think it's far too late. We've already bought a house."

"I can't wait to get into the house, but I'm going to miss my tractor."

"That's it? Only the tractor?"

"I might miss a few other things, but mostly I'll miss the tractor."

"I'm sure Cameron will let you come and visit it anytime you want."

"He will probably even let me do some work with it. He's selfless like that. I bet Cameron and Spencer are excited. Tomorrow, they truly take over the business and the house becomes their home."

"This has been their home for a long time, Brendan."

"Yes, but now they own it. With us gone, it will truly feel like their home. I'm excited for them."

"Maybe they'll adopt. This is a great place to raise kids."

"Don't pressure them."

"Me?"

"Yes, you."

We snuggled together and soon fell asleep.

***

Brendan and I caught the scent of bacon frying as we walked downstairs the next morning.

"I was going to cook breakfast," Brendan said.

"That's very thoughtful, but we want your last breakfast here before you move to be a pleasant memory," Spencer said as he worked at the stove. Brendan's lack of cooking ability had been a running joke for decades. He was a master on the grill, but his talents in the kitchen were less than stellar.

"Am I allowed to pour tea?" Brendan asked.

"Well... I suppose we can risk it," Cameron said.

"When do the movers get here?" Spencer asked.

"They should arrive at 9:30."

"We could have moved everything for you," Cameron said.

"You have more than enough to do running the tree farm," I said.

"True and now we're losing our free help."

We soon sat down to a breakfast of French toast covered with blueberries, walnuts, butter, and syrup, with bacon. Spencer was an excellent cook and Cameron was rather good too.

The farm already officially belonged to Cameron and Spencer. Brendan and I had given it jointly to Clint, Cameron, and Conner. Clint and Conner had sold their shares to Cameron. We were only taking Brendan's Corvette, my Prius, and what furniture and other items would fit into the three-bedroom ranch we had purchased in Bloomington.

"I am going to miss this place, but I won't miss all the work it takes to keep it up," Brendan said.

"I'm going to miss you doing all that work," Cameron said.

"Yeah, good free help is hard to find."

"Well, I do have Spencer."

"I think that's what he likes best about me," Spencer said.

"Hardly." Cameron and Spencer smiled at each other.

Just as we were finishing breakfast, a truck with "College Moving & Junk Hauling" painted on the side arrived.

"It looks like they're here for our junk," Brendan said.

"Right on time. Brendan, let the movers load the furniture. They are young college guys and they can handle it. You leave it alone," I said.

"He's so bossy," Brendan said. "Spencer, do not let Cameron boss you around the way Casper does me. He's been doing it nearly fifty years!" Cameron and Spencer laughed.

"I meant what I said, Brendan," I warned. Brendan was quite strong and accustomed to farm work, but he wasn't used to lifting heavy furniture and I didn't want to take any chances.

"See what I mean? Okay, Casper, I will let the young guys do the work."

The movers came in and I pointed out what needed to be loaded. I had everything very organized, but it still took over two hours to load the truck. As soon as it was loaded, the college boys departed.

"We need to head out since we have to beat them to Bloomington," I said.

"We'll miss you guys, but we'll see you before too long," Brendan said, hugging and kissing both Cameron and Spencer.

15

"Call when you get there, Dad," Cameron said.

"We will," I said, then hugged and kissed them too. Spencer had become like another son to us. He was very good for Cameron.

Brendan and I stepped outside and took a last look at the farm and farmhouse before departing. We would miss this place, but we were both eager to begin the next phase of our lives.

"We'll be back to visit," Brendan said, gazing at me. He knew I was very attached to the farm.

I nodded. "We had better head out. Don't speed too much. Your Corvette is a speeding ticket magnet."

"I never drive faster than the car can go."

I fixed Brendan with a stare and he grinned. I could still see the high school boy I fell in love with when I gazed at him.

Brendan climbed in his Corvette and departed. I waved to Cameron and Spencer, climbed into my Prius, and followed him.

Sadness overwhelmed me as we pulled away from Verona, but I reminded myself that there was a time I had called Bloomington home. Since those days, Brendan and I often made trips to Bloomington to visit Brandon, Jon, and Marc and to eat in the Tudor Room. Now, we would live in Bloomington as we did during our college years, and drive to Verona to visit everyone and eat in Café Moffatt.

The sadness passed along with the miles. Brendan and I needed a change. Our life in Verona was pleasant, but had developed a predictable sameness. We were, perhaps, beginning to stagnate, and that wasn't wise for guys our age. I knew Brendan was absolutely thrilled to take over the IU football program. I would enjoy being back in Bloomington and having a much smaller home and yard. Without Cameron, Brendan and I would have had to move out of the huge farmhouse years ago. Our new home in Bloomington was quite large, but manageable.

Brendan and I loved the Bloomington house the first time we viewed it so much that we immediately made an offer above the asking price. Later that day, our offer was accepted. We were delighted.

Finding a home in Bloomington had been difficult. We had looked at seven different houses before purchasing ours. We wanted something very close to campus, but every available home was not only extremely expensive, but needed extensive renovations. The rental market around campus is so fierce that homes can be rented out for unbelievable amounts. Money was not a problem, especially with Brendan's new job, but we did not want to bother with more renovations than absolutely necessary. Even so, we made an offer on a Craftsman style home not far from the stadium that needed a fair amount of work and despite offering more than the asking price, we were outbid. It was a disappointment, but I told myself we were not meant to have that house. Less than two weeks later we found a home.

The home we purchased was near North High School and directly across from the Cascades Golf Course. Brendan had timed the trip to campus and it was only seven minutes from the house. He could make it to the stadium in less than five. We could drive to everything on the east side in ten minutes or less and to everything on the west side in even less time. It wasn't as convenient as our old east side apartment in The Crossing, but the location was great. It almost felt as if it was in the country and yet if it wasn't for the trees, we could have seen the stadium from our front yard. The home was built in 1960, but needed no renovations. It was completely updated and move-in ready, which was a huge plus. I had plans for the back yard, but those could wait.

We beat the movers to the house, but just barely. Brendan arrived before me and pulled his Corvette into the yard. I pulled in behind him. The easiest way to move furniture into the house was through the garage so we needed our cars out of the way for the truck.

Brendan and I went inside to hit the restroom and have a quick look around. The home looked empty. It was empty, of course, but the previous owner, Tina, was still living in it on the day we viewed it so this was the first time we'd seen the house without her furniture. Tina was eighty and taking care of it had become too much for her, but she was the one who had seen to the renovations during her years here. I have to say she had great taste.

The movers arrived and I began directing the placement of furniture. All the boxes were stacked in the smallest bedroom to keep them out of the way and everything I wasn't sure where to put was placed in the large living room.

I had looked at the listing photos several times since we'd purchased the house, but they didn't do it justice. I liked the home even more than I remembered. The style was modern, but our antiques fit in well. The kitchen was plenty big without being too large. I loved the French doors that led from the kitchen directly to the brick patio and back yard.

The college boys unloaded the truck, placed the furniture and set up the beds in about two hours. Brendan paid them, gave them each a tip, and then, for the first time, we were alone in our "new" home.

"How do you like it now?" Brendan asked.

"I love it, but even if I didn't, I am not going through the house buying or moving process again. I have days of unpacking ahead of me yet."

Brendan smiled. "I think this will be perfect for us. We have all the room we need and it will be much easier to keep up the house and yard. I bet I can mow the yard with a push mower in forty minutes."

"It doesn't need it now, so you get to help me unpack. Only unpack the boxes marked Brendan."

"You don't trust me with the other boxes?" Brendan asked with a grin.

"I trust you, but I intend to organize as I go along. The boxes filled with things in your domain are marked Brendan. The rest are things in mine."

We set to work. I had put a red sticker on all the boxes that contained items we would need the most quickly, like dishes, towels, washcloths, shampoo, and similar items.

I started in the kitchen first. I set up the microwave and then unpacked the boxes that contained glasses, dishes, silverware, pots, pans, and miscellaneous kitchen items. There was much more to unpack in the kitchen, but after I unpacked the boxes with red stickers, I moved onto the bathroom where I put up the shower curtain and liner and unpacked all our shower items. Unpacking and organizing everything would take days, but once I had unpacked all the boxes tagged with a red sticker we would have all the basics, except for groceries.

"I'm starving," Brendan announced some two hours later as he walked into the kitchen.

"Now that you mention it, I am too. We have nothing other than Pop-Tarts and tea so let's go out. Where would you like to go?"

"I'd love to go to the China Buffet."

"That closed in 2017 if I remember correctly."

"You asked where I wanted to eat, not where we could eat. How can you remember such things?"

"I remember because of how disappointed you were when we drove down to eat there and it was gone."

"That was depressing. I loved that place. Both locations of the Scholar's Inn Bakehouse are gone too. So is Casa Brava."

"Yeah, Casa Brava closed at the end of 2018," I said. "Things change and it's been a long time since we lived here. There are other restaurants. Pick one."

"The Tudor Room is already closed for the day so how about Fazoli's? It will be great to live close to it again."

"That works for me, but let's not walk there like we did when we lived at The Crossing."

"Yeah, it would be quite a hike from here.

We locked up and headed to the east side in my Prius. From our new home it took under ten minutes to arrive by car, which was much better than the hour drive from Verona to the Fazoli's in South Bend.

"One thing I love about being back is that everything is so close," Brendan said.

"I was just thinking about that."

"Yeah, I love Verona, but other than Ofarim's and Café Moffatt, there isn't much there."

"When we get too old to drive, we can give up our cars and use buses and taxis."

"Give up my Corvette? Are you mad? I want to be buried in it, sitting behind the wheel."

I laughed. Brendan loved his vintage Corvette. He had owned it most of his life.

When we arrived at Fazoli's, Brendan ordered ultimate spaghetti, which came with lots of mushrooms and meatballs. I ordered three-cheese tortellini Alfredo.

"Is it just me, or is this Fazoli's better than the one in South Bend?" Brendan asked as he bit into a bread stick.

"I think it's better, but I think it's more the memories associated with this location than the food."

"I am going to enjoy eating out more often."

"Me too, although I'll be too busy to do it much for a while. It takes a while to set up a house. I'm sure I'll need to make multiple trips to Kroger and Target until I get us properly stocked up."

"We can stop by both after we're finished here," Brendan said.

"No. I'll do that tomorrow while you're at practice. There is a lot I want to get done at the house before bedtime."

Our food arrived. That's something I love about Fazoli's. The service was fast.

"I love being back in Bloomington. I could have happily remained here after college," Brendan said.

"Now you tell me! We could have saved all the packing!"

"I think we would have missed out on a few things."

"It's too bad we can't be in both places at once. We will miss out on things in Verona now."

"True, but we'll have experiences here we would not have had if IU hadn't offered me a position."

"I'm glad they did. You came so close to playing pro football. If it weren't for that injury your senior year in college, I have no doubt you would have. Personally, I think coaching at IU is better, but then what do I know about football?"

"Plenty, from being around me all these years. I agree with you. Coaching at IU is better. I would have loved to play pro ball, but I also loved coaching at Verona High School. No one can do everything."

"Personally, I am looking forward to slowing down. We had the boys to help us with the farmhouse, but it was still a lot of work. I swear that by the time I finished vacuuming and dusting it was time to start again."

"Yeah, and I wasn't around to help much."

"Well, you did have that teaching and coaching thing going on and you helped me in the summers."

Brendan and I kept talking while we ate in the easy way we had developed over the years. We knew each other so well there was little need to ask the other's opinion on any topic, but we did anyway.

Neither of us ate all of our food, likely because we ate so many breadsticks, so we asked for to-go boxes. The girl at the counter gave us more breadsticks too. Now, we would have some food at the house, at least temporarily.

We returned home and unpacked and organized until we grew tired, then pulled out two lawn chairs and sat on the patio behind the house with glasses of iced tea. We didn't have the expansive view we enjoyed back at the farmhouse, but we had a nice fenced in yard, not too small and not too big. I was already planning to plant a snowball bush and a lilac bush like Ardelene had planted years ago on the Selby Farm, as well as other flowering trees and shrubs.

"You're landscaping, aren't you?" Brendan said, grinning at me.

"Yes."

"I knew it. We haven't even finished moving in and you're already thinking about making changes. I think we need something to block the view of the neighbor's house directly behind ours."

"Ha! You're landscaping too."

"A little. I think it would be nice to sit out here without being on view."

"We can put that on our list of things to do. I think it will number 114."

Brendan laughed. "We don't need to do it all at once."

"Thank goodness."

***

"This reminds me of my college days," Brendan said as he bit into his raspberry Pop-Tart the next morning at breakfast.

"Yes, but not your freshman year. These aren't burned."

"Hey, toasters are complicated."

"Of course they are."

"If I didn't have you to cook for me I would have starved long ago."

"You would have survived on steaks, hamburgers, hot dogs and anything else you could grill."

"True, but I think I would have gotten tired of all that. I better get going. I don't know when I'll be back, but I do know I won't be here for lunch." Brendan kissed me.

"Now that reminds me of our college days," I said.

Brendan departed. I set up our Amazon Echo in the opening between the kitchen and living room so I could create my shopping list while I was working. I remembered when such things existed only on *Star Trek*. I had even set the wake word to "Computer" instead of "Alexa." There was no more creating a list with pen and paper for me.

The amount of unpacking I had to do was overwhelming, but I would do it over a period of days. I concentrated now on unpacking more kitchen items, all the while adding items to my shopping list.

I was nowhere near done in the kitchen at 11 a.m., but I stopped and headed for Kroger. I had an enormous list and knew I would probably be making a few trips to the grocery in the next few days.

There was actually a Kroger very near us, but it was much smaller than the Kroger on the east side. I would likely use the nearby Kroger for quick grocery runs, but planned to do my serious shopping at the east side location. That's where Brendan and I had shopped when we lived in Bloomington during our college years. I guess one could say I was being nostalgic.

The bypass gave me very quick access to the east side, but instead of heading straight to Kroger, I took a detour past our old apartment on Pete Ellis Drive. Memories came rushing back as I pulled into The Crossing. It didn't look the same and yet it didn't look all that different. I slowed as I passed our old apartment, 3136, remembering the days when we had cookouts out on the small patio. I could see red roses cascading over the fence in the corner and wondered if it was the bush I had planted long ago.

I continued on my way, reminding myself that we needed to have Brandon, Jon, and Marc over soon. I wanted to get the house in shape before we did and I'd have to find out when Brendan wasn't busy. I was almost certain he would be busier here than he was at VHS.

Kroger had changed, but I was not surprised. Brendan and I visited Bloomington now and then, but I hadn't been inside Kroger for some years.

Despite the changes, it seemed the same. I almost felt as if no time had passed and I would be returning with groceries to the apartment in The Crossing, instead of our home in Fritz Terrace across from the Cascades Golf Course.

My cart filled up quickly. Other than the Pop-Tarts and a few varieties of teas, Brendan and I had brought no grocery items from Verona. We had left everything for the boys. Our cabinets here were bare and the refrigerator contained only tea, water, and Fazoli's leftovers.

I picked up milk, bread, sugar, Parmesan cheese, cereal, bagels, cream cheese, and on and on. I was extremely thankful for my shopping app. The items I had added by talking to the Echo device in my kitchen were on my smart phone. Things had truly changed since I was a college boy. I could remember when no one had a computer and when phones were attached to the wall with a cord. Clint's twins thought that was funny. They were growing up in a technologically advanced world that was science fiction when I was their age.

I missed Dax and Drew. When my brother had asked Brendan and me to care for his boys after the death of his wife so many years ago, I didn't know if we could handle it, but we had turned out to be great dads. It was hard to believe that Clint, Cameron, and Conner were old enough to have their own kids now. The boys still called us "Dad." Thankfully, Dax and Drew usually called Brendan and me by our names instead of calling us "Granddad." I was sixty-one now, but I didn't feel old enough to be a grandfather. In any case, I missed taking care of kids, even though Dax and Drew hadn't been around all that often, especially in recent years. It was hard to believe they were teens. It seemed like no time at all since I was their age.

I stopped shopping when my cart was so full, top and bottom, that there was no room for more. There were still items on my list and I was sure I would add others, but what I had gathered was enough for now. I checked out, loaded the back of the Prius, and headed home.

I felt a very strange sense of déjà vu as I unpacked the groceries in the kitchen. It was so much like my first days in Bloomington my freshman year it was almost scary. Brendan was busy with football practice back then, so I took care of the apartment. Now, he was back out on that same football field and I was still taking care of everything at home.

I was excited about our new house and our new life, but I must admit I was a little lonely. That reminded me of my freshman year too. The situation had improved back then once classes started and I got involved with campus activities. I ceased being lonely when I met Aiden, and Brendan and I took him in. I smiled when I thought of Aiden. That homeless boy was now a professor at IU.

I liked my new kitchen and the modern cabinets with pullout shelves. The previous owner had completely renovated the entire house and paid special attention to the kitchen. The trash and recycling bins were hidden away in the cabinets and so were the washer and dryer.

Our antique step-back cupboard looked great in the kitchen. I had worried that it might clash with the modern interior, but it fit well. I planned to put stoneware jars and gray graniteware on the top of the cabinets, but it would be awhile before I unpacked items that were merely decorative.

There was so much to do! The backyard was nicely landscaped, but I wanted to bring some peonies and starts of black-eyed Susans from the farm. I had already told Cameron I planned on moving a few to Bloomington. Over time, I planned to make the entire backyard a garden of perennial flowers, using the flowering shrubs as accents. By the time Brendan and I were too old to mow, there wouldn't be any grass left.

I ate my Fazoli's leftovers for lunch and continued unpacking boxes and organizing. Even if Brendan hadn't been busy on campus, it's something I wanted to do. I was the one who needed to know where everything was located and I was far more organized than Brendan. His organization scheme was a pile for everything.

I listened to one of my Audible audio books as I put things away. The narrator kept me company. That's something else I didn't have back in my freshman year of college. There were audiobooks, but no technology like the Echo that started and stopped by voice command. I sometimes felt as if I was living on the Enterprise.

My day was not exciting, but it was productive. I kept working right up until Brendan got home just after 7 p.m. He greeted me with a kiss.

"What's that I smell?" Brendan asked.

"Lasagna."

"Great, I'm starving. Let me shower real quick. I was sweating like crazy on the field."

"Think of the poor players."

"I do, mainly that I'm glad I'm not one of them anymore."

"Come on, you know you'd love to play again."

"If I could have the body I did in college I'd be all for it, but not now."

"There is nothing wrong with your body."

"There's one thing wrong with it—it's sixty-three years old!"

"You're in great shape."

"Yes, I am—*for my age*. I'm smart enough to know I shouldn't play football anymore."

"I'm very happy about that. It was bad enough when you were in high school and college," I said and kissed him.

"Worry not. These days I stay on the sidelines."

While Brendan showered, I pulled the lasagna out of the oven and put in garlic bread to toast. I had picked up the lasagna and garlic toast during my morning trip to Kroger. The only part of our meal that required any real effort was the cooked apples and I had been more than glad to sit down and cut them up in the mid-afternoon. It was a great break from unpacking.

By the time Brendan returned, the garlic toast was done and I had the table set. Brendan poured us glasses of iced-tea and then we sat side-by-side on one of the benches so we could gaze out at the back yard as we ate

"It feels good to sit down," Brendan said.

"I bet."

"How was your day?"

"It was filled with excitement. I shopped for groceries, which is why we have something to eat, and I spent the rest of the day unpacking and organizing."

"Everything looks great so far. Do you think you'll ever get done?"

"Oh, we'll be unpacked by Christmas." I grinned. "Another few days will probably do it. I'm very glad we didn't bring more than we did."

"Yeah, we had too much stuff."

"Yes, like your clothes from high school."

"Hey, those are back in style. Drew and Dax were thrilled with them. What if I had thrown them out?"

"We would have had less boxes stored in the attic."

"Well, I turned loose of them, didn't I? The only thing I kept from high school was my letterman's jacket."

"You did very well—finally."

I wasn't lonely anymore. All I truly needed was Brendan.

Chapter Two
Scott

The door buzzed. The guard pushed it open and I passed through. I was free at last, but dreaded where I might be headed next. I wondered how long it would be before I was back in the Juvenile Correction Center, better known as Juvie.

My steps faltered as I spotted Nicole standing a few feet away, gazing at me with an expression that was a mixture of pity and disappointment.

"You came for me? I figured they'd send me somewhere else. I figured you were tired of me and glad to be rid of me."

"Tired of you? Never. I missed you, which isn't easy with a house full of kids. Disappointed. Yes. We had a deal."

"I'm sorry, I fucked up big this time."

"Scott."

"Sorry, I screwed up."

"Yes, you did and now you have a record. It will be expunged if you keep out of trouble during your probation. If not, I'm not sure how long will judge will put you in detention next time. You were very lucky to get off with six weeks." I nodded. "You and I are going to have a talk."

I swallowed hard. Nicole could be stern and frightening when she wanted. This was one of those times. She didn't so much as raise her voice, but I dreaded the talk as much as I'd dreaded anything.

Nicole hugged me and mussed my hair. I hugged her back tightly. I hadn't received many hugs in my life.

"Come on."

I followed Nicole out to the beat-up van she and Megan used to transport their foster kids. There were seven of us, including me, the extra. Today, the van seemed huge with only Nicole and me inside.

We rode in silence as Nicole drove to the house she shared with her wife. It didn't bother me that they were lesbians. I just didn't get what two women could do naked together. I guess it didn't matter. Nicole and Megan sure liked each other.

I followed Nicole inside when we arrived at the house. As always, it was crowded. My foster brothers and sisters barely noticed me as I passed through on the way to the kitchen. I was used to not being noticed, unless I did something royally stupid like I did in May.

"Sit," Nicole ordered.

I sat at the kitchen table. She sat across from me.

"We had a deal. You broke it. You do it again and you are out. Is that clear?"

"Yes."

"If you bring drugs into this house, I will drag you down to the police station myself."

"I never brought any..." Nicole's stern gaze silenced me.

"You need to stay away from those friends of yours and I do not want them here, especially that Blaze."

"Yes, ma'am."

"You so much as step out of line and you will be one very, very sorry boy."

"Yes, ma'am."

I could feel my face going pale. Nicole had never been quite this fierce before.

"I'm sorry that Megan and I can't spend as much time with you as you'd like or need, but we have jobs and seven kids to care for."

"I know."

"Do we understand each other?"

"Yes ma'am."

"Enough said then. Welcome back."

"Thanks." I smiled slightly.

"Now get out of here. I have to start supper."

I took my backpack and walked to the room I shared with my three foster brothers. Cliff's stuff was all over my bottom bunk. I scooped it up and moved it across the room to his bunk. Cliff was nine and the youngest of my foster brothers.

"Hey, dip shit," Nicolas said as he entered. "I heard you were getting out today. You're a real dumb fuck, you know that?"

Nicolas was sixteen and the oldest boy. He didn't like me much, but he wasn't all that bad. He didn't pick on any of us and even looked out for Bennie and Cliff.

"Yeah, I screwed up."

"You screwed up all the way to Juvie. Anyone give it to you up the butt in there?"

"Shut up."

"Are you sure you want to bother unpacking? I'm willing to bet you'll do something stupid and be sent right back."

"I'm not going to do anything stupid."

"I'll be surprised if you don't. Megan said you're on probation."

"Yeah, I am."

"So if you're caught tagging a building or doing any of the other delinquent stuff you do, you'll be right back in Juvie."

"I'm not going to do any of that."

"I hope not."

I looked at Nicholas. I could tell he meant it.

"Thanks."

"Why the hell were you messing with drugs? It was your boyfriend Blaze, wasn't it?

"He's not my boyfriend."

"You and him have something going, right? It's fine if you do, I don't care about that shit, but if you cause any more trouble for Nicole and Megan I will fuck you up."

I looked at Nicolas again, this time paling a little. He meant that too. He could be violent and he considered himself the man of the house.

"I won't cause them any more trouble and I'm done with drugs."

"You better be, dumb ass."

I sighed. Everyone was on my ass and had been since I landed in big trouble. I wished I could talk to Brad, my Big Brother, but he had graduated from IU. He was gone, but at least he had come to say 'goodbye' when I was in Juvie. I could tell he was disappointed in me. Everyone was, including me. That's what I was—a disappointment.

"Oh yeah, I forgot to tell you something," Nicolas said.

"What?"

"Welcome back."

"Thanks," I said, grinning for a moment. Yeah, Nicolas wasn't so bad, but he'd be watching me—everyone would.

Chapter Three
Casper

"If you are open to getting more involved, we have a boy who truly needs help. Have you ever considered taking care of a foster child?"

The question threw me. It was now July and Brendan and I had been in Bloomington a month. At first, I was busy setting up the house, but soon I had very little to do. I thought of a part-time job, but we didn't need money. I applied to become a big brother at Big Brothers & Big Sisters. I thought I could put my experiences to good use and help a boy who needed some direction, but I was not expecting the question just put to me.

"Brendan and I did something like that years ago. We raised my brother's three sons."

"I know that a foster child is probably not on your radar, but there is a boy in our program that is in serious need of help."

"Brendan and I are getting a little old to raise a kid, even on a temporary basis. My gut reaction is to flat out say, 'No.' I definitely can't promise anything and it's not my decision alone, but tell me about him."

"I understand completely. His name is Scott. He's fourteen. He was abandoned by his parents when he was eight." I winced. "He's been in and out of foster homes for the last few years. Some were not good environments. Others were, but none of the foster parents could or would take him on permanently. The only stable force in his life has been the Big Brothers & Big Sisters program. Unfortunately, his latest big brother graduated from IU in May and now lives in another state. Scott has been in trouble in the past for minor offenses, such as vandalism, but near the end of the last school year he got himself in some real trouble. He was busted for possession of drugs and placed in juvenile detention. He's out now on probation. He's truly not a bad kid, but his life has no stable influence. It's been one temporary home after another. The one he is in now is overcrowded. I very much fear that if Scott doesn't get some real stability in his life, he'll end up in prison. I know that's not a very rosy picture of him, but I have to be honest with you. If he can have a stabilizing influence in his life, someone he can count on, it will make all the difference."

"You're really putting me in a difficult spot," I said, chewing my lip.

"I'm sorry, that's not my intention, but when I see a kid who needs help, I try to do everything I can for him or her. We have very limited resources. Our main resource is people like you who come in and volunteer to give their time to children. That's a truly wonderful thing. I don't expect you to say "yes," but I wouldn't be doing my best for Scott if I didn't ask."

"Let me think about it. While I'm doing so, perhaps I could be Scott's big brother, although I'm sure he's expecting someone much younger."

"Most of our big brothers and sisters are younger, but not all. What all of these kids need is guidance, an example to follow, and simply someone in their life who will spend time with them and pay attention to them."

"That I can do. As I'm sure you've read in my application, I did a lot of volunteer work at the high school in Verona and I was involved with the gay youth center there. I also raised three kids with Brendan."

"Yes, you have extensive experience working with kids, far more than most of our big brothers. Let's pair you with Scott and see where things go."

"What's his family situation like now?"

"He's with a wonderful lesbian couple, but they took him on as a personal favor to me. They already have six foster kids so they truly don't have room for him. As you can imagine, he's quite a handful on top of the others. I've promised to place him elsewhere as soon as possible."

"Wow, that is a lot of kids."

"Yes, you can see the predicament."

"When can I meet him?"

"I'll see if I can set up something for tomorrow."

I nodded. We moved onto paperwork. As with everything, there were forms to sign and these were on top of all the information I had already provided when applying. I wasn't surprised. The safety of kids was involved.

Brendan arrived home at around 7:30 that evening. I could usually expect him about then and if he was going to be later, he called.

"You're grilling tonight. I have chicken breasts thawed in the refrigerator," I said after Brendan greeted me with a kiss.

"You wanted the evening off from cooking, huh?"

"You know how lazy I am."

"You are anything but lazy. Do I smell baked beans?"

"Yes, and I baked brownies, just the way you like them with cranberries and walnuts."

"Then you aren't very good at taking the evening off."

"I put them in the crockpot this morning. It wasn't too taxing."

"I didn't know you could make brownies in a crock pot!"

I cocked my head. "Even you know better than that," I said.

Brendan laughed. "Baked beans and brownies with cranberries and walnuts, what's the occasion?"

"I have been assigned a little brother." I grinned.

"Great. You can tell me about him while we eat. I'll plug in the grill."

I began working on a salad while Brendan heated up the grill and worked his magic on the chicken breasts. Brendan usually did all the grilling. He was a disaster in the kitchen, but he was the master of the grill. I don't know what he did, but everything he grilled tasted better.

I was content as I moved about the kitchen and Brendan stepped in and out to check on the chicken breasts. Brendan had been a part of my life for so long I couldn't imagine life without him. I hoped I never had to experience it.

We ate at the kitchen table and gazed at the backyard through the French doors. I had moved a few plants from the farm in Verona during the last month and purchased others at the Saturday farmer's market downtown. The black-eyed Susans and purple coneflowers were doing nicely. Both were already beginning to bloom.

"Are you looking forward to meeting your little brother?" Brendan asked as we ate.

"Yes. His name is Scott, he's fourteen, and I'm told quite a handful."

"He sounds like Cameron when he was young." Brendan laughed.

"Scott is even more of a handful. He was recently in juvenile detention for drugs."

"Oh. You couldn't pick an easier one?"

"He's the one who most needs a big brother. Trevor, who runs the Big Brother/Big Sisters program, even asked me to consider taking him in as a foster child."

I gazed at Brendan. He looked back at me. "What did you say to that?"

"I told him my gut reaction was to say, 'No.' I said I would consider it and that I'd have to discuss it with you."

"Casper, we're getting too old to take care of a kid. Remember what it was like with Clint, Cameron, and Conner? We were a lot younger then. I don't know if we could handle even one kid now, especially one with problems like Scott."

"I know."

"Are you seriously considering it?"

"I'm... keeping an open mind." Brendan nodded. "Is it something you would be willing to consider?" I asked.

"I'm not at all enthused by the idea. My instinct is to say I don't want to take on a foster kid, but I'll keep an open mind as well. I'm not saying, 'Yes,' but we can see where things go."

"I'm really... I don't know... I'm not completely averse to the idea, but I have a feeling this kid may be a lot of trouble and we are getting older. This isn't like taking in Clint, Cameron, and Conner. Scott isn't family and yet..."

"You can't help but care." I nodded. Brendan reached out and took my hand for a moment. "That's one of the things I love about you."

"Don't worry. I will make no decisions without you. I'll be honest, I'm not enthused about taking in a foster kid either, but I am excited about being his big brother."

"If he's into sports, you can bring him to the stadium and I'll give him a tour. Just let me know in advance."

"That can be a future activity if I think he'll enjoy it. I don't know too much about him, except that his parents abandoned him when he was eight and he's been in foster homes ever since."

"That's truly sad. You know, that could have been the boys if we didn't adopt them. I hate to think where Cameron would be now," Brendan said.

"Instead of what might have been, he's running a Christmas tree farm."

"Did you ever think that would happen when he arrived?"

"Never. He is the last I would have picked for getting into farm work. Our boys turned out okay, didn't they?" I said.

"Yes they did. Your brother did as well. I remember when I wanted to kill him."

"Yeah, and now he owns Walberg's Farm Store."

"Has anything worked out as we thought it would, Casper?"

"Yes. We're still together. It won't be long before we've been together fifty years."

"Damn, how did we get so old? I could swear I was playing high school football a couple of weeks ago."

"We're not old, we're just middle aged."

"We're not, you know! Middle means the middle of life! People don't live to be 120!"

"I think we should watch *On Golden Pond* again soon," I said, laughing. Brendan was quoting the movie, more or less.

"I don't know. I think I'm slowly turning into Norman Thayer, Jr."

"Well, I'm not turning into Katherine Hepburn, no matter how much I like her. There is no way you can turn into Henry Fonda. You're never crabby like Norman."

"I bet I could do it. *Who the hell is in this picture?*" We both laughed.

"That's not a bad Henry Fonda impression."

"Maybe I should have been an entertainer."

"I think you'd best stick with football."

Brendan and I kept talking while we ate. We had lived through some very rough times and some wonderful times, but I always knew we would be okay as long as we were together.

***

I walked up the steps of a large 1930s bungalow and knocked on the door. A nice-looking blond woman in her 30s answered.

"I'm Casper."

"I'm Nicole. It's very nice to meet you. Just a moment. Scott, your big brother is here!" she called out.

A surprisingly muscular boy with curly blond hair and blue eyes and the look of a skater soon appeared. He eyed me warily.

"You're my big brother? You're old."

"I'm sure I look ancient to you. If you would rather not hang out with me..."

"Let's get out of here."

Scott walked past me, across the porch, and down the steps.

"I guess we're going. I'll have him back in two or three hours. It was nice meeting you."

I walked to car. Scott climbed in the passenger side. I slipped behind the wheel.

"My last big brother was awesome. We went to movies and did a lot of cool stuff together. He went to IU, but he graduated."

"I moved here in June. I'll be sticking around," I said as I pulled away from the curb.

"Are you married?"

"I'm the same as married."

"Shacking up, huh? Good for you."

I laughed. "I would exactly call it that, but yes. Brendan and I have been together almost fifty years."

"He's a guy?"

"Yes. Does that bother you?"

"No. I have two foster moms now. They're cool. I wish I could stay with them but they've taken in too many strays already. So... what are we going to do?"

"Since we don't know each other well yet, I thought we'd eat and talk. We can figure out what to do in the future, if you decide you don't mind hanging out with an old guy."

Scott gave me a sideways glance, but didn't respond.

"This is the university campus," Scott said, when I parked in a space on 6th Street near Indiana Avenue a few minutes later. "We're eating here? Brad usually took me to Burger King or someplace like that."

"He was a college student. The advantage to an older big brother is that I have more money to spend."

We got out of the car, crossed Indiana Avenue, walked along it to the Sample Gates, and then entered the old part of campus.

"I used to walk here with Brad."

"I bet you miss him."

"Yeah. I do. It sucks that he left, but I understand. He lives in Connecticut. It's not like he could take me with him. I would have gone with him if he'd asked, if I could that is... but... you know."

"You two must have been close."

"Yeah, very close. He even said he wished he could take me with him and I think he meant it."

"He likely did, but at his age he couldn't properly care for you."

"I can take care of myself."

"Yes, but I'm talking about money. It takes an enormous amount of cash to raise a teen."

"You sound like you have experience."

"I do. Brendan and I raised my brother's three sons. They cost us a fortune and it was worth it." I smiled. "A boy like Brad, who is just starting out, couldn't begin to afford that."

"Yeah, I guess you're right."

We walked along the edge of Dunn's Woods, turned left, and headed for the IMU.

"Where did you go to college? Oh, sorry... maybe you didn't. I know a lot of people didn't go to school in the olden days."

I laughed. "Brendan and I both attended IU."

"Really? Cool."

We entered the massive student union building and walked through the hallways, crossing the South Lounge with its fireplace. I gazed at the dancing flames as we passed. This place brought back so many memories.

I paused just beyond the South Lounge to look at the painting *When Skies Are Blue* by T.C. Steele.

"This was here when I was a student. It's one of my favorite paintings," I said.

"It was here way back then?"

"Yeah, way back in the 1980's. We didn't even have electricity or indoor toilets then."

Scott cocked his head at me and almost smiled. We continued on and turned into the Tudor Room.

"This looks fancy," Scott said, looking down at his tank top, running shorts, and sandals.

"It is, but not stuffy. Students often wear sweat pants in here. I've even seen them in pajama bottoms."

Scott glanced at my cargo shorts and sneakers and relaxed.

"We have a reservation for Casper Westwood," I said as we reached the stand at the front.

We followed the hostess to a small table by a window.

"This is a buffet," I said. "There is a salad bar with soup along the wall, near it is the main buffet, and I'm sure you noticed the dessert bar at the front."

"I can eat anything and as much as I want?"

"Yes, but save some room for dessert. The Tudor Room has a rule that no one is allowed to leave before trying at least four desserts."

Scott eyed me skeptically. "I can handle that."

We hit the buffet. I selected almandine rainbow trout and sundried tomato parmesan risotto. I was determined to follow my own advice and save room for dessert.

"What do you want to drink?" I asked when I saw our waitress approaching. "You can have as many different drinks as you like. They have all the usuals and stuff like cranberry juice and orange juice."

"Hello, I'm Mary. Would either of you like something to drink besides water?"

"I would like iced tea and hot jasmine green tea," I said.

"Could I have a Coke and cranberry juice?" Scott asked.

"I'll be right back."

"This place must cost a fortune," Scott said when she had gone.

"No. It's less than $15 a person and everything is included."

"I love all-you-can eat places. Brad used to take me to Denny's and we both got the all-you-can-eat pancakes."

"Well, I hope you didn't bankrupt them. I like Denny's."

"We tried, but we couldn't do it."

"What are your interests? Skating perhaps?"

"Yeah, I'm a skater. How could you tell?"

"You look like a skater."

"Are you into skating?" Scott asked with a mischievous grin.

"I can't say that I am. I wasn't much good at it even when I was younger. There is a skate park very near where I live."

"Oh, you live by the Cascades Golf Course then and North High school."

"Yeah. Do you go to North?"

"I will next month. I'll be a freshman."

"North isn't far from our house. It's within easy walking distance."

Our conversation was limited because we were eating and because words don't come easy between those who have just met. We knew very little about each other.

Scott went back for another plate before I finished my first.

"You are saving room for dessert, right?" I asked when he returned.

"Oh yeah. I can eat a lot."

"We have plenty of time."

"You know, you're not so bad for an old guy. What are you... like seventy-five?"

I choked and sputtered on the iced tea I was unfortunately drinking at the time and then laughed.

"I'm sixty-one."

"Really? I actually thought you were older than seventy-five, but I was trying not to make you feel old." His words only made me laugh more.

"Yes, I am really sixty-one, which I'm sure seems very, very old to you. It's fine. I don't mind."

Scott released a long breath. "Whew, I was afraid I'd screwed things up."

"Does that mean that spending time with me isn't so bad?"

"It isn't so far. I guess you aren't into any sports stuff."

"I like swimming and I'm good at bowling, although I'm not sure that can be considered a sport. Otherwise, I leave the sports to Brendan."

"How old is he?"

"He's sixty-three."

"Oh."

"Most people think he's much younger, although perhaps you won't. He's very athletic. You'll meet him sometime, unless you decide I'm too old for a big brother."

"Well, you're more like a grandfather or a really old dad."

I couldn't help but laugh yet again and it made Scott laugh too. There was no malice in his words, only honesty.

We hit the dessert bar together. I placed slices of key lime and pecan pie on my plate, along with a no bake cookie. Scott chose chocolate cake, a lemon bar, and some bite-sized cheesecake.

"This is so good. Thank you for bringing me here," he said when we returned to the table and he tried his lemon bar.

"You're welcome. Does it beat Burger King?"

"Yes!"

"I like Burger King too. There used to be one in The Commons on the floor below us."

"Back in the olden days, huh?"

"Yeah way back in the distant time known as the 1980's. You might have studied about it in history class."

"Actually, I like vintage 1980's stuff. That was the golden age of summer movies. *Raiders of the Lost Ark*, *E.T.*, *Back to the Future*, *Ghostbusters*, *The Goonies*, and *The Karate Kid* all came out then."

"Brendan and I watched all those at the theatre."

"Wow. That is cool. I've watched them on DVD. They must have been something on a huge screen."

"They were."

"You are so lucky to have lived back then. That's when *Wham*, *Michael Jackson*, *A-Ha*, *Tears for Fears*, *Survivor*, *Journey*, and all those other cool artists were making music."

"I suppose we were lucky, but we didn't know it at the time."

"It's cool talking to someone from my favorite time period."

"I do know a lot about the '80's. I was there. I never thought that time would be considered historic, but then I never thought I would someday carry a computer in my pocket."

"Did you have computers back then?"

"Barely. They were very primitive compared to today's computers, very expensive, and not that many people owned them. Any smart phone can do much more than the computers in the 80's."

"I don't have a phone."

"We didn't have them when I was your age either. When we finally did get them, all they did was make phone calls."

"I saw one of those in the historical society museum once." I raised an eyebrow. "Really! I did! I swear. It was an exhibit on the evolution of technology."

"I believe you."

Scott grinned, but then frowned.

"I guess they told you I'm trouble. I just got out of juvie."

"I heard, for vandalism and drugs."

"Vandalism. Yeah right. That makes it sound like I go around tearing things up."

"What did you do then?"

"I got caught tagging buildings downtown. I did it a lot before they caught me."

"Tagging?"

"Graffiti. I like painting things on buildings. What really got me in trouble was the drugs. I got caught with pot and a few pills."

I nodded. "I was told you're making a real effort not to repeat your past mistakes."

"I am. If I don't, I'll be right back in juvie. I still smoke, but just cigarettes."

I didn't comment. I didn't want our first meeting to include a lecture or disapproval.

"You don't seem like trouble to me."

"You don't know me yet. I have a tendency to screw things up." Scott's expression and tone of voice made it seem as if he was challenging me.

"I don't know you yet, but I would like to get to know you better."

Scott gazed at me suspiciously. "What does that mean?"

"It means I would like to spend more time with you, learn more about you, and do more things like this with you."

"What do you get out of it?"

"Your company and perhaps the opportunity to help you with things the way a big brother would."

"It doesn't sound like a good deal for you."

"You underestimate yourself. I've had a great time talking to you."

Scott shrugged and still seemed suspicious as if he suspected there was a catch or that I wanted something from him he wasn't willing to give. I tried to draw on my experience with Cameron to figure Scott out, but he was quite a different boy. The two were alike in some ways, but more unalike.

"I am so full," Scott said after a second trip to the dessert bar.

"Are you sure you don't want another piece of cake?"

"I might spew."

"It's probably best if you don't have another then."

I paid our check and left a tip. We walked out into the hallway together.

"Someday I'll take you for ice cream at the Chocolate Moose in The Commons, but ice cream doesn't even sound good right now."

"Don't even mention food."

"Whenever I eat lunch at the Tudor Room, I usually don't eat much the rest of the day."

"I may never eat again."

"So, what do you think? Would you like to do something again next week or would you rather try for another big brother?" I asked as we walked back through the South Lounge and then down the flights of steps on the north side of the IMU.

"We can do something next week. You're not so bad," Scott said, smiling mischievously.

"Good. I've enjoyed spending time with you today."

We didn't speak much the rest of the way to the car. We were both busy taking in the scenery. Scott eyed the shirtless college boys playing Frisbee on Dunn Meadow, but I couldn't tell if he was attracted to them, sizing himself up against them, or both. It didn't matter either way, but the more I knew about him, the better I could help him.

I drove the few blocks to Scott's foster home and stopped the car.

"Thanks for lunch. It was great and I liked talking to you, especially about all the '80's stuff."

"You're welcome and I have lots more to tell you about the '80's. Think of me as a time traveler from the past."

"I like that. See you next week."

"I look forward to it."

I smiled as I pulled away. I liked Scott. I had feared hostility, but all things considered I thought our first meeting had gone very well.

That evening, Brendan and I sat out on the patio eating salami sandwiches and barbeque chips. Brendan had insisted on fixing supper and this was his idea of cooking. It was fine by me. Even at nearly 8 p.m. I wasn't terribly hungry.

"So what did you think of the kid?" Brendan asked.

"I like him. He wasn't what I was expecting. I thought he might be a little bad ass, but he seemed a lot like the kids I worked with at VHS a few years ago. I'm not naïve. I know he has problems and has been in trouble, but he's not the hardcore case I feared. He was in Juvenile Detention for drugs, which concerns me. He's also been in trouble for tagging buildings."

"Tagging?"

"Really, Brendan, you need to keep up with the times. Tagging means creating graffiti."

Brendan eyed me. "You had to ask him what it was, didn't you?"

I smiled. "Yes. Oh, he thought I was about eighty or eighty-five."

Brendan laughed. "He's a kid, they think anyone over twenty is old and anyone over thirty ancient."

"He's very into the olden days, which he defines as the 1980's. It gave us something to talk about."

"I miss those olden days, but I'm happy right here too."

"Yeah. I get nostalgic for past parts of my life. It's not that they were better, only different. I miss Jack and Ardelene too."

"Me too, but they both made it to a hundred. Not many people do that and they were both healthy to the day they died. That's how I want to go—in my sleep."

"Well, I'm not finished with you yet so don't even think about taking a permanent nap." Brendan smiled.

Chapter Four
Scott

I whipped my arm around my back at the sound of footsteps.

"Oh, it's you," I said, as Benny, my twelve-year-old foster brother came around behind the garage. I pulled the cigarette to my lips and took another puff.

"I thought you weren't supposed to smoke."

"I'm not. I'm going to quit, but I'm only having one and it's just a cigarette."

"Lemme try it."

"No."

"Why not?"

"Because it's bad for you and it will kill you."

"Then why are you smoking it?"

"I need it. You wouldn't understand."

"Come on. Let me try it."

"You won't like it."

"Come on. You owe me for not telling on you."

"You won't tell on me, you're not a rat."

"Right, so gimme."

I reluctantly handed the cigarette over to Benny. He took a drag and began coughing violently. I took it back before he dropped it.

"That's horrible!" Benny said when he could once again speak. "Why do you smoke those?"

"Because I was stupid and let someone talk me into it and now I'm hooked. Don't start smoking, Benny. Once you start, stopping is really, really hard. I'm trying to stop, but..."

Benny grabbed the cigarette, threw it on the ground and smashed it under his sneaker. He looked at me fearfully, but I laughed instead of getting angry.

"Yeah, don't start, Benny, or you'll need a kid to snatch your cigarettes away to keep you from smoking."

"I'm not gonna start. That was nasty."

"Do not tell Nicole or Megan I let you try it or I'll be in huge trouble."

"I won't. Nicolas said you're on probation. Would you get in trouble for smoking?"

"Not for smoking a cigarette."

"What's prison like?"

"I wasn't in prison. I was in juvenile detention. There aren't cells with bars. We had rooms instead, but there are all kinds of rules and it isn't a nice place. You don't ever want to go there. Don't do the stupid shit I did."

"If it was stupid, why did you do it?"

I looked at Benny. He wasn't being a smart ass. From him, it was an innocent question.

"You wouldn't understand and I'm not going to tell you. It's complicated. Just don't get into drugs. It's not worth it."

"Nicholas said not to listen to you. He said you're a bad influence."

I sighed. "He's right. I am a bad influence, but you tell him what I've told you and I think he'll tell you to listen to me this once."

"Nicholas always looks out for me."

"You're lucky to have such a good big brother."

"You a good big brother too, mostly."

"I'm not so good. Don't get used to me being around. I won't be here long. I'm temporary. There isn't room for me."

"I wish there was."

"Me too."

I went inside with Benny, but didn't stay long. It was too crowded in the house and I always felt like an outsider there. Nicole and Megan were nice to me, nicer than I deserved. My foster brothers and sisters didn't give me much trouble, but they were all permanent. I wasn't. I was the extra kid, taken in out of pity because no one else would have me.

I went out and walked down the front steps, then up the sidewalk, with no particular destination in mind. I passed one family home after another. I wondered what it was like to have a real family. I wondered what it felt like to live somewhere and know that no one would ever come and take you away to somewhere else. Someday, I was going to own a home. It might be small or crappy or even just a trailer, but it would be mine. I'd decorate it with movie posters from the 1980's and everything would be just as I wanted it. Best of all, no one would ever come and tell me I had to go live somewhere else. I wouldn't have to wonder where I would sleep next month, or tomorrow.

I had to get my act together if that was going to happen. I couldn't keep doing stupid things that got me into trouble. Houses cost money, even crappy travel trailers cost money and I wasn't going to have any if I blew it on cigs and drugs. I'd never actually had to pay cash for the drugs. Blaze shared with me, but I paid for them just the same.

I kept walking. I liked being outside. I liked public places because they were always there. I had lived in a lot of different houses in Bloomington, but the public places remained the same. No matter where I lived, I could go to the library and use the computers. I could go to the parks and on the IU campus and none of it ever really changed. I liked that. I liked things not changing. If things hadn't changed when I was very young, I'd have a home and a mom and dad, but most things changed. There was no stopping it and I hated it.

I ended up on the IU campus. I walked though Dunn's Woods, which I liked doing because it was quiet and peaceful. It was right in campus and close to busy Kirkwood Avenue and yet when I was there I felt as if I was deep in a forest. I didn't like quiet for too long, but it was nice sometimes.

I entered the huge IMU and followed the path Casper and I had so recently walked. I stopped and gazed at the painting he said was there when he went to school here. I liked that the painting had been there all those years. It was something else that never changed.

I walked past The Tudor Room. It was closed now, but eating there had sure been nice. I felt out of place in there at first, like a street kid in a fancy restaurant, but Casper was right, students ate there wearing sweat pants. There was one boy who wore a tank top, worn out shorts, and scruffy sandals. He sure wasn't dressed up. I remembered that guy. He had nice muscles. I liked older guys because they had muscles.

I missed Casper as I walked the places I had walked with him. Now, I felt like... like I had stayed at a party too long and everyone else was gone. It was the same place, but felt empty. I was disappointed when I first saw Casper. I wanted another big brother like Brad, not some really old dude, but Casper was kind and he took me to the Tudor Room. I had never been anywhere so nice before.

I wondered about Casper. He seemed nice from the start, but maybe a little too nice. It was odd that an older guy like him would want to be a big brother. When I asked what was in it for him, he said my company and a chance to help me, but there had to be something else. People weren't kind for no reason. They didn't do something for nothing. They always wanted something. There was always a price.

I wondered what Casper really wanted. I figured he'd put his hand on my leg in the car and try to grope me, but he didn't. I didn't catch him checking me out either. Maybe he wasn't into boys like me, but when older guys are nice, they usually want something. I wanted to spend more time with Casper, but I was going to keep my guard up. I had learned long ago that I had to take care of myself.

Chapter Five
Casper

"It looks like the new neighbors are moving in," I announced as I walked into the kitchen. "They must have a large family. The moving van is big."

"They can't have too large a family. That house is about the size of ours," Brendan said, going to the front window to look out. "Oh my god. I can't believe it. No way!"

"What?"

"You are not going to believe who is moving in next door."

Brendan was already on his way out and I quickly followed. My eyes widened as I walked across our yard toward the home just to the north of ours.

"It's about time you showed up to help," Brandon said.

"Why the hell didn't you tell us you bought the house next to ours?" Brendan asked.

"We didn't want to give you the chance to move away."

"We?"

A car pulled into the yard. Jon got out.

"You guys? Living together?" I asked incredulously.

"Why not? We did it before."

"Yeah, in college. That was a long time ago," Brendan said.

"It makes sense. We're both widowers and our kids are out of the house. Neither of us much liked living in a big empty house alone."

"He begged me on his knees to buy this place with him," Jon said as he approached.

"You are as full of shit as ever, Jon Deerfield, and don't think for a moment you're getting the big bedroom," Brandon said.

I grinned. Brandon and Jon had not changed in all the years I'd known them and that was a lot of years.

"We'll flip for it," Jon said.

"Okay, you guys can be honest with us. You're a couple, aren't you?" I asked.

"Yeah, you got us, Casper. We both got married and had kids to throw you off, but now we're willing to admit the truth. We're a couple. Jon has been madly in love with me all these years and he's my little bitch," Brandon said.

"In love with you? Ha! It's only on a good day I can stand the sight of you! As for being your bitch, if we were a couple, you would be my bitch!"

"Ha! Everyone can tell by looking that you'd be the bitch if you were gay. Of course, you'd have to pay for sex just like you did in high school."

"I never once paid a girl for sex," Jon said.

"Okay, you only paid guys for sex."

"I did not have sex with guys or pay them."

"Oh, that's right. Guys and girls paid to not have sex with you," Brandon said.

Jon growled.

"They'll never change," Brendan said, looking at me.

"If we changed it would a loss to the entire world," Brandon said.

"That's right. Hey, we need to tell the movers where to put everything. If you were good neighbors, you'd invite us over for supper since we don't have anything unpacked."

"Are we good neighbors?" I asked Brendan.

"I guess we could take pity on them. Come over later and I'll grill steaks."

"I told you moving next door to them would have perks," Jon said.

"See you two later," Brandon said.

Brandon and Jon disappeared into the house and Brendan and I returned to our home. We walked into the kitchen and sat down.

"That did just happen, didn't it?" Brendan asked.

"I'm not sure. I think I might be dreaming."

"Neither of them said a word!" Brendan said.

"That is a very Brandon and Jon thing to do. You know, I always pictured them living next door to each other bickering over the fence, but I never thought about them living together."

"It does make sense. They've been best friends for almost fifty years, their wives are gone, and their kids grown up. Brandon's youngest is twenty-six, right?"

"Yeah. Little Casper isn't so little anymore either. Jon's youngest is twenty-five."

"This is awesome! Maybe we can get Ethan and Nathan to buy the house on the other side of us."

"Ha! That will never happen. They will die on their farm."

"True. They'll never leave the Selby Farm. Damn I'm surprised about Jon and Brandon moving in next door, but I'm thrilled."

"Me too, but we can't let them know that."

"Never!" Brendan and I laughed. We were both exceedingly content. It was as if a part of our youth had returned to us.

"We do have steaks, right?" Brendan asked.

"Yeah, but I need to get them out of the freezer. I'll do it right now. We have sweet potatoes I can bake. Hey, will you run to Kroger and pick out a cake?"

"I can handle that. Do we need anything else?"

"Pick up some milk while you're there. I think we're good on everything else."

"I'll be back in a few."

I pulled steaks out of the freezer while Brendan ran to the store. We used the north side Kroger for quick grocery trips. It was great to have it so close for times like this.

I thawed the steaks in the microwave, while I washed sweet potatoes and punctured them. I laughed while doing so because I suddenly remembered Brendan blowing up a potato in the microwave once. That wasn't as bad as the time he tried to microwave an egg. What a mess.

I was as happy as I was surprised that Brandon and Jon were moving in next door. We had been friends since high school. During our college years, they lived in the apartment above ours in The Crossing. It would be like old times; except we were now a lot older and we all had kids.

It was odd how things worked out. I would never have guessed when we were all in high school back in Verona that one day we would live next door to each other 150 miles away. I would also never have guessed that Brendan and I would raise three kids or run a Christmas tree farm. Life was full of surprises. Not all of them were good, but for the most part, I was happy with the way our life had worked out.

Brendan returned a few minutes later with a large sheet cake and a gallon of milk. He seemed very pleased with himself.

"What did you do?" I asked.

"I had the cake especially decorated for our new neighbors."

I took one look at the cake and laughed. The bottom half was decorated with two lawns side-by-side. The one on the left was neatly mowed while the one on the right was completely overgrown. The letters at the top of the cake read, "No, you can not borrow the lawn mower."

"Come on, Brandon and Jon will never ask to borrow our lawn mower. They'll ask us to mow their lawn," I said.

"Maybe we can get them to mow ours."

"Good luck with that!"

"I'm going to go over and see how they are doing," Brendan said.

"Okay, I'll finish up here. There isn't much to be done until it's time to grill the steaks."

I could tell Brendan was excited. He was like a kid sometimes. It was odd. We were both in our sixties now and yet I felt as if we hadn't changed since high school. I think everyone had an age that they identified with the most. Perhaps it was the age that they truly became themselves. If that was true, then most everyone felt as they did when they were young.

It was two hours before Brendan returned, which was not a surprise.

"I'm going to plug in the grill. They'll be right over," Brendan said.

I pulled the steaks out of the refrigerator where I'd kept them since they thawed and then set the kitchen table. It was rather hot and steamy out so I figured the guys would want to eat inside.

Brandon and Jon soon arrived and plopped down on the benches on either side of the kitchen table.

"I'm exhausted just from watching those boys carry all our furniture," Jon said.

"You are an old man," Brandon said.

"You are the same age as me."

"Yeah, but I'm still fit and hot."

"You keep telling yourself that buddy," Jon said.

"Are you sure living together is a good idea?" I teased.

"I can put up with almost anything, even Jon," Brandon said.

"Ha! I am a delight to live with—you, on the other hand..."

"Look at all that smoke out there. I hope Brendan isn't burning our steaks. We didn't invite ourselves over for burnt steaks," Jon said.

"You know Brendan is a master on the grill. He grilled yellow squash a few evenings ago. It was great."

"Squash?" Brandon asked, wrinkling his nose.

"Yeah, it was wonderful."

"I'll take your word for it."

I fixed the baked sweet potatoes in the microwave while Brendan grilled the steaks. It wasn't long before we were all seated around the kitchen table, eating.

"When did you buy the house next door?" I asked.

"The day it came up for sale, which was a day or two before you moved in here. We had been looking for a place for a few months. We checked it out and liked it."

"It has the added bonus of us next door," Brendan said.

"Eh, well... you can't have everything," Jon said.

"You kept a secret that long? I'm impressed," I said. "What are you doing with your separate houses?"

"They are both sold. Property is snatched up fast in Bloomington, especially near campus," Brandon said.

"Yeah, we missed out on a couple of houses when we were looking," I said.

"The kids were kind enough to take what furniture I didn't need off my hands," Jon said.

"Mine too!" Brandon said.

"Restore is coming to pick up everything the kids don't take. I like that the money they raise goes to Habitat for Humanity. The house will be empty in a few days," Jon said.

"I'm doing the same. That way I don't have to deal with it," Brandon said.

"You guys always were good at getting out of work," I said.

"It's a skill," Jon said.

"It's tough moving out of a house after living there so many years, isn't it?" I asked.

"Yeah, Denise and I raised four kids in that house. It's difficult to leave because of the memories, but that's also why I wanted to leave. Everything there reminded me of Denise. It was too much of a reminder of what I'd lost. I shouldn't have waited so long to move. The last few years have been rough," Brandon said.

"Brandon talked me into buying a house with him and it didn't take much convincing. Sharon has been gone a year, but I still kept expecting to see her when I came into the kitchen or returned home from teaching."

"I think living together will be good for both of you," Brendan said.

"Yeah, the boys worry far too much. They act as if I'm an old man," Brandon said. Jon started to open his mouth. "Shut it, Deerfield."

"Merely arguing will keep you guys young," I said.

"It was time for a change and I can think of worse things than living with Jon and next door to you."

"We're glad to have you," Brendan said.

"I hope you don't ruin our football team," Brandon said.

"When I'm through with them, they will be better than ever," Brendan said.

"We brag to everyone that we know the head football coach for IU," Jon said.

"Hmm, a compliment. They must want free tickets," I said.

"Well..." Jon said.

"I'll get you some and for your boys too."

"It's taken decades, but putting up with Brendan has finally paid off," Brandon said.

"Yeah, football tickets and free steak. This isn't starting out badly," Jon said.

"Maybe Brendan can cook Italian food some evening," I said.

"Oh, uh... we're busy that night," Brandon said. Jon nodded.

"Everyone has made fun of my cooking for fifty years!" Brendan said.

"You're good at everything else. That's all we've got," Brandon said.

"Except bowling. Brendan is, without doubt, one of the worst bowlers in the entire world," Jon said.

"Yeah, I am the worst. I'm number one!" Brendan said, making everyone laugh. "I also have trouble with miniature golf."

"Everyone does, Brendan," I said.

"Let's have dessert. I baked a cake just for you guys," Brendan said.

"If you really baked it, I'd claim I have to leave now, but I know you didn't so bring it on," Jon said.

"Yeah, if you baked, the house would be filled with smoke," Brandon said.

"There would likely be a fire truck out front too," I said.

"Wait until you see it," Brendan said.

Brendan took the cake from the counter, removed the lid and showed it to Brandon and Jon. They immediately started laughing.

"Well, there goes that idea," Jon said.

"I'll have you know we have two mowers," Brandon said.

"Yes, but will you use them?" Brendan asked.

"Hmm, maybe I could make one of my soccer players mow the lawn," Brandon said.

"I swear you get lazier every year," Jon said.

"It's my retirement plan."

I pulled the vanilla ice cream out of the freezer. Cake was nearly always better with ice cream.

We hadn't actually spent much time with Brandon or Jon since we'd moved to Bloomington. It was good to catch up. What was better was the knowledge they would be right next-door.

"You could have your kids mow your lawn. Pretend you're old and feeble," I said.

"Jon doesn't have to pretend. He *is* old and feeble," Brandon said.

"I'm young enough to kick your ass, Hanson," Jon said, then grinned. "The boys are all so busy. They offered to help us move, but it was easier on everyone to hire movers."

"My boys helped me pack and sort. What a job," Brandon said.

"Mine did too. That is where I truly needed them. I couldn't believe the amount of stuff in that house."

"We had it easy. We took what we wanted and left," Brendan said.

"You always were a slacker," Brandon said.

"I think you'll find that having less stuff is a relief. Our smaller house is much easier to clean too," I said.

"I bet Brendan leaves you with all the cleaning, doesn't he? Jon asked.

"I do most of it, but Brendan does have that coaching thing he does. In Verona, my job was working on the tree farm, but here I don't have a job outside the house."

"You're so loyal. Brendan doesn't deserve you," Brandon said.

"No, I don't, but I'm glad that I have him," Brendan said.

"God dammit, Brewer, how are we supposed to say nasty things about you when you agree with us?" Brandon said.

"He's obviously trying to ruin our fun," Jon said.

"The bastard," Brandon said.

"Yep, ruining your fun is my goal. Besides, you have each other to pick on and you do it so well," Brendan said.

"We've had plenty of practice."

"You know, it's kind of odd that the coaches for the North and South high school soccer teams are living together," Brendan said.

"We can spread rumors they're a gay couple," Casper said.

"That would just make us seem even cooler to the kids," Brandon said.

"We definitely don't want to spread that rumor then," Brendan said.

"This has been great. We'll have you guys over once we get organized, which will take a while," Jon said.

"We spent over a week unpacking boxes," I said.

"I bet by *we* you mean *you*," Brandon said.

"I did most of it, but only because I wanted to organize everything where I could find it."

"I was allowed to unpack my own stuff and then Casper exiled me to the yard," Brendan said.

"I guess he's good for something," Brandon said. "Thanks for supper. Everything was wonderful and this was a great break from unpacking, but we should get back to it."

"You get back to it and I'll stay here and talk," Jon said.

"Oh, no you don't, Deerfield!"

"It was worth a try."

"I'm so glad you guys moved in next door," I said, hugging first Brandon and then Jon. "I'll send some of this cake home with you."

The guys departed soon after, toting half of the remaining cake. Brendan helped me clean up, then we sat down at the kitchen table and looked out over our back yard.

"Having Brandon and Jon live next door is like having a little bit of Verona here, isn't it?" Brendan asked.

"It certainly is," I said, smiling.

***

"Is this dressed up enough?" Scott asked when he stepped out his door.

"You look great. I just didn't want you to wear sandals."

"I'm not so sure about going to a play."

"It's Sweeney Todd: The Demon Barber of Fleet Street. It's about a barber who murders his customers and shoves them down a chute to Mrs. Lovett who uses them to make meat pies to sell on the street."

"That's twisted. I like it."

"I thought you would."

We walked to the Prius and drove the short distance to IU, where I parked in the lot just across Indiana Avenue.

"I've never been to a play, except at school. Some of those are kind of good."

"This one will be better. It was revived on Broadway a couple of years ago and is now touring the country."

Scott nodded. He looked very handsome in his solid blue Henley and jeans, but seemed a little uncomfortable in them as if he wasn't accustomed to wearing them.

We followed the path between Dunn Meadow and the Jordan River, passed the IMU on the right, then the old gym on the left.

"There sure are a lot of people," Scott said as he noted all the others walking along with us. Campus buses were unloading even more people in front of the auditorium across the arts square.

"It's a popular show and has most of the original Broadway cast. It's sold out."

Scott looked at the large banner over the entrance doors to the auditorium.

"Dorian Calumet? Wow! He is my favorite actor! I've seen him in so many movies. He's really here?"

"Yes, he's playing Sweeney Todd."

"This is awesome!" I smiled at Scott's enthusiasm. I had almost forgotten what it was like to experience things through the eyes of a kid.

We walked up the steps and entered the auditorium. Scott gazed up at the enormous murals above depicting scenes from Indiana history.

"Those were painted by Thomas Hart Benton, weren't they?" Scott asked.

I turned and stared at him for a moment.

"Yes. He painted them for the 1933 Chicago World's Fair."

Scott gazed at them in wonder and if I wasn't mistaken, admiration. It gave me an idea, but there was no time to think about it now.

We waited in line and a short time later an usher escorted us to our seats right down front.

"Whoa! How did you get these seats? This is front row center!" Scott said.

"I have my ways."

The auditorium quickly filled and a few minutes later the show began.

I hadn't attended a show at the IU Auditorium for years. I had forgotten it was such a wonderful experience. Brendan and I needed to start coming, if he had the time. Unfortunately, he couldn't make it tonight.

I smiled when Sweeney Todd appeared. It had been quite a while since I'd seen Dorian. He was a major Broadway and film star now and had been for years, but I still remembered him as a high school boy.

I was soon completely lost in the performance. I had worked with several high school productions, so I knew the work that went into a play or musical. A Broadway show was on a whole other level, but I could imagine what it took to put it together.

Dorian was brilliant. He was so talented that he completely disappeared and was replaced by Sweeney Todd. I wasn't aware it was Dorian up on the stage until the cast took their bows. In my opinion, he was the finest actor ever, but I was a little biased.

Scott began to get up when the rest of the audience did at the end of the show, but I held him back.

"Let's wait until it clears out."

"That was so awesome! Thanks for bringing me. I'll admit, I wasn't that excited when you told me we were going to a play."

"I'm glad you liked it."

"This night could not get any better."

"Are you sure?" I asked.

"I'm pretty sure. I could watch this play over and over. I'm not usually into musicals, but all the songs fit. Sweeney looked so maniacal and crazed."

"I imagine a lot of murderers out for revenge look that way, not that I've met any."

"I would hope not!"

We kept talking about the play until the auditorium had mostly cleared out, then I led Scott to the side of the auditorium and proceeded up the stairs at the side of the stage.

"Here, you'll need this," I said, turning to him when we reached the top and handing him a pass to clip to his shirt.

"We're going backstage?"

"It looks like it."

I led Scott around behind the curtain and then up the side stairs. Security parted for us when they spotted our passes. We soon arrived at our destination.

"Wow, this is incredible. There he is—Dorian Calumet. You think I can get his autograph?"

"I'm sure of it."

We walked closer. Dorian turned, spotted us, and quickly crossed the distance between us.

"Casper! I'm so glad to see you!" Dorian gave me a big hug, which I returned. Scott stared with his mouth open.

"This must be Scott," Dorian said, reaching out to shake his hand, which flustered Scott even more.

"Yeah, I'm Scott." Turning to me he asked, "You know Dorian Calumet?"

"We went to high school together and Dorian came back to help when I was working with the drama department there later."

"Wow. I've seen all your movies. You are my favorite actor," Scott said. He stared at Dorian wide-eyed.

"That's wonderful. I haven't even seen all my movies."

"Hey, can I get a picture with you?"

"Of course."

I pulled out my camera and took a few shots of Dorian and Scott together.

"I'll get prints of these made for you," I said.

"Thanks!"

"Come back to my dressing room with me. I need to get out of this costume and makeup."

Scott swallowed hard. He looked like he suspected he was dreaming.

We followed Dorian to a large dressing room. He pulled off his wild black wig to reveal his hair, still blond and long after all these years.

"That thing itches under the lights," he said. "How is Brendan?"

"Oh, he's great as always."

"I knew you guys had moved to Bloomington. I wouldn't mind moving here myself, but I spend so much time traveling I'd never be here anyway. So, did you grow up here Scott?"

"Yes."

"It's a great place. I went to college here."

"Yeah, I know."

"How did you get involved with this guy?" Dorian asked, indicating me.

"He's my big brother."

"You're lucky."

"Yeah. I thought he was too old at first, but this is the second time we've spent time together and he's pretty cool."

"He is pretty old. We're the same age."

"You don't look old," Scott said.

"You just became my best friend."

We kept talking while Dorian removed his makeup and changed. About the time he finished, hot tea and cookies arrived.

"Please join me. I requested plenty for all of us," Dorian said. "I always like hot tea after a performance and I'm always hungry after, too."

Scott asked a lot of questions as we sat and ate, but Dorian and I had time to talk too. It was wonderful to catch up with him. He was so busy it was difficult to contact him.

Scott was in heaven. He kept looking at me as if he wanted me to confirm this was really happening. Scott definitely wasn't shy. He did most of the talking.

"Hey, my car will be here soon. I have to leave for Chicago where we're playing tomorrow night," Dorian said after about half an hour.

"Don't you ever get to sleep?" Scott asked.

"I have a driver so I sleep while he drives. I'll check into the hotel the moment I arrive too."

"Can I have your autograph?" Scott asked.

"Of course, I'll sign some photos for you."

Dorian not only did so, but also signed a copy of the Sweeney Todd CD and gave it to Scott.

Dorian and I hugged and then Dorian hugged Scott.

"It was so nice to meet you, Scott. Try to keep Casper in line."

"Meeting you is the highlight of my life, and I will."

"I hope you have greater highlights that this in the future," Dorian teased.

"I don't think anything can top this."

Dorian smiled. "Say 'Hi' to Brendan for me. I'm sorry he couldn't make it."

"Yeah, he is too. He sends his love."

The three of us walked outside together. Dorian bid us goodbye once more, then climbed into the back of a white Rolls Royce.

"That's was stupendous!" Scott said as we walked down the sidewalk.

"So you had a good time?"

"Are you kidding? This is the best day of my life! Why didn't you tell me you knew Dorian Calumet?"

"You didn't ask."

"Grr."

I laughed.

"Thank you so much." Scott surprised me by grabbing me around the middle and hugging me. He was strong and I could barely breathe. I hugged him back.

Scott released me and we continued on our way across the arts square. The evening air was cool and the sound of the falling water of Showalter Fountain was soothing. Being with Scott reminded me of taking care of Clint, Cameron, and Conner when they were young.

Scott talked about Dorian all the way to his house. I had never seen him so lively or excited. He leaned over and hugged me again before he got out of the car. I couldn't help but hug him back.

Brendan was home when I arrived a few minutes later. He was sitting at the kitchen table drinking hot tea and looking extremely tired.

"Tough day?" I asked.

"Not so much tough as long. How was your evening?"

"It was a smashing success. It turns out that Dorian is Scott's favorite actor. Dorian sends his love by the way."

"I'm sorry I couldn't be there but the university expects big things for big bucks."

"I'm sorry you couldn't too. You have to meet Scott soon. He hugged me tonight, twice. He reminds me so much of Cameron."

"I'd like to meet him. You certainly think highly of him."

"He's not without his problems and emotional baggage. I'm not naïve, but I want to help him, Brendan."

"I think history is repeating itself. Didn't we have this conversation in college about Aiden?"

"I know... I like to take in strays."

"True. I'm amazed every time I walk in and don't find a dog or cat here. The next logical step is for me to meet him. We'll have to arrange it around my schedule, but I'm sure we can make it happen soon."

"Thanks, Brendan," I said, hugging him.

Chapter Six
Scott

"What I want to know is why *you* got to meet a movie star," Nicolas said as he gazed at my signed photo of Dorian Calumet.

"It's all in who you know," I said airily.

"Your Big Brother is being awfully nice and spending a lot of money on you. You know you need to be careful around older guys, right?"

"Yeah. I'm not stupid you know."

"I mean, he may be okay, but he might not be. I know you like guys, but he might do things to you that you don't want."

"I know. You warned me about Brad, too, and he was okay."

"Yeah, but just remember they aren't all okay."

I nodded. Nicholas had had a bad experience in a park at night. Two college guys tried to force him to do something he didn't want to do. He got away, but he was suspicious of any older guy and his motives. Nicholas was not into guys, but that didn't matter. I was, but I didn't want to be forced to do anything I didn't want to do.

Nicholas still looked apprehensive. I appreciated his concern. It was way better than him not giving a shit or worse, forcing me to do things himself.

"I think he's okay. I hope he is. I like him. He knows everything about the 1980's."

"He should. He was there."

"Yeah, but I like his stories. I figured an old guy would be boring, but he's not. I feel like... like he cares about me too."

Nicholas smiled at me sadly. "Be careful, and don't let yourself get hurt. He's just your Big Brother, not your dad."

"I know that!" I snapped.

"You don't have to get angry. I'm just saying you shouldn't expect too much. I'm not saying he doesn't like you, but you know it probably won't last. Don't set yourself up to get hurt."

"I know. Nothing is forever, but I want to enjoy it while I can. I miss Brad, but we had a lot of fun together. I have the memories."

Nicholas suspected something was up, but then he tended to be overly suspicious. I wasn't letting my guard down, but the more time I spent with Casper, the more genuine he felt.

"So, you got photos with Dorian too?" Nicolas asked.

"Yes, Casper is going to make prints for me."

"Life is not fair. I should have met him, not you."

"Yes, it really isn't fair, is it?" I said and grinned.

"Shut up."

"Your jealousy only makes it better."

"In that case, I'm not jealous. I don't care at all. I'm glad you met him instead of me. I don't even know who Dorian Calumet is. I've never heard of him."

Nicolas made me laugh.

"What's funny?" Cliff, my nine-year-old foster brother asked as he stood in the doorway.

"Don't come in or Scott will tell you all about meeting Dorian Calumet. It's a boring story!" Nicholas said, rolling his eyes. I stuck my tongue out at him.

"You did not meet him. He's a movie star."

I turned my autographed photo so that Cliff could see.

"Where did you get that?"

"From Dorian Calumet when I went backstage last night to meet him," I said.

"And here we go. I'll be at my desk, holding my hands over my ears," Nicholas said.

Nicholas did move to his desk and began looking at a magazine, but he didn't cover his ears. I told Cliff all about the night before—from the beginning.

***

Summer was slipping away. The time to return to school was growing ever closer. I wasn't sure what I thought about that. I was no longer suspended, but I was still banned from all athletics. That meant no football, no baseball, and no anything else I liked. I had always been involved in sports. No matter where I lived or which school I attended, I was on a team, but no more.

I knew why I was banned, but it didn't seem like a smart move on the part of the school system to me. If I attended practices and played, I'd be less likely to be out smoking pot with friends. I thought I might try to plead my case at North High School. If I did, I'd use that argument.

I didn't know if I could handle not playing sports. I'd be willing to attend practices and not play in any games. That would be something at least. Hell, I'd be the team manager or the water boy just to be involved. School was going to suck if I couldn't get the ban lifted.

I didn't let myself think about it. All things considered, I was okay. I was out of Juvie and did not intend to go back. I still smoked my cigs, but I was determined to stay away from drugs, which meant I had to stay away from Blaze. I could most definitely not hang out with him. He could talk me into anything. Blaze was much harder to resist than the drugs. He was like a drug himself. He was addictive and I needed a fix.

I pushed Blaze out of my mind too and took out a cigarette and lit it up. I was trying to cut back, but it was extremely difficult and sometimes, like now, I really needed a smoke.

Even as I took a drag, I wished I could quit smoking. For one thing, a pack of even the cheapest smokes was hella expensive and I was perpetually short of cash. I also had to talk someone older into buying them for me and that wasn't easy.

I guess it didn't matter if I smoked or not. If I couldn't play sports, what did it matter if got winded fast when I ran? If my life was going to suck anyway, what did it matter if I died young from lung cancer?

Damn. I was in one dark, doom and gloom mood. I needed to shake it off.

I turned and walked in the direction of the Building Trades Park, which was located between 2nd and 3rd streets. There were basketball hoops there. I didn't have a basketball, but maybe I could catch some guys playing and join in.

I arrived at the park a few minutes later. It was right behind the police department, which made me a little edgy, but I wasn't doing anything wrong. My cigarette was long gone and the rest of my precious pack was deep in the pocket of my cargo shorts. Even if I was caught with them, that would not violate my probation.

Three shirtless boys were playing basketball. They looked a little younger than me, which was fine. Sometimes, older boys wouldn't let me play, but younger probably would. I walked over and watched them until they stopped for a moment.

"Can I join?" I asked.

"What's in it for us?" asked the cocky blond with the best build of the three.

"You get to pick up amazing basketball skills from me."

The boy grinned, showing a gap in his front teeth. "Come on, I was just messin'. You know how to play Horse?"

"Who doesn't?"

We began to shoot baskets from different spots around the free throw line. It was easy stuff for me and not difficult for the younger guys. The game got interesting when we began to devise more difficult shots. I did one over the shoulder without looking at the goal that the others could not duplicate. Blondie did a long distance shot that only he and I could perform. The smallest boy, with black hair, tripped everyone up except me with a bizarre two-hand shot from between the ankles.

We laughed at the crazy shots we tried. The others missed one here and there. When the kid with curly brown hair was knocked out, I still hadn't missed. Blondie did his best to come up with shots I couldn't handle, but he only succeeded in knocking his buddy out of the competition.

"It's you and me, Blondie. Now shit gets real," I said.

"Prepare to be annihilated," he said.

"Says the boy who already has H-O-R."

Blondie stuck out his tongue, then devised a difficult one hand shot from the side. "Suck on that," he said as it went in.

I took the ball and duplicated his shot.

"Ah, man! Don't you ever miss?"

"Never," I said.

It was hot, so I took off my shirt and stuffed it in the side of my shorts. I took a few steps back, bounced the ball off the pavement, and ricocheted it off the backboard and into the net.

"Suck on that one," I said, smiling.

"Grr."

I noticed Blondie steal a look at my chest as he set up to make his shot. I don't know if my muscles distracted him or if he just couldn't make the shot, but he missed. He ricocheted the ball off the backboard, but it bounced off the rim.

"Dammit!"

"H-O-R-S," I said.

"If you weren't bigger than me, I'd punch you," Blondie said with a grin.

Blondie continued to check out my chest and abs. He even stole looks of the bulge in my shorts. I wondered if he was attracted to me or was merely checking me out in the way younger boys do older. I liked to think I was attractive, but I'd never been quite sure.

I duplicated Blondie's next shot with ease, then did a two-handed, between the legs shot while facing away from the basket. Blondie completely missed. I won.

"You're pretty good," I said.

"I'll be as good as you when I'm older, taller, and stronger."

"Yeah, but by then I'll be even older, taller, and stronger than I am now."

"The universe is against me!"

I laughed. I liked this kid.

"I gotta go," the boy with curly brown hair said.

"We're done then. It's his ball," Blondie said.

"Thanks for letting me play guys."

"You're only saying that because you won," the smallest boy said.

"That does make it better, but thanks."

I exchanged a fist bump with each the boys and they departed.

I turned to see Felix, one of my old crowd, watching me. He walked toward me.

"So, you're hanging out with kids now?"

"What better way to make sure I win?"

"We haven't seen you around in forever."

"You know I was in Juvie, right?"

"Yeah."

"That's where I was most of the time. I'm on probation now."

"Blaze has been looking for you."

I shrugged. I didn't want to come out and say I was avoiding Blaze and his crew. I should have told Felix I didn't want to hang out with him, Blaze, and Ace, but couldn't bring myself to do it. I wasn't afraid of Felix, but I couldn't get the words to come out of my mouth.

"I've been busy and my foster moms are on my ass."

"I bet. We'll see you around I'm sure. I'll tell Blaze I saw ya."

"Yeah, do that."

Felix departed. We had never been real close. I had the feeling he didn't like me all that much. I had feeling he had a thing for Blaze and was jealous because it was me that Blaze took off alone. If Felix knew what happened when we were alone he might not be so eager to take my place. Then again, maybe he would be. It was fine with me if he did. I had to avoid Blaze if I was going to stay out of Juvie.

***

"A museum? Why have you turned on me? Why do you hate me?" I asked Casper as I rode in the passenger seat of his Prius.

"Perhaps you should become an actor, Scott. You're certainly being dramatic enough for one."

"You're a riot! Museums are boring."

"You'll like this one."

Casper parked the car on 6th Street near campus.

"I thought you were dragging me to a museum against my will?"

"I am."

"There are no museums near here."

"There's more than one, actually, but I'm taking you to one on main campus. Surely, you've noticed it?"

"Nope."

"We walked right by it the other night."

"We did?" I asked.

"Are you putting me on, Scott? You really didn't see it?"

"I didn't. There's a museum on campus?"

Casper looked as if he did not believe me. We walked across Indiana Avenue and followed the path between the Jordan River and Dunn Meadow. We walked past the IMU and on toward the auditorium. There was nothing here but classroom buildings. I began to suspect Casper was putting *me* on.

"There it is," he said, pointing.

"Where?"

"Right in front of you. Come on." Casper led me across the street to a fairly large sign. "Read that for me."

"Indiana University Art Museum. This is an art museum?"

"Have you never read the sign?"

"Well, no."

"I would think that giant sculpture out front would have tipped you off."

"There's stuff like that all over campus."

Casper growled. "Come on."

My excitement level intensified. While I did not care so much for museums in general, not that I'd seen many, I did love art. It was one of the passions of my life, not that I'd admit it to most people.

We walked into a huge open space with a glass roof far overhead. Casper led me to the left and he opened a door and motioned me inside.

"Wow," I said. Hanging only a few feet away was a very, very old painting that put me in mind of something by Raphael. "Look at those colors. I would ask if this is real, but it must be real."

"It's real. I believe that one was painted in the 16th century."

"This is amazing!"

"You *really* didn't know this was here?"

"Are you kidding? If I knew, I would have lived in here!"

Casper grinned at my enthusiasm. "See what reading a sign can get you?"

"Okay, I get your point. There are so many paintings!"

"Yes. There is a Monet in here, as well as a Picasso, and a Jackson Pollock."

"Seriously? Here, in a museum in Bloomington?"

"Yes, and upstairs is painted ancient Greek pottery."

"Wow."

I wanted to stand and stare at the first painting, but I was pulled forward by the next and then the next and the next. The paintings slowly moved forward in time. I didn't know the names of most of the artists, but that didn't matter. The paintings were magnificent. Eventually, we came to the painting by Claude Monet, The Seine at Argenteuil, 1874. I had read about Monet and looked at photos of his paintings in books, but I never thought I would see an actual Monet.

"I can't believe this," I said, gazing at Casper, grinning.

"Think of all the times you have walked by this building with no idea of what is inside," Casper said.

"Don't rub it in, but thank you for bringing me here."

Casper did not rush me, but let me gaze at the paintings as long as I wanted.

"I've read about a lot of these artists. Did you know that Monet could hear color?" I asked.

"I've never heard about that."

"He said he could and I believe he could because I hear it too."

"What does color sound like?" Casper asked.

"It's not a specific sound so much as it is a frequency. Each color has its own... I guess you could call it tone. I don't know, but I thought I was imagining it until I read about Monet."

"I wish I could hear what you hear," Casper said. He did not disbelieve or even doubt me. I liked that.

"I wish I had his talent," I said.

"Perhaps you have it and only need to discover it inside yourself. A little practice would help too."

"I draw, but canvas and oil paints are expensive. I've taken art classes at school and plan to take all I can."

"I think that's wise. You should pursue what you love," Casper said.

"Is that wise old man advice?"

"Yes, it is."

"I think I'll follow it."

When I reached the end of the gallery, I started all over again and noticed things I had not before. There was a painting of a truly beautiful boy called simply, "Portrait of a Boy" by Philips de Koninck who was from Amsterdam. It was painted in 1673. I loved the boys long reddish blond hair. I wondered who he was and what his life had been like. Did he grow old or did he die shortly after the painting was created? I knew next to nothing of this boy, but thanks to the artist, here he was in 21st century. It was a kind of immortality.

"We are growing short of time and there is one piece I want to show you upstairs and somewhere else I want to take you before I drive you home. We can return here again and, of course, you can come on your own. There are other galleries with artifacts from different cultures."

I reluctantly followed Casper out of the gallery and up the weird angled stairs. We entered another gallery, but this one was filled with really old stuff. I wanted to stop and look more closely as some of the painting on the Greek pottery, but I obediently followed Casper. Soon, we stood before a flat stone, pointed at the top and broken at the bottom. A young nude boy holding a small bird was carved upon it.

"This is Brendan's favorite piece. It's called the Stele of Apolexis."

"It's beautiful. Did you know most ancient stuff like this was originally painted?"

"No. How did you know that?"

"I like to read about art. This looks like a tombstone."

"It is."

"I wonder where he lived, when he died, and why."

"Well, the name is Greek and this says it dates to the late fifth to early fourth century BCE, so he lived about 2,400 to 2,500 years ago."

"He looks like someone I could meet at school, except for being naked. He actually looks a lot like me."

"I was going to remark on that. He looks like a younger version of you. I'd say he's about twelve or thirteen. Maybe you are his reincarnation."

"That would be cool. It sounds weird, but I feel a connection to him."

"I can believe it. Brendan said he's been drawn to this piece since he was a college student."

We departed from the museum. I was determined to return and soon. I wanted to explore it from top to bottom.

"That was as good as meeting Dorian Calumet and that was the highlight of my life," I said.

"See? Old guys aren't so bad."

"No. They aren't."

We walked back to the car, but Casper passed it. I had no idea where he was taking me until he turned into Pygmalion's Art Supplies on North Grant Street, about a block from where we had parked.

"I thought I should buy you some art supplies," Casper said.

"Oh. That's... too much."

"No. It's not. I want to buy you some art supplies and I'm going to do it, so no arguing," Casper said.

"Thank you so much."

"Could you help us?" Casper asked the handsome college guy behind the counter. "We need a set of oils for a beginner, as well as brushes, canvases, and an easel."

My eyes widened.

"Sure, I'll be glad to help you."

"Do you go to IU?" Casper asked.

"Yes. I'm in the arts school, as you might guess. I'm Clarke." He smiled and my heart fluttered. He was *really* handsome.

We walked around the store. Clarke made suggestions and each time Casper picked the more expensive option. He wasn't satisfied with a small set of oil paints. He bought me a big, nice quality one. Instead of cheaper brushes, he picked out the best. He bought me several canvases of different sizes, as well as paint thinner and other supplies. My eyes widened at the total.

"I can't believe you bought me all this stuff," I said as we departed the store. Both of us were loaded down with bags and boxes.

"I only bought you what I thought you needed."

"Thank you so much! All this is great and I appreciate it, but you don't have to buy me stuff. I like spending time with you."

"I'm not trying to buy your friendship."

"Oh, I didn't mean that exactly. It's just that I want you to know that I'll be happy to spend time with you if you never buy me another thing. I look forward to our time together."

Casper smiled. "I do too, Scott."

Chapter Seven
Casper

"Scott. This is Brendan," I said as Brendan walked up to us in The Commons in the IMU.

"Hi, Scott. Casper has told me a lot about you."

"Uh oh."

"It was mostly good."

"Whew!"

Scott looked Brendan over. I could tell Brendan wasn't what he was expecting. Brendan was 6'1" with broad shoulders and he was muscular. He wasn't the typical sixty-three-year-old.

"Are you guys hungry? I'm starving."

"I'm always hungry," Scott said.

"I thought the Crimson Grill would be good. I know you love their burgers," I said to Brendan.

"After you guys," Brendan said, motioning us to the grill, which was mere steps away from where we stood.

Brendan and Scott ordered double cheeseburgers with fries, but I went for a regular sized burger with cheese, lettuce, and tomato with onion rings. Our wait was not long since The Commons was not busy in the later evening hours. It was also easy to find a seat. We chose a table by a window that overlooked the patio below.

"Hey, Coach."

"Hey," Brendan said and nodded to a college boy passing by. It wasn't the last time he was greeted as we ate. Nearly everyone on campus knew Brendan. He was better known now than he was when he was a quarterback.

"Wait..." Scott said after a few minutes. "You're the head football coach. I've seen your picture in the newspaper."

"Yes, I am."

"Why didn't you tell me he was the head football coach?" Scott asked me.

"You didn't ask."

"Grr! That's what he said when I asked him why he didn't tell me he knew Dorian Calumet!"

Brendan laughed. "Yeah, Casper is like that. Do you like football?"

"I love football. I played at Tri-North last fall, but I... uh... got kicked off the team. I'm sure Casper told you why."

Brendan nodded. "Getting kicked off is rough, but staying out of trouble is a requirement, especially at the college level."

"Yeah. I did some stupid stuff. Tagging buildings wasn't so bad I guess, but the rest was a huge mistake."

"We all make mistakes. The trick is not to repeat them."

Scott nodded. "I do stupid things sometimes. I don't know why. I just do. Maybe it's because I'm stupid."

"I have to disagree with that. I've been around you long enough to know you definitely aren't stupid," I said.

Scott shrugged.

"Even tagging buildings wasn't such a great idea. I didn't think about it much when I did it. I just wanted to create something and who wants to look at the boring wall of a building?"

"Blank walls are often improved with art, but it's best to obtain permission first," Brendan said.

"Yeah, I learned that the hard way. Casper bought me a bunch of art supplies recently, so I stick to painting on canvas now."

"That is wise. Do you like any other sports?" Brendan asked, likely to change the subject.

"I like all of them."

"You're my kind of guy."

"I think I'm outnumbered," I said.

"You didn't do *any* sports back in school?" Scott asked.

"I ran track. I was fast when I was kid, mostly because I had to outrun bullies. It was either run fast or get my butt kicked. I was a scrawny little guy."

"You don't look like you were ever scrawny."

"Oh, I was. When I was your age I doubt I weight a hundred pounds."

"Wow."

"Luckily, I soon had Brendan to protect me. He was football player then and he was built. No one dared mess with him and soon no one dared to pick on me because of him, except for my brother."

"So you guys *have* been together a long time. That's cool."

"Yes, and the years have gone by too quickly," I said.

"That's what old people always say. Oh, Sorry."

"We are getting old and to you I'm sure we're ancient," Brendan said.

"Not ancient... merely... experienced?" Scott said, causing us to laugh and him too.

"Time does seem to pass faster when you're older. I remember not believing that when I was your age, but it does. I think it has something to do with a year being an increasingly smaller percentage of one's life. When you're four, a year is a quarter of your life. When you're ten, it's 10%. When you're our age, it isn't even 2%," Brendan said.

"I never thought of that. Man, coaching football must be great."

"It is. I coached at a high school for decades and now I'm here. I can't think of any place I would rather be."

"I don't know what I want to do when I get older, but being a football coach is a possibility. I doubt that will ever happened. I'm banned from all athletics because of... you know."

"Hopefully, that ban won't be permanent and you can play again. I'm sure not playing is rough. I would have thought it was the end of the world."

"That's kind of how I see it. I really screwed things up."

"Casper will have to bring you to practice sometime soon so you can see what it's like close up."

"Really?"

"Of course."

"That would be awesome!"

"We will arrange it then," Brendan said.

Scott grinned. I looked across the table at Brendan and he smiled at me. I could tell he liked Scott a great deal.

"You know, Brendan almost went pro," I said.

"Yeah? Why didn't you?"

"I was injured near the end of my senior year. It ended my playing days."

"That must have been horrible."

"It was heartbreaking to get so close and then have my hopes dashed. The injury itself was no picnic, but the disappointment of not getting to play pro ball was what hurt. I got over the disappointment soon enough. I had always hoped to coach after my pro career, so I went straight to the second part of my dream. One good thing about not having a pro career was being able to remain with Casper. If I played pro ball, I would have been living in another city while he finished school here. Even after that, I wouldn't have had much time with him. Looking back, I think the way everything worked out is best."

"I wish I could say that about my life," Scott said. "My life is one big train wreck."

"I think life often puts us where we belong. Sometimes events which seem bad at the time, such as my football injury, are the universe's way of getting us where we need to be."

Scott shrugged.

"It's something to think about," said Brendan.

"I feel like life screws me over every chance it gets," Scott said.

"I can see why you feel that way. You have had a difficult life, but don't think you're stuck in that life. Casper and I both had some very rough times when we were young. When my parents discovered I was gay, they sent me to a conversion center against my will. I was dragged out of my home by police officers and held prisoner in that center. I was drugged and tortured there."

Scott's face paled. He looked at me and I nodded.

"What happened?"

"I escaped, and Casper and I ran away. We had nothing and went through some very rough times but eventually we ended up in a little town up north called Verona where we found a home and people to love us. Casper can tell you his own story sometime. His life was far more difficult than mine, but we ended up together and we've lived a wonderful life. I'm not saying our lives are without problems. There is no such thing as living happily ever after, but for the most part, we've been happy."

I smiled at Brendan. Scott looked at me and knew it was true.

"I figured you had a perfect life. I figured you were a popular jock in school with parents who were proud of you."

"Well I was a popular jock and my parents were proud of me until they discovered I was gay. Mom and I made amends a few years later, but my father and I never did. When he died, I didn't even go to his funeral because the dad I knew as a boy had ceased to exist the moment he put me in that center."

"Damn."

"Don't make the mistake of thinking everyone else has a perfect life. It's an easy mistake to make. I coached and taught in high school for years and some of the kids you would have thought had it all were dealing with serious issues. There was one boy who was handsome, extremely athletic, and very popular, but he had a heart defect and he knew he was going to have a short life. He died when he was seventeen. Everyone has problems, Scott. I'm not making light of your problems, but you are not alone."

Scott nodded. We were silent for several moments.

"This burger is really good," Scott said to break the silence.

"They're a step above the usual fast food burgers. When Brendan and I went to school here, there was a Burger King where The Globe is down at the other end of The Commons. We ate there all the time, but the Whoppers were not as good as the burgers from the Crimson Grill."

"They had Burger King back then?" Scott asked, mischievously.

"Yes, we had Burger King back then," I said.

"The burgers were cooked over an open fire. Grills hadn't been invented yet," Brendan said.

"Don't encourage him."

Brendan winked at Scott and he laughed.

"What do you two have planned after this?" Brendan asked.

"Bowling," Scott said, watching for Brendan's reaction.

"I don't know if I'm allowed to bowl with amateurs. It might affect my pro status," Brendan said.

"That's not what Casper told me! He said you're a horrible bowler."

"Bowling? Seriously?" Brendan asked, looking back and forth between us.

We nodded.

"I think the two of you just want to laugh at me. It's been a very long time, but okay."

After we finished eating, we walked the few steps to the Back Alley, the bowling alley that had been located at the end of The Commons as long as I could remember. For all I knew, it had been there since the 1930's. We rented shoes and Scott picked out a lane.

Scott began with a strike. I was able to take out seven pins and then it was Brendan's turn. Scott and I watched as his ball went into the gutter twice.

"Perfect!" Brendan said as if he was pleased.

"Perfect?" Scott said. "Your ball went in the gutter both times!"

"Exactly. Look at that. I didn't knock over a single pin. Perfect."

"You're supposed to knock down the pins!"

"Really?" Brendan said, acting surprised. "So you did that on purpose? I didn't want to say anything, but I thought you were really bad at this."

"I'm good at this. You really are a horrible bowler, just like Casper said."

"Hmm, and here I thought I bowled a perfect game that time back in college when I didn't hit a single pin."

Scott grinned. He knew Brendan was putting him on.

We continued bowling. Scott was an excellent bowler. I was very good. Brendan was terrible. He did knock down a few pins, but he could never manage to hit many.

"How are you holding the ball?" Scott asked. He examined Brendan's fingers in the ball. "Hmm, you're holding it right and you're doing everything else right. How can you possibly miss so many pins?"

"Everyone has a hidden talent, Scott."

"Yes, but they're usually good at something, not bad."

"Don't try to understand it, Scott. Brendan is good at all sports, except this one. Apparently the gods of bowling have it in for him."

"That's the answer! Bowling isn't a real sport," Brendan said.

"It's a sport," Scott said.

"If you can eat a hot dog while competing, it's not a sport. Try to think of a sport where it's possible to eat a hot dog while competing."

Scott concentrated for a few moments. "Diving."

"Diving?"

"Yeah, you can eat a hot dog on the way from the diving board to the water. It is necessary to eat it quickly because the bun gets very soggy if you don't finish before you reach the surface."

"Okay, you've already spent too much time with Brendan," I said. Scott laughed.

We bowled a couple more games before I needed to take Scott home. Scott was the victor of both and Brendan was the big loser. Scott had a great time and Brendan obviously liked him a great deal.

"I'll see you at home," Brendan said, giving me a hug. "It was nice to meet you, Scott. I hope to see you again soon." Brendan shook Scott's hand and headed out.

"He's truly that bad at bowling?" Scott asked when Brendan had departed and we headed out into The Commons and then outside.

"Oh yeah. That was not an act. Brendan is terrible at two things; bowling and cooking."

"Cooking?"

"I could tell you horror stories, like the time he tried to make scrambled eggs and ended up with a black sticky mass with egg shells in it. Then, there was time he managed to burn frozen lasagna to charcoal. Some of the stories are too gruesome to repeat. He's great on the grill, but in the kitchen he's scary."

Scott laughed. "I like him."

"I do too!"

I drove Scott home and then drove to the home Brendan and I shared.

"So what do you think of Scott?" I asked as I entered.

"He's a great kid. If you want to take him on as a foster son, I'm for it."

"Seriously? You don't want to discuss it? You weren't at all enthusiastic about the idea when we talked about it before."

"Seriously. I've been thinking about it since we first talked about him and after meeting him, I'm sure. I know he has problems and I know it will be difficult. There will likely be times I'm sorry I agreed, but I think we can help him. We are what that boys needs. I just plain like him, too."

I gave Brendan a hug. "I hoped I could convince you. I want him here with us. He's been shifted around for far too long. He needs us and maybe I need him too. You have your job, but all I do is take care of the house."

"That's quite a job in itself and you cook as well as run errands for me when I can't."

"I know, but I need something more."

"Now you can add foster dad to the list. I'll do my part, but you know my schedule. This will mostly fall on you."

"I raised three boys before and ran a farm. I can handle one."

"It's settled then. Get the ball rolling."

***

I parked the Prius in the lot on the east side the stadium. Scott and I got out.

"Excited?" I asked.

"Yes! I've never even been inside the stadium before."

We walked to the nearest entrance. I took out my card and unlocked the door. We made our way to a long hallway. Scott took in everything, gaping at the huge photos of IU players who had gone on to play pro ball. Soon, we came to a large set of glass doors that led directly onto the field. Practice was in session and the field was filled with players.

"Wow," Scott said as we stepped onto the field. "The players are so huge. This whole place is huge!" Scott turned in a circle, taking in the vast tiers of seats that went up and up, the press box, the suites & stadium club, and the Henke Hall of Champions.

We watched the players for a few minutes as they passed footballs back and forth, worked with tackling dummies, and ran scrimmages. There was action all over the field.

"There are so many players!"

"There are around 120."

"At Tri-North we had nineteen." Scott laughed, but then grew sad. "It sucked getting kicked off the team. I was good."

"I'm sure it was very hard, but that is the past. It's best to look to the future."

Brendan noticed us after a while and trotted over.

"Hey, I'm glad you could make it. I'll be busy with practice for a while, but I'll have Trey show you around. He's one of our quarterbacks, but he's getting over an injury so he isn't allowed to do anything strenuous for a few days." Brendan turned toward the stands on the other side of the fields, cupped his hands, and yelled. "Send Fitzgerald over!"

Another coach relayed Brendan's message and soon a player walked toward us.

"This guy is good. You'll see him play this fall," Brendan said, then turned to his player, "Trey, this is Casper, my partner, and this is Scott. I want you to give Scott the VIP tour. Show him everything, including the locker room."

"Sure thing, Coach."

"I'll catch up with you guys at the end of practice," Brendan said.

"Let's head inside," Trey said.

"What's that rock?" Scott asked as we crossed into the north end zone.

"That's Hep's Rock. It's a limestone boulder found in the practice field. It was moved here to the end zone and Coach Hoeppner started a tradition of every coach and team member touching The Rock before running onto the field for a game. The team enters the field on game days through the doors just behind it. Coach Hoeppner died of brain cancer and The Rock was renamed Hep's Rock."

"That's really cool," Scott said.

"Many people don't know it, but the Memorial Stadium is also known as The Rock. Let's go inside."

We entered the glass double doors into the vast weight room. I had been inside before when Brendan gave me my own tour, but Scott's eyes widened and his mouth dropped open. There were heavy-duty weight machines everywhere.

"This is fifty times the size of the school weight room!"

Trey grinned. "Yeah, it's impressive. My eyes bugged out of my head when I entered this room the first time. This is the athlete gym. There are others on campus for all the other students."

"Wow," Scott said. It was a word I would hear often during our tour.

Trey took us into the pressroom, showed us private tutoring rooms, the team meeting room (which looked like a lecture hall), and all through the vast complex that was the stadium. Scott was particularly interested in the locker room.

"I had no idea all this was here," Scott said.

"Most people don't. There is only a hint of it from the outside," Trey said.

Our tour continued and Scott was fascinated by everything. He spent a good deal of the time gazing at Trey, who was an impressive young man with broad shoulders and lots of muscle. Trey was wearing his practice uniform, which particularly impressed Scott. I think the idea that he was walking next to an actual college quarterback was almost overwhelming for him.

Practice was just ending when Trey returned us to the field. I seriously think he had shown us everything.

"Thank you so much. That was great!" Scott said.

"My pleasure," Trey said as Brendan approached.

"Thanks, Trey. Two more days and you can get back on the field. It won't be long now," Brendan said.

"Two days is an eternity. It was nice meeting you, Scott and Casper."

Trey departed.

"Let's get a better view of the field," Brendan said.

He led us inside, through the hallways, and up flights of stairs until we finally emerged in the Henke Hall of Champions, which we had toured a few minutes earlier. It was a vast space for public functions with showcases of artifacts connected with IU Athletes who had gone on to become famous.

We exited through the glass doors and stepped back out into the stadium, but now we were standing above the field, looking out over the seating at the north end zone. These were the good seats. It cost plenty to sit here during games. Brendan and I looked at each other. He nodded.

"Scott, Brendan and I want to talk to you about something," I said.

Scott's face paled. "Oh... you don't want to be my big brother anymore, do you? That's what this is about. You got me a tour of the stadium because you wanted to let me down easy."

"That's not it at all. Brendan and I would like to know what you think about becoming our foster son."

Scott's head jerked up and his eyes widened more than they had when we entered the athlete weight room.

"You mean it?"

"Yes. We know the foster home you have now is crowded and temporary. We would like you to come and live with us. We want to know what you think of the idea," I said.

In answer, Scott hugged me tightly around the middle and then buried his head in my chest. When he pulled away, he had tears in his eyes, but did not cry.

"I would love that," he said, then hugged Brendan too.

"There is one condition," Brendan said in a serious tone that made Scott stop smiling. "If you live with us, you don't smoke and you don't do drugs. None."

"I won't. I haven't done any drugs since I got arrested. I don't want to do that anymore. I'm trying real hard to quit smoking. I've cut down to only one cig every few days. I want to quit, so I'll stop completely before I come to live with you. I promise. I won't do any drugs and I won't smoke."

"Good. Then we've said enough about that."

"There will be lots of paperwork and inspections, so it won't happen right away," I said.

"I know. I've been through this before."

Sadly, that was all too true.

"We'll start the process tomorrow," I said.

"This has been the best day ever!" Scott said, coming back to life.

I gazed at Scott. His eyes were shining. I didn't think he could quite believe this was happening.

"I'm hungry. Who is up for Steak 'n Shake?" Brendan asked.

"Me!" Scott said. I nodded.

"Want to ride in my Corvette, Scott?"

"Yes! No offense to your Prius, Casper," Scott said.

I laughed. "I'll see you guys there."

I walked back to the Prius and then headed for the Steak 'n Shake on North College, the one nearest our home and the closest to the stadium. I arrived a short time later. Brendan and Scott were waiting on me.

We went inside and got a booth. A waitress took our drink orders and we browsed the menus.

"I'm getting a western barbeque and bacon burger," Brendan said.

"I want a Frisco melt," Scott said.

"I'm going to order a double Steakburger. How about a milkshake, Scott?"

"Good idea!"

Our waitress returned with our drinks, iced tea for Brendan and me and a Coke for Scott. We placed our orders, including a birthday cake shake for Scott.

"Do I get my own room?" Scott asked when our waitress had departed. "I don't mind sleeping on a couch if I don't."

"We have a nice bedroom for you. It's not large, but it will be all your own," I said.

"Awesome! I haven't had my own bedroom since I was little. I share a room with Nicholas now and it's small."

"We have a fenced in back yard too," I said.

"I can't wait."

"It will be a few weeks yet, I'm sure. It's not a simple process," I said.

"Yeah, but maybe they'll hurry since I'm an extra with my foster moms. They don't really have room for me."

"Trevor at Big Brothers & Big Sisters said Nicole and Megan were full up, but took you in anyway," I said.

"Yeah, they're nice, but... they're women. They don't understand boy stuff."

"We do have the advantage of once being boys ourselves, a few centuries ago," Brendan said.

"Just don't tell me that thing about having to walk five miles to school and ten miles back, uphill both ways, in the snow."

Brendan laughed. "Well, there goes that one."

"You will be walking to school since it's so close," I said.

"Someday, when I'm old, I can pretend it was really far."

Our food soon arrived and we kept talking. Scott was very excited. I was glad he knew how the process worked. I wished we could take him home with us immediately, but these things took time. Brendan and I needed time to prepare as well. It had been a long time since we'd raised a boy.

I began the process the next day. There was a load of paperwork, followed by home inspections, and unnecessary red tape. The entire process went smoothly, but seemed almost endless. Weeks passed before it was finished. The summer quickly slipped by and it was nearly time for Scott's freshman year to begin at North High School before he could come to his new home.

Chapter Eight
Scott

"Hey look, it's the quitter."

I turned. Dexter and Harley walked toward the bench where I was sitting outside the library.

"I didn't quit," I said.

"We had a great season, until you left. You ruined everything."

"It wasn't my choice to leave. I was kicked off the team and out of school. Remember?"

"Yeah, but it was your choice to become a druggie."

"I'm not a druggie."

"Hmm, he was busted for possession of drugs. That sounds like a druggie to me. Isn't that what it sounds like to you, Harley?"

"I don't do drugs anymore."

"Ha! Once a druggie, always a druggie."

I had never liked Dexter or Harley much. They tended to be jerks. They were my least favorite baseball teammates.

"Hey, I've got an idea. Why don't you two fuck off?" I said, setting my book down on the bench and standing up.

Dexter and Harley looked at each other. There were two of them, but I was probably the strongest boy in my grade. I figured I could take them both if they attacked me.

"Pfft! We don't have time for losers like you. That's what you are—a loser. Why don't you go shoot up and lay in a gutter somewhere," Harley said.

"Your opinion means nothing to me," I said flatly.

Harley snarled, but he and Dexter went on their way. I sat back down, opened the book I had borrowed from the library, and tried to lose myself in it gazing at the impressionist paintings. I especially like Monet and could hardly believe I had seen one of his paintings. I liked the way he painted water. I wish I could paint like he did in his painting *Bain à la Grenouillére*, whatever that meant.

I looked up from my book and gazed across Kirkwood Avenue. I was a loser. I was a great first baseman last spring and the reason we won so many games. I was the master at tagging guys out. After I left, the team didn't win a single baseball game. It was near the end of the season when I was kicked off, but we had a shot at a championship. I ruined that.

Maybe my parents sensed I was a loser. Maybe that's why they didn't want me. Many animals abandoned weak or inferior young. Maybe that's what happened to me, I was abandoned like a runt piglet or a deformed kitten. Maybe none of my foster parents ever kept me long because they discovered I was a loser. I wondered if Casper and Brendan would be different, or if they'd figure out I was loser and pass me on to my next foster family.

I sighed. I wished I was eighteen so I could set out on my own. Maybe I could get a job and my own place then. It would be a crappy place at first, I'm sure, but maybe someday I could have something better. Then again, the thought of being on my own was scary. Bloomington was reasonably safe, but even here they were dangers. I wasn't ready to be on my own. Maybe this time would be different. I hoped so. There weren't that many foster homes and it was hard to place a reject like me. I really thought Casper was going to tell me he didn't want to be my Big Brother anymore at the stadium. I almost could not believe he and Brendan wanted me for a foster son. I was not going to screw this up.

I closed my book, stood, and headed toward the farmer's market over on Morton Street. It was only 11 a.m. on a Saturday, so the market would still be going. I was more interested in the people than the market itself, but there were usually musicians performing for whatever money passersby would give them.

I walked through the town square, past the huge courthouse and then on. Soon, the market came into view. It was crowded as usual.

I strolled through the market, looking at tomatoes, squash, apples, peaches, flowers, and all kinds of other stuff. I tasted a sample of cheese, and watched the shoppers. I stopped to listen to the musicians. One was an old man playing a fiddle. He had a little puppet hooked up so that it played its fiddle as he did. There were three older teen boys playing guitars and singing. They were talented and also handsome. Another performer was a girl with down syndrome, who sang and danced. She wasn't especially good, but I admired her courage. Others obviously did as well because she had quite a bit of money in the box in front of her. If I had musical talent, I'd come and perform to get some cash too, but no one would give me money to sing. Perhaps I could get them to give me cash *not* to sing. The thought brought a smile to my lips.

I sat down, pulled out a sheet of paper and began to sketch a booth that sold eggplant, squash, and sunflowers. I tried to work like an impressionist, with rapid strokes to quickly get the scene down, but I only had a pencil with me. I sketched the booth and the vegetables first and then tried to capture a young couple as they browsed. They weren't there long, so that's where sketching quickly came in.

My attempt was sad, but then again I had never tried to draw like this before and I was using a pencil instead of paint. I thought I could do better with paint. Perhaps next week I'd come better prepared.

I took out another sheet of paper and placed it on top of the book I'd borrowed from the library and tried again. I didn't sketch quite as fast this time. The booth, squashes, and eggplants weren't going anywhere so I didn't have to be in such a rush. I picked up my pace when a small boy stopped and gazed at a large eggplant. I quickly sketched in his outline and the features of his face. He moved on after only a few moments, but I held his image in my mind and concentrated on sketching only him.

When I finished drawing the boy, I looked back toward the booth and worked on details. This sketch was turning out much better than the first. I definitely had to bring my paints and easel next time.

I kept working. I probably wasn't truly doing the impressionist style, which is what I'd set out to do, but the sketch was pretty good. I had always liked to draw, everything from comic strips to animals to landscapes. One of my art teachers told me I had talent, but I had to move again and switch schools after that.

I stiffened slightly when the woman in the booth came out and walked toward me. I hoped she wasn't mad because I'd been staring at her booth for so long. I thought about hiding my sketch as she came closer because I'd drawn her in the booth, but before I could decide she was beside me and looking down at my sketch.

"I had to come and see what you were drawing. That's wonderful."

"I was trying to draw like an impressionist.   I kind of got away from that."

"It's charming. Would you be insulted if I offered you $10 for it?"

"Uh... no. You really want to give me money for it?"

"Yes, I love it. Will $10 be okay?"

"Certainly."

"You must sign it," she said.

"Oh, I will." I did so as she reached into her belly bag and pulled out a ten. I handed her the drawing and she handed me the money.

"You're very talented. I'm going to frame this."

"Thank you."

"I need to get back to my booth. You should keep drawing. You could be a professional artist."

"I will. Thanks."

I was a bit overwhelmed as I sat there. No one had ever wanted to buy my art before. I seriously didn't think it was that good. I smiled. I had ten whole dollars now. That was a vast improvement on the thirty-five cents I had when I arrived.

The market was beginning to close up, so I headed out. I was tempted to take my cash and find someone to buy me cigarettes, but I had made a promise to Brendan and Casper. I wasn't living with them yet, but I had to quit smoking. I had rationed out my last pack so that I smoked only a single cigarette every three or four days. I ran out almost a week ago and I wanted one bad, but purchasing more would only making quitting harder.   I absolutely, positively had to quit so it would be stupid to waste my cash on what I should not buy anyway.

I was hungry so I headed for Taco Bell instead. The food there was cheap.   I could get something good and still have money left over.

Taco Bell was only a few blocks away. It was well after noon so there were only a few customers inside.   I ordered a $5 Chalupa Cravings Box, which came with a chalupa, two tacos, cinnamon twists, and a drink.

I sat in a booth so I could watch traffic on North Walnut Street as I ate. I took my time because I didn't have anything to do and as long as I sat there, I could get free drink refills. I had never before in my life eaten a lunch that I paid for with money I earned. I felt proud of myself. I was also very pleased that someone thought enough of my art to buy it!

The food was extra good. I started with Pepsi, but when my cup emptied I switched to Sierra Mist, then Gatorade fruit punch, and finally to Tropicana pink lemonade.

I took my time in Taco Bell. It wasn't busy, so no one cared if I lingered. I wasn't in a hurry to return to the overcrowded house. I wondered what having my own room would be like after sharing one for so very long. I wondered what living in a house with only two others instead of eight would be like too. It had to be an improvement. I surely wouldn't have to wait so long to get in the bathroom. More than once, I'd had to run outside and pee in the bushes because I couldn't hold it anymore. I'd probably miss my foster brothers and sisters a little at first, but only a little. I had always been an outsider in that house.

Things were going to be different when I moved in with Brendan and Casper. I was tired of being a loser. I wasn't going to let anyone talk me into doing drugs again, not even Blaze. That meant I had to stay away from him because that boy could probably talk me into jumping off the top of the parking garage I could see across the street. Splat! I wasn't going to smoke another cigarette either. I wanted one badly right now, but I wasn't going to give in to the craving. Smoking was stupid if I was going to be a serious athlete anyway. Perhaps, after a year or so of good behavior, I could get the ban lifted and play football and baseball again. I'd like to try swimming, soccer, and wrestling too. Actually, I'd like to try every sport. Damn! I wished I hadn't screwed everything up.

I sighed. There was no use in lingering over past mistakes. I had fucked up and now I was paying the price. I needed to learn from those mistakes and focus on what I had instead of what I did not. I couldn't wait to move in with Casper and Brendan.

Chapter Nine
Casper

Scott hugged Nicole and Megan.

"Thank you letting me live with you," he said.

"You're welcome. We enjoyed having you here. Don't cause your new foster dads any trouble. I mean it," Nicole said, pointing at him.

"I'll do my best." Scott turned to us. "I'm ready."

Brendan, Scott, and I walked to the Prius. Scott opened the back door and tossed his bag in. Brendan climbed in the passenger side and I slipped behind the wheel. Scott gazed at the bungalow as we pulled away. I couldn't tell if he was sad about leaving or not.

I drove north through town and then west on the bypass for a block and then turned right. We passed the Kroger and the small strip mall that included Subway and Avers Pizza and then entered a residential area. Soon, the skate park appeared on our right and as we turned the corner, the golf course. The whole trip took well under ten minutes.

Scott gazed eagerly out the window as I pulled into the driveway of our home.

"This is nice," he said as we got out.

With Brendan's salary as head football coach we could have afforded something much bigger, but we were tired of living in a too large home.

"I think you'll like it," I said.

We entered and the three of us walked to the bedroom Brendan and I had fixed up for Scott. There was a single bed, a dresser, desk & chair, and a small closet.

"This is awesome!" Scott said, taking in his bedroom, which was next to the room I shared with Brendan.

"It's your own private space. We took everything off the walls so you can put up your own stuff. We expect you to keep your room reasonably neat, so no trash and dirty clothes on the floor. I want to be able to vacuum in here," I said.

"I'll keep it picked up. I promise. Thank you."

Scott looked overwhelmed and also a little frightened, as if what he was seeing might suddenly disappear.

"There are hangers in the closet. We'll leave you alone so you can settle into your room," I said.

Brendan and I walked into the kitchen.

"Well, we've done it," Brendan said.

"Once again. Will we ever learn?" I asked and smiled.

"I hope not."

Scott stayed in his room for quite a while and then came out. Brendan was in the living room reading, but Scott joined me in the kitchen.

"That is one big back yard," he said, looking out the French doors.

"Yeah, I like the space, but wouldn't want it to be any larger," I said. "Are you getting hungry?"

"Yeah."

"We're going to have the neighbors over for a cookout. We're just grilling hot dogs. They're old friends of ours from high school."

"Do they have kids?"

"Yes, but they are older and don't live with them. They're names are Brandon and Jon."

"So they're a gay couple?"

Brendan laughed from the living room. "Yes!"

"Don't cause trouble, Brendan. No, they aren't gay. Brandon is a teacher and soccer coach at North. Jon does the same at South."

"Why do they live together? Are you sure they aren't a gay couple?"

Brendan laughed again.

"I'm sure. They are very good friends, best friends, although they love to bicker. They're very entertaining."

"It still seems odd. Hey, are there kids in this neighborhood?"

"Yes, I've seen kids out in surrounding yards. There are a lot that walk past the house, but they may not live here. They may be coming or going to the high school or the skate park."

"Cool."

"I'm going out to plug in the grill," Brendan said and stepped into the garage.

"I'll sure you'll make friends and you'll have your friends from Tri-North. They'll be going to North too."

Scott nodded, but seemed uneasy.

My cell phone rang. "Just a second," I told Scott, then answered.

"Casper, Jared and Mark stopped by. Mind if they come to the cookout?"

"Of course we don't mind, but Brandon, you live next door. Are you so lazy you couldn't come over and ask?"

"I think we both know the answer to that. Yes!"

"See you guys soon." I disconnected and looked back to Scott. "That was Brandon next door. We're having two extras for the cookout, Jared and Mark."

"I'll be surrounded by old guys."

"Jared and Mark are old from your point of view, but younger than the rest of us. They're both thirty-one."

"That's still pretty old."

"Everyone is old to you," I said, grinning.

"Well... yes."

"That's because you are very young. I know you don't feel like it, but you are. I was the same when I was your age. I felt like I was completely grown up. It wasn't until later that I realized I wasn't. The older I get, the more I realize I wasn't grown up even when I was thirty and forty. As old as I am, I'm probably not even grown up now. Perhaps none of us ever are."

"O-k-a-y," Scott said.

"Too much, huh?"

"A little. Damn, I need a cigarette."

"I know."

Scott raised an eyebrow.

"What?"

"I didn't expect you to say that. I expected you to tell me I don't need one or that I can't have one so I might as well forget it."

"Nicotine is a physical addiction. I've never smoked so I don't know what it's like, but I do know your body wants it. I can understand that you feel you need a cigarette because that's what your body and mind is telling you."

Scott eyed me curiously. "You're different from the other foster parents I've had. Some didn't care if I smoked. They only yelled at me if I took their cigarettes. Others hit me if they smelled cigarette smoke on me. My foster moms told me not to smoke, but they were too busy to do anything about it if they smelled smoke on me."

"Brendan and I will not allow you to smoke, but we won't hit you. That's not acceptable. Yelling doesn't accomplish much either. We made an agreement and we expect you to live up to it. It's as simple as that. I know it's hard, but there is nothing good about smoking."

Scott nodded. "I still need a cigarette. Keeping off drugs hasn't been so bad, but I constantly want a smoke. You probably think I'm stupid for ever starting."

"No. It's easy to get pulled in. You've made some bad choices, but we all do that. You haven't had anyone in your life that you can look to for guidance in a long time, so you're bound to make mistakes."

"I'm glad you don't think I'm stupid."

"I know you aren't, and Brendan and I expect you to do well in school."

"Oh, uh... I might be a little stupid!"

"Nice try."

Scott grinned. "That must be them," he said, looking out the French doors where Brandon, Jon, Jared, and Mark were stepping onto the patio.

"Yeah, we'll introduce you in a minute. Will you fill some glasses with ice while I grab up plates and other stuff we'll need?"

"Sure."

Scott and I worked together. I hoped being busy would help him keep his mind off cigarettes. I knew it wasn't easy to quit. Uncle Jack had once told me he smoked as a young man and even though he'd quit decades before, sometimes he still yearned for a smoke. I smiled then I thought of Jack. He would have liked Scott.

Brendan was pulling out more lawn chairs as Scott and I stepped out onto the patio. We placed everything on the glass top table.

"Everyone, I would like you to meet Scott. Scott, that's Brandon, Jon, Jared, and Mark."

100

"Believe nothing Brendan and Casper have told you about me," Brandon said.

"No, believe everything they told you about him, but nothing they told me about me," Jon said.

"Well, they said you were smart, handsome, and witty, but don't worry. I don't believe any of it," Scott said to Jon.

Everyone began laughing.

"I like you, Scott," Brandon said. "No one mess with this kid. He's sharp."

Jon crossed his arms and glared, but then he smiled.

Brendan began grilling hot dogs, while the rest of us poured ourselves iced tea, Coke, or Coke Zero and lounged in the lawn chairs.

"You have him trained well, Casper. I wish I could train Jon like that," Brandon said.

"The grill is Brendan's territory."

"At least he's good at something," Jon said.

"Hey, I'm good at everything, except cooking."

"And bowling," Scott said.

"Zip it, Scott," Brendan said, making Scott laugh.

"Oh yeah! I had forgotten about that. Brendan is bad at bowling and I mean *bad*. Have you witnessed that?" Brandon asked.

"Yeah, we went bowling on campus. He rarely hit a pin and he tried to claim he thought the goal of the game was to miss all the pins," Scott said.

"He must like you if he agreed to bowl with you."

Scott nodded.

"You play any sports, Scott?" Jared asked.

"Football and baseball."

"Those are good, but soccer is better."

"Ha! I don't think so," Scott said. "I do like soccer. I like all sports."

"Well, I guess you're okay if you like soccer," Mark said.

"I like it. I prefer football. I like knocking guys down."

"We did some of that in high school, but we got red carded," Jared said.

"Soccer is far superior to football," Jon said.

"I rarely agree with Jon, but he's right," Brandon said.

"Yeah, Casper told me you guys are soccer coaches." Scott eyed Brandon and Jon for a minute and then turned to me. "Are you sure they aren't a gay couple?" he said.

Jared spewed the Coke he was drinking and Mark began to laugh. I saw Brendan grinning and trying to hide it.

"Did you put him up to this?" Brandon asked me.

"No. I told Scott about you two and he thought you sounded like a gay couple."

"They aren't handsome enough to be gay," Brendan said.

"Hey, we are so, at least I am!" Brandon said.

"You sure you're not a gay couple?" Scott asked. "I mean, it's totally cool. No one cares about that now."

"If I was gay, I could do much better than him," Jon said, pointing to Brandon.

"You would be lucky to have me!"

"You'll have to get used to Brandon and Jon. They are known for having totally pointless arguments," I said.

"Our dads really aren't a gay couple, but we are," Jared said, taking Mark's hand.

"Hmm, so they're your dads?"

"Yeah, Jon is my dad and Brandon is Mark's."

Scott nodded, but I could tell he was trying to work it all out and make sense of it. I could understand his confusion. I could see where he could easily confuse Brandon and Jon for a gay couple. If they were, that would make their sons dating rather odd.

"Everyone come and get hot dogs," Brendan said.

Soon, we sat around eating hot dogs grilled to perfection, potato salad, Cool Ranch Doritos, salt & vinegar chips, and brownies with icing.

"I want everyone to know I cooked everything today," Brendan said.

"Yeah, Kroger makes great potato salad," Brandon said.

"Remember our wiener roasts on the Selby Farm," Jon said.

"Watch out, you're about to hear about the *old* days," Jared warned Scott, who smiled.

Jon glared, but then continued. "Remember when that chicken came up behind Dorian and he screamed like a girl?" Brendan, Jon, Brandon, and I laughed.

"Wait. Are you talking about Dorian Calumet?" Scott asked.

"Yes. The way he reacted you would have thought a bear was after him. We razzed him about that for years. I still do by email now and then," Jon said.

"You would," Brendan said.

"Dorian is awesome! Casper introduced us."

"Scott is a big fan," I said.

"To us, he's just Dorian the chicken boy," Brandon said.

"Maybe we should sell that story to the Enquirer," Jon said.

"Don't do that," Scott said.

"He's kidding. We all love Dorian," I said.

"I've seen all his movies."

"He is extremely talented. He always was," Brandon said.

"Yeah, the school auditorium was always packed when he was in a play," I said.

"And he was in every play," Jon said.

"That must have been something to see him before he was famous," Scott said.

"You do any acting?" Mark asked.

"No, not me. I just do sports."

"That's pretty much the way we were in high school. We were all about soccer and didn't care much for anything else," Mark said.

"We were very competitive with each other. We didn't even like each other at first," Jared said.

"We actually hated each other at first, but that changed later."

"It must have," Scott said.

"The biggest adjustment was mine. I had to get used to a Deerfield in the family," Brandon said.

"I thought the biggest adjustment was mine, getting used to a Hanson," Jon said.

Scott laughed.

I noticed that Scott didn't seem to think anything about Jared and Mark being gay and a couple, just as he accepted Brendan and me. Even his amazement that Brandon and Jon weren't a couple wasn't prejudiced in any way. I wondered if that was because Scott was gay or bi, or merely because sexual orientation wasn't a big deal to the younger generation. He had said that no one cared about that anymore, so perhaps it was the latter.

"This is cool. I didn't think hanging out with old guys would be much fun," Scott said.

"Who are you calling old?" Brandon asked.

"You. You're our age. You're old. Get over it," Brendan said.

"We aren't old, eighty is old."

"I bet when you reach eighty you'll say ninety is old," I said.

"That's the plan."

"No offense, I like old guys. They're interesting," Scott said earnestly.

Jared and Mark tried not to laugh, but couldn't help themselves.

"I like you, Scott," Jared said.

"You'll be our age next week, just you wait and see," Jon said.

"The elderly have a strange concept of time," Mark said to Scott, who grinned.

"You're not too old for me to bend you over my knee! Well, I guess you are," Brandon said.

"Like you ever spanked your kids," Brendan said.

"There were days..." Brandon said.

"He's talking about my brothers. I was a perfect angel," Mark said.

"Sure you were, Mark," I said.

"Did you guys ever smoke?" Scott asked.

"Never," Jared said.

"I tried it once, nearly coughed to death, and never tried it again," Mark said.

"This is news," Brandon said.

"Okay, I wasn't quite an angel, but close."

"I've quit, but it's hard," Scott said. "I want a cigarette right now."

"I'm sure it's extremely hard, but think of the money you'll save over your lifetime. I'll tell you something I did. I wanted a vintage 1987 Cutlass Supreme. I found one a few years ago for $15,000 and I bought it with the money I would have used on cigarettes," Jared said.

"I was smoking a pack a week, which isn't too bad, but that is a lot of money. They're about $8 a pack, times 52... wow, that's over $400 a year."

"Yeah and over a period of several years it adds up into the thousands. Think of what you could buy with that."

"I like thinking of it that way."

"I'll tell you what, in addition to your allowance, which we haven't discussed yet, I'll put $10 in a savings account for you every week you don't smoke. When you're eighteen, it's yours," Brendan said.

"Seriously?"

"Seriously. I wouldn't have said it if I didn't mean it."

"Thanks! Put it in one of those online savings accounts that pay the best interest," Scott said.

We talked for quite a while after we finished eating. Jared and Mark headed out, and then Brandon and Jon departed for their home next door.

"What did you think of the guys?" Brendan asked as we carried things inside.

"Brandon and Jon are funny. It's still hard to believe they aren't a couple, but I do believe it. I like the way they argue. Jared and Mark seem cool. I like that none of them treated me like a kid."

"At the risk of treating you like a kid, we need to go buy your school clothes and supplies tomorrow," I said.

"Ack! No! Don't say that word!"

"You mean school?"

"Yes! Nooo!"

Brendan and I laughed. We knew Scott was putting on an act.

"I always loved school when I was a teacher. I enjoyed tormenting my students and giving them lots of homework, especially before weekends and holidays," Brendan said

"I knew it! I knew teachers were evil."

"I think it's rather cruel that the back to school sales start in July. What kid wants to be reminded of school?" I said.

"Exactly," Scott said. "I actually don't mind going back to school too much. Being banned from athletics is what sucks. That's the worst part of getting busted, even worse than Juvie and that was plenty bad."

"All actions have consequences. I kicked players off my teams for using drugs and would do it now. You are making a positive change in your life, Scott. You're leaving drugs behind. I'll look into the situation and see what I can do," Brendan said.

"Thanks!" Scott said with genuine gratitude. "If you can get the ban lifted, I promise I'll be an angel!"

"Never make promises you can't keep, Scott. No one can be quite that good."

"Well, I'll come as close as I can. Can I watch TV?"

"Of course you can. Use the headphones behind the TV. We always use them so the sound doesn't disturb anyone else in the house," I said. "We don't have cable, but we do have Amazon Prime. The remotes are in the drawer of the table between the chairs."

"Sweet."

I resisted telling Scott how to operate the TV and headphones. He was fourteen. I would probably be going to him for help with such things.

Scott watched TV most of the rest of the evening. It was odd having a boy in the house, but it reminded me of the days when Clint, Cameron, and Conner were young. I was sure Brendan and I would adjust.

We all stayed up until 11 p.m. Brendan and I would have to think about what time we wanted Scott in bed once school began, but for now it didn't matter much. I knocked on Scott's doorframe before Brendan and I turned in.

"I wanted to say 'good night.' Did you brush your teeth?"

"Yeah."

I looked around Scott's room. He had almost no possessions.

"You need a computer for school," I said.

"Really?"

"Yes, and a printer. We'll have to add that to the list. You and I are going to do a lot of shopping tomorrow. Don't worry;

I'll let you pick out your own clothes. I'm sure I'm out of touch with what high school kids are wearing now."

"Thanks," Scott said. I could hear the gratitude in his voice.

I crawled into bed with Brendan a few minutes later. He kissed me and almost immediately fell asleep. Coaching football was not easy and I was sure he was tired. Tomorrow night, I'd likely drift off to sleep instantly after a day of shopping with Scott.

I couldn't hear Scott in his room, but I was aware of his presence. The house had never felt empty and yet now that Scott was here, I think it would without him. I hoped everything worked out.

Scott was still in bed when Brendan and I woke up the next morning. I always got up to have breakfast with Brendan and see him off to work. He put in a full day and more, but I was accustomed to that. It was the same at VHS.

This morning, I made cinnamon toast. We sat and talked quietly while we ate our toast and drank iced tea. After we finished, I hugged and kissed Brendan and then he departed.

I was putting the plates in the dishwasher when Scott walked into the kitchen wearing only boxers. I was struck by how well built he was for his age, even more than I'd thought previously. He was quite muscular and defined.

"How about some breakfast? I'll make you cinnamon toast."

"I've never had cinnamon toast."

"I think you'll like it. If you want to shower, the towels and washcloths are in the linen closet right by the bathroom."

"Yeah, I like to shower before breakfast."

"I'll wait until you're finished to begin your toast. It doesn't take long."

Scott returned a few minutes later with damp hair, this time wearing shorts and a t-shirt. Both were quite worn. The boy needed clothes.

I prepared Scott's cinnamon toast and then he sat down at the table to eat.

"This is great! I think I have had this before. I think my grandmother used to make it, but she died when I was little."

"My grandmother used to make it too. She lived to be a hundred."

"Wow."

"Are you registered for school yet?"

"Yes."

"Okay, I thought of that last night. After you finish breakfast, we'll head to the mall. What kind of computer do you think you'd like, a PC or a Mac?"

"Well, I'd like a Mac, but they're expensive so a PC will be fine. I've never had my own computer, but I've used them at school."

"I think we'll go to the Mac store on campus. I can use Brendan's discount."

"You guys are too nice to me. I don't deserve all this," Scott said, looking down at his lap.

"Yes, you do." Scott looked up. He looked a little teary, but nowhere near ready to cry.

"No one else has ever thought so. My parents didn't. The women at my last home were good to me, but there wasn't much money to go around. I didn't mind that. I liked that they were kind to me."

"They seemed like a nice couple."

"They are. I miss them... but I'm glad to be here," Scott added quickly.

Scott finished his toast.

"One rule we have here is to clean up after yourself. Always put your dirty dishes in the dishwasher," I said.

Scott nodded, put his plate in the dishwasher, and then disappeared into the bathroom. He soon reemerged.

"Are you ready to head out?" I asked.

"Yeah."

We locked up and walked out to the Prius. Ten minutes later, we entered College Mall on the east side. In my college days, the Sears was next to the entrance, but it was long gone. Sears was a thing of the past.

"Where would you like to shop for clothes?" I asked as we walked through the mall.

"Target is good or we can go to Goodwill. I'm fine with secondhand."

"There's nothing wrong with either, but I was thinking about something that will last longer. See what interests you as we walk through the mall."

I subtly watched Scott as we passed one store after another. I thought he might be into Hot Topic, but instead he gravitated toward American Eagle. He gazed at it almost longingly, but didn't make a move in that direction.

"Let's look in American Eagle," I said.

"Really?"

"Yeah. They have nice stuff, unless it's not your thing," I said.

"No, that's great!"

We entered. I could tell Scott was going to be shy about buying clothes and that I'd need to encourage him.

Scott was most interested in t-shirts, but eyed the boxer briefs in different colors too. I thought we might start there.

"You definitely need underwear," I said. "What colors do you like or should I ask what colors do you not like?"

"No pink. Otherwise, I like them all. Teal is my favorite color."

"What size?"

"Medium."

I began picking up boxer briefs in every color but pink. Scott looked overwhelmed.

"I don't need so many."

"You can never have too much underwear. How about shirts? Start picking some out."

Scott examined the shirts carefully. He found two with a lot of teal in them.

"Can I get two?" he asked.

"I think twelve would be better. Do you think I want to do laundry *every* day?" I teased. "You should get some polo shirts as well for more dressy occasions."

"Twelve? Seriously?"

"Yes. Get to it. We have a lot of shopping to do."

Scott did so and soon had a dozen t-shirts picked out. We moved to polos. He picked out one that was teal and another that was hunter green.

"Jeans and shorts," I said when he'd finished.

We spent well over an hour in American Eagle. Our pile on the counter was quite large. By the time we finished, I had Scott well clothed, at least until winter, but we'd purchase winter clothing for him when the time came.

Scott's eyes widened at the total and he swallowed hard. I don't think anyone had ever spent so much money on him. We headed straight to the car with our purchases. There were so many bags and they were so large that they were all the two of us could carry.

"We should hit Target next. You'll need deodorant and other such things," I said as we once more headed inside.

"This is like Christmas, but Christmas as I dreamed about it—not as it ever was."

"I thought kids hated clothes for Christmas."

"Hey, I'm fourteen. I'm not a kid."

"My mistake. When you hit sixty, everyone under thirty seems like a kid. It's one of those old people things." Scott grinned.

We were in Target quite a while purchasing necessities and school supplies for Scott. It was time for lunch before we departed with several bags.

"Where would you like to eat lunch?"

"Can we go to KFC?"

"Of course."

We added the Target bags to the others in the back of the Prius and then drove the short distance to KFC, which was just across the street. We both ordered boxes, Scott's with chicken strips and mashed potatoes and mine with a breast and slaw. We soon sat at a table.

"I love KFC," Scott said.

"It is good. I rarely bother to fry chicken. It's such a mess and this is better. In college, Brendan and I had an apartment just up the street. We used to walk here."

"They had KFC back..."

"If you say, 'the olden days' I'm going to smack you with a wet nap."

Scott laughed. "I don't think that would hurt much. I was going to say, 'back then.'"

110

"That's better. Yes, KFC was here back then, it goes way back. It feels good to sit down for a while. Shopping is hard work."

"Yeah. It's going to take me forever to put everything away when we get home," Scott said.

"You have your work cut out for you."

"When I have to leave someday, do I get to take my clothes with me?" Scott asked, chewing his bottom lip.

"Everything Brendan and I buy you is yours to keep, but who says you have to leave someday? Well, you will go off to college, but you won't have to leave."

"I just... I figured you'd get tired of me. I tend to get in trouble. I try not to, but trouble finds me. I'm going to try my best, but..."

"Let me tell you about Cameron..." I said.

The tale of Cameron's boyhood took up the rest of lunch and continued on the short journey to campus. I smiled while I related some of Cameron's exploits, even those that were the cause of some of my gray hairs.

"How did you keep from smacking the crap out of him?" Scott asked.

I laughed. "There were times I had to walk away for a while to maintain control. That boy could be infuriating. His older brother pounded him a few times. Cameron was absolutely certain Brendan and I would grow sick of him and send him away. It took him a long time to realize that wasn't going to happen.

"I know that you've just began to live with Brendan and me, but you don't have to fear us sending you away to another foster home. I understand that you may find that difficult to believe. You haven't been around very many adults you can trust and you have no reason to think we're any different. In time, I hope you'll come to understand that we are different. We won't abandon you."

Scott looked like he very much wanted to believe me, but I knew that belief would take time.

We entered the IMU by way of the north entrance, walked through the Commons, past the food court and Sugar & Spice and entered the bookstore, where the Apple store was located.

"What do you think about a laptop? You might want to take it to school or the library sometimes."

"A laptop would be great."

I relied on Scott and the expertise of the college boys working in the Apple Store to set Scott up with what he needed. I knew computers well, but I wasn't acquainted with what a teen might need in one.

We departed half an hour later with Scott toting his new laptop.

"I can't believe I have my own laptop. This is incredible! I've always had to share old computers when there was a computer at all. This is like... like driving a junker that is falling apart and suddenly getting a Ferrari."

"Well if you think you're getting a Ferrari, forget it," I said, grinning. Scott laughed.

We headed back home. Scott and I carried all his things into his room and then I left him alone to set up his laptop and organize all his stuff. I knew he both wanted and needed some time to himself. I was certain that adjusting to his new home was not an easy task.

I hoped Scott would grow to feel at home here. He had been moved from one foster home to another for too many years. There was no stability in his life and nothing he could count on. I had tried to explain that he could count on Brendan and me, but I knew that telling him wasn't enough. He had to learn it for himself.

Chapter Ten
Scott

I looked up from the kitchen table as Brendan entered, trying and failing to hide my apprehension.

"How did it go?" Casper asked.

"You are no longer banned from playing sports in the Monroe County School System," Brendan said, looking at me.

"Yes!"

"You are on probation. Any drugs at all and you're out permanently and you will likely be randomly tested for drugs. I had a long talk with the principal and with the head football coach. When you start at North you'll be starting with a clean slate, except for the probation. This is your second chance. You will not get a third. If you repeat the mistake you made in middle school, there is nothing I'll be able to do to get you back on the football team or on the baseball team in the spring."

"I won't screw things up this time. I won't touch any drugs. I promise," I said and meant. "I won't even take a Tylenol."

"You still have to earn a spot on the team. Open tryouts are after the first day of school."

"I'll get a spot. I'm good. I was the quarterback of my 8th grade team." Brendan's right eyebrow went up.

"You could try a new sport," Casper said.

"Oh no. Football is *the* fall sport. I probably play baseball in the spring, unless I think something else is more interesting, but I have to play football. It's the best!"

"I have to agree," Brendan said.

"I thought you might," Casper said.

"Can I go to the skate park? I have very few days of freedom left," I asked.

"After supper," Casper said.

"I'm not that hungry." It wasn't true, but I was so hyped up I needed to get out and do something physical.

"After supper."

"Grr."

"We're having spaghetti. It's nearly ready. All I have to do is toast the garlic bread."

I endured the wait. The spaghetti did smell good and when we began to eat at the kitchen table, I discovered I was hungrier than I thought. Skating could wait for a few minutes.

"Now can I go?" I asked when I'd finished.

"Yes."

"Thanks!"

I hurried into my room, grabbed my skateboard, pads and helmet and headed out.

I had lived with Brendan and Casper for less than a week. Doing so still felt weird, but good. I could not believe all the money they had spent on me. Just yesterday, they had taken me to Peralta's Bike & Skate shop and bought me a skateboard, helmet, and pads. I had rushed straight to the skate park when we got home. The place was deserted, which kind of sucked, but also didn't because I hadn't skated in a long time and needed a little practice.

So far, living with Brendan and Casper was great. Casper had been my Big Brother for several weeks. I wasn't quite ready to let my guard down, but he seemed cool. Neither he nor Brendan had made any moves on me. They were just as nice to me as they had been before I became their foster son. I didn't especially distrust them or expect them to have an ulterior motive, but I've learned it's best to be wary. So far, they were exactly as they seemed. I sure hoped nothing changed. Everything was going so well it was almost scary. What if the universe was giving me all this because it knew something bad was coming?

I had to put that thought out of my mind. Instead, maybe the universe had realized how much my life sucked ass and decided to give me a break. I certainly hoped so.

I felt like a huge weight had been lifted from my shoulders. I almost couldn't believe Brendan had been able to get my ban lifted. I absolutely had to keep from fucking things up this time. I had to avoid the drugs and to do that I needed to avoid my old drug buddies. That wouldn't be the easiest thing to do. Avoiding Blaze would be especially hard. He and I did things together that... well, I really wanted to do again.

It didn't take long to walk to the skate park. That was one of the many cool things about my new foster home. I had never been so close before, not that it mattered during the last year and a half. My crappy board had busted so I had to skate on a borrowed board when I could get one. My new board was sweet!

114

There were three guys skating as I approached. They were older, college age, but didn't look likely to give me trouble. Skaters were generally cool with each other, but there were exceptions.

I put on my helmet and pads and began skating on the basketball court first. I was still getting my skills back. At one time, I'd been good, but I wasn't up to my old level and I was still growing accustomed to my new board.

I eyed the older guys as I skated. They were definitely college age. One was even wearing an IU tank top. He had nice muscles. My eyes were mostly drawn to the shirtless one with spiky black hair. He was the best built of the three and had muscles in all the right places. I wanted to look like him and yearned to run my hands all over his body.

After I warmed up, I entered the actual skate park through the gate. The older guys nodded to me. They were skating in the big bowl, which was the largest in the entire state, so I headed for the bigger area to the right and did my thing.

I never lacked for confidence on a board, but I grew bolder as I skated. Skating always made me feel like a bad ass. I needed to keep that in check. Feeling like a bad ass often got me in trouble. I did not want to screw up what I had going in my new foster home.

I skated for a few minutes and then walked over to the college boys, eyeing their bodies in the least obvious way possible. The shirtless one nodded to me.

"Hey, I'm Cade."

"Scott," I said.

"That's Mike and Sly," he said pointing. "Want to join us?"

"Sure! I mean, sure," I said, toning down my excitement.

Cade moved back and nodded toward the bowl. I took off, shot down into the bowl, then up the far rim, turned while airborne and skated back down the side. Cade, Mike, and Sly all joined me in the bowl. It was more challenging with other skaters, but more fun too.

I had a blast skating with the big guys. They seemed impressed with my abilities. I'm a great skater if I do say so myself and I was getting my skills back fast. I'll admit I still have plenty to learn. Every skater can always improve.

I was amazed with Cade's ability to ride the top of the ledge. It's something I hadn't quite mastered. He saw me watching him intently and gave me a few pointers. It allowed me to check him out from close up. He had the most amazing muscles. I yearned to reach out and touch them, but controlled myself. You don't just go and touch another guy like that.

We skated until dark. I knew I should probably go home, but Brendan and Casper knew where I was and I couldn't tear myself away. I almost never got to spend time with college boy skaters. I was in Heaven.

Eventually, Cade, Mike, and Sly decided to leave. Cade gave me a fist bump and I couldn't help but check out his sexy chest once more. Sly caught me at it. I swallowed hard, but all he did was wink as they departed.

I walked home thinking about Cade. Being near him made me breathe harder. Sometimes, when he looked at me, I thought I detected a hint of attraction, but why would he be attracted to a boy like me? If he wanted to touch my body I would have let him. All the time I was near him, a part of me wished he would touch me, even while another part feared he would.

I put all that out of my mind. I hoped I could find other skater friends in the future, maybe even some regular buddies. My time for skating would be limited. School was about to start so I'd be busy. I was determined to make the football team and excel at it once I did.

***

I walked into the kitchen on Monday morning to find Casper cooking breakfast.

"Mmm, pancakes," I said.

"I thought you deserved something special for your first day of school."

"I love pancakes."

Brendan entered, pulling on his shirt. I got a glimpse of his stomach. He had some serious abs! Even wearing a shirt, he was obviously muscular, but this was the first time I'd seen any part of his bare torso. I didn't realize he was ripped. I'd never seen a guy his age with a body like that. Most were flabby or fat. I wondered if it was because he was gay.

"Oh, pancakes," Brendan said.

"You two get your drinks and sit down. They're almost done."

Soon, we were all seated with plates of pancakes and bacon and iced tea in cobalt blue tumblers. Brendan and Casper used real butter, which made it extra good.

"Are you excited about your first day of high school?" Brendan asked.

I gave him my "please" look. "Is anyone ever excited about the first day of school?"

Brendan laughed. "I guess not. Let me alter my question. Are you excited about football tryouts?"

"I can't wait. I know high school football is tougher. Middle school football is kid's stuff compared to it."

"It's more advanced, but your past experience will be very valuable."

"I intend to make the team."

"I'm sure you will."

I smiled. Brendan meant it. He had faith in me. I didn't know if anyone had ever had faith in me before.

"So what do you have planned while I'm working and Scott is at school?" Brendan asked Casper.

"You know me. I'll lounge around, nap, and watch TV."

"Yeah right. What will you really be doing?"

"Laundry, mowing, errands..." Casper continued with a long list.

"That's what I thought. Hey, maybe Scott will switch with you. He can do all that and you can go to school."

"Suddenly, school seems like fun," I said.

Breakfast was incredible. I had never had a foster home where someone actually made pancakes. The closest I came was living with Nicole and Megan. They microwaved frozen pancakes, which weren't bad, but were nothing like Casper's.

When we finished, Brendan departed for the IU campus and I brushed my teeth. I also made sure to get my hair just right. First impressions are important. Most people make up their mind about you in the first seven seconds.

I checked myself out in the mirror and smiled. I actually looked good. Never before in my life had I worn new clothes. Before Casper and Brendan became my foster dads, everything I wore was second hand and often not in the best shape. I remember one foster home where they actually tried to get me to wear a pink My Little Pony shirt. I refused.

Today, I was wearing khaki shorts, new, cool sneakers, and an IU football t-shirt Brendan had brought home for me. I looked like a college boy. Well, I guess not. I was fourteen and too short for a college boy, but I looked good.

"I'm leaving," I said when I walked into the kitchen with my backpack slung over my shoulder.

"Have a great day and good luck with tryouts," Casper said.

"I don't need luck. I'm good," I said then grinned.

"Okay, Mr. Confidence. I'll see you after tryouts."

"Bye."

I headed out the front door and walked north up the sidewalk. North High School wasn't far away. It wasn't real close, but I figured I could walk there in fifteen minutes. I was glad I didn't have to ride a stupid bus.

Cascades Golf Course was on my right the entire way, even when North Kinser Pike turned sharply to the left. I passed one nice home after another. Fritz Terrace was a really nice neighborhood, the nicest I had ever lived in.

North looked big when it came into view, a lot bigger than it had when I came to register. It was a lot busier too. There were buses, cars, and kids walking. It was as if all of Bloomington was entering the doors.

I did not know my way around. I didn't know the teachers. I didn't know how things worked here. I didn't know most of the students. All the 8th grade students from Tri-North would be here, but we were only a small part of the total population. There were students from Tri-North I did not want to see either. I was trying hard to make a new start and I couldn't hang out with my old friends because I knew they'd want to smoke, get high on hydros, and get into mischief. I was also not excited by the thought of seeing any of my old baseball teammates. They did not think highly of me.

All that went out of my mind when I spotted *him*.

I didn't know his name, in fact, I had never seen him before, but he was hot and not just any kind of hot, he was my kind of hot. He was about my age. His dark hair was super short on the sides with a Mohawk about three or four inches tall running over the top of his head. He was very good-looking, obviously had a nice body and instead of the punk look one might expect with a guy wearing a Mohawk, he was dressed smartly in an open pale green button-down shirt with a tight white shirt underneath. He wore somewhat tight jeans and nice work boots. The whole effect was super sexy.

He was out of sight in moments, but he was permanently etched in my mind. I had to meet him.

I continued on my way to the lockers. I found mine with little difficulty and opened it on the first try. We were issued books in our classes, so I pulled out a notebook and hung my backpack in my locker.

I felt small as I walked through the hallways to my first class. At Tri-North, I was one of the big 8th graders. Now, I was a freshman and there were guys here much bigger than me. I spotted a few that I figured were football players or wrestlers. They were really big. I was suddenly less confident about making the team, but I was sure as hell gonna try.

Classes didn't seem all that different. I was an okay student and made pretty good grades, but I had never put out too much effort. Why bother? I knew I was ultimately going nowhere. I was destined to stand behind a counter and ask, "Would you like fries with that?" Now, things had changed. Casper had mentioned college as if it was a foregone conclusion I would attend. Brendan and Casper were different from all my other foster parents. They were from a different world. They acted as if they were going to keep me around forever.

Don't get your hopes up. You're only their foster son. You know what that means. You're expendable. When you start screwing up, they'll get tired of you quick enough.

I willed the little voice in my head to shut up. I wasn't going to screw up—not this time.

When my lunch period arrived, I stepped into the cafeteria trying to appear more confident than I felt. Since I was avoiding my old friends, I had nowhere to sit. It was a bad situation, especially on the first day of school. I didn't want to look like a loser who had no friends.

I moved through the line, getting hungrier by the second. By the time I walked out with my chicken drummies, potato wedges, carrots, fruit cocktail, and chocolate chip cookie, I was hungry enough I thought I might even eat the carrots.

"Watch it, freshman!" said a boy twice my size as he pushed past me on the way to a table.

I avoided that table, but made my way to another where the kids were more or less my age. I sat down with them as if I belonged and nodded. No one gave me any trouble. Maybe they even thought I was a sophomore. I had more muscles than most freshmen, although the guy who yelled at me sure pegged me for one.

I concentrated on eating since no one was talking much. I didn't know any of these kids. I made sure not to be too friendly. Friendliness could be mistaken for weakness.

As I sat there, I became determined to make some new friends and find myself a table where I belonged. With any luck, I would have a place among the jocks.

During the afternoon, I caught sight of Felix and Ace, two of my former toking buddies, but I didn't spot Blaze until nearly the end. He didn't see me, luckily, because I feared what would happen if I looked into his eyes. It was Blaze who taught me how to smoke pot. It was Blaze who sold me hydros and the powdery drug that sent me to the hospital. Blaze was most definitely trouble, especially now that I wanted and needed to get away from all that. It was going to be difficult to resist him. Blaze had taught me other things too and the mere sight of him made my penis stiffen in my shorts.

I pushed Blaze out of my mind as best I could and continued with my day until, at last, it was time for tryouts.

I won't bore you with the details of tryouts because they're all the same. It was mostly skills tests with some scrimmages thrown in. By the time it was over I was confident I had proven I could pass, receive, and block. I had also proven my strength by holding my own against older guys. If the coaches here were truly giving me a second chance, I would surely make the team. My fear was that they weren't sincere and that my past would ruin the new future I was trying to create.

A few of the guys on my middle school team tried out too, but they seemed unsure about me and made no effort to be friendly. Everyone at Tri-North knew I'd been kicked off the baseball team, suspended from school, and sent to Juvie. I was officially stamped a loser and it was going to take time to get past that.

I walked home alone, partially because of my isolation, but mostly because most students rode a bus. North was huge so kids came in from a large area, even way out in the country.

Walking home, even alone, was much preferable to riding a bus. School buses were too loud and the city buses took too long to get anywhere. I could easily be home in the time it took to wait for a bus to arrive.

I liked my new neighborhood. Most of the houses were well kept and all of them had fenced in yards. Directly across Kinser Pike, the green grass of Cascades Golf Course made it look like a park. The fifteen-minute walk home was quite pleasant.

"Hey, Scott. How was school?" Casper asked from the kitchen as I walked in the front door.

"Fine."

"Nope. One-word answers are not allowed. Let's try this again. How was school?"

I grinned slightly. "Classes weren't bad. I had nowhere to sit at lunch so I ate with kids I don't know. Football tryouts were great. Some of the guys trying out were huge, but I think I still have a good shot at making the team. If I do, I'll sit with the team at lunch."

"That's a much better answer. I'm glad tryouts went well."

"How was your day?" I asked.

"Great." I crossed my arms and glared. Casper laughed. "Believe it or not, I was busy all day cleaning, running errands, paying bills, and taking care of all the details no one thinks about but must be done. It was not an exciting day, but it was productive."

"That's a much better answer," I teased. "I'm starving."

"Supper won't be for a couple of hours yet, so you'd better grab something from the refrigerator. Don't stuff yourself. I'm grilling squash and making fried potatoes and cooked apples for supper."

"Squash? Who grills squash?" I asked, wrinkling my nose.

"Wait until you try it. I brush it with olive oil and butter and add a few herbs. You will love it."

"I don't know about that."

"Hey, I said you will love it," Casper said as if it was an order, but I knew he was joking.

"Okay, I'll love it... even if it's horrible!"

I grabbed a leftover chicken leg and a huge dill pickle from the fridge.

"I'll be in my room. My sadistic teachers all made assignments today."

"Hey, give them a break. They've gone all summer with no kids to pick on," Casper said. "Do you know how rough that must be for them?"

I smiled. Casper wasn't at all like any of the other foster parents I'd had in the past.

Brendan and Casper had Amazon Prime, which gave me access to tons of music. I turned on my playlist and began my homework in my room. Most people thought I wasn't very smart. Okay, I did do some stupid things, but that didn't mean I was dumb. Most people wrote me off as a druggie and they hadn't always been wrong about that, but my grades were usually good. If I made the team, I had to keep my grades up to play. I also didn't want to screw things up in my new foster home, so I was going to make more of an effort than I had in the past. That was my real problem. I had never tried that hard before. I put in only the minimum effort necessary to be eligible to play sports. I had to do better. Not everything in life is fun.

One nice thing about starting in on homework the moment I got home is that it was finished by supper. In the past, I had put things off, so assignments hung over my head for long periods of time, but today, everything was done and I could forget about school entirely. That was a huge bonus.

The squash wasn't bad. It was kind of good actually. I would prefer a hamburger or hot dog any day, but the squash wasn't horrible like I feared. I hoped Casper didn't cook a lot of weird stuff. I sure as hell didn't want any sushi. I was not eating raw fish! Yuck!

After supper, I watched clips of Ohio State football games with Brendan. He often stopped the playback, went back, and reviewed the play again, pointing out the strengths and weaknesses of the Buckeyes. I thought I knew football, but I was learning a lot.

"This is like... your homework, isn't it?" I asked.

"I guess you could say that. Coaches do a lot of research on the teams they'll be up against."

"Hey, I'll trade you my homework for yours."

"No deal, kiddo. That's like offering to trade an apple for a chocolate chip cookie."

"Come on, you like apples."

"Yeah, but not as well as cookies."

"It was worth a shot."

I liked watching football with Brendan. What I liked even more was that he discussed plays with me. He didn't treat me like a kid, but like a player who knew a thing or two about football. Nothing was the same here as it had been in my past foster homes.

I lay in bed that night more at ease than I had been in a long time. I was pretty sure from the beginning that Casper and Brendan had no ulterior motives and I became more certain of that as the days passed. I wasn't ready to completely let my guard down, but in the past, if something bad was going to happen, it had started pretty quickly. Bad stuff didn't happen in every foster home. It hadn't in my last two, but I'd been in more than one home where I never felt safe, especially at night. I was beginning to feel safe here. I hoped I wasn't in for a letdown.

***

I made the team! Yes! I was pretty confident I would if the coaches gave me a chance, but I wasn't sure because the guys at tryouts were way better than the players in middle school. There were some really big guys too. A lot of the older players were already on the team and that meant there were only so many spots available. I could relax now. I could also sit with the other players at lunch.

I liked school better after I saw my name on the list, but making the team meant I had to be even more careful now. I could not screw up as I had in the past. I thought I could avoid drugs without too much difficulty and yet a part of me... Well, I wasn't going to do that anymore. Giving up smokes was hard. Damn, I needed a drag.

At lunch period, I headed straight for the football table with my fish sandwich, cole slaw, and hush puppies. I spotted only three guys I remembered from my 8th grade team. None of them look particularly pleased to see me so I ignored them. The guys I didn't know were indifferent. I guess I looked enough like a football player they figured I belonged. I doubted anyone who wasn't on the team would dare try and sit with the players.

I didn't talk much. Instead, I observed and listened. It didn't take me long to figure out which guys were the top dogs. From their size, I figured they were seniors. It made sense that seniors ruled. They were older, more experienced, and... they were seniors. I was a lowly freshman, so I'd have to prove myself and watch my step. I wanted these guys to like me. I needed them to like me and value what I did on the field.

I nodded to the guys when the lunch period ended and everyone headed out. I didn't want to appear too eager to please or too timid to interact with guys I didn't know. Nodding was the perfect middle ground.

I strolled leisurely toward my next class. In the past, I had rushed to finish homework or study for tests in the breaks between classes. That's how ill prepared I had been in middle school. I guess there was a value to finishing my homework right after I got home from school.

Felix, Ace, and Blaze all spotted me in the hallways during the afternoon. Felix and Ace were together when our paths crossed, but Blaze was alone. Luckily, there was no time to talk. I pretended not to see Felix and Ace at all, but Blaze was not so easy to ignore. The mere sight of him made me breathe harder. Was it my imagination or was he hotter than he was before I went to Juvie?

Blaze had blond hair like me, but it was short on the sides, long on top, and spiked to stand straight up. It made him look fierce and dangerous. He also had brown eyes instead of blue, eyes I could never gaze into for long without doing whatever he wanted. He didn't have much muscle, but his body was sexy and what he had in his shorts was especially big.

I let out a long breath and did my best for forget about him. My mind did an okay job of that, but other parts of me were not so successful.

I spotted Mohawk boy right after school. I had hoped he'd be in some of my classes, but no such luck. I thought he might be a sophomore, but then again this was a big school so it wouldn't be unusual that we had no classes together even if he was a freshman. I so wanted to meet him, but he was gone so quickly I would have missed him entirely if I wasn't looking in his direction.

I successfully dodged my old friends and survived the school day. Finally, it was time for practice. This was the best and most important part of the day. I sat on the bleachers with the other guys as the coaches gave us a long talk; similar to those I'd heard in middle school. Next, the team manager, a good looking but very slim and small guy who almost looked too young to be a freshman, handed us our uniforms as the coach read off our names.

I couldn't help but grin as I accepted my practice and game uniforms and walked toward the locker room. Inside, I claimed one of the vacant lockers in the football bay and wrote my name on the strip of athletic tape on the door. I stripped naked without hesitation. I was accustomed to being naked around other guys and even though most of those around me were bigger, I knew I had a nice body. I was definitely the best-built freshman and was even more muscular than some of the sophomores.

I began to feel complete as I pulled on my maroon and gold uniform. I loved the deep maroon jersey with gold lettering. I glimpsed at myself in the mirror. I looked good.

The locker room was a little intimidating. In middle school, I was the best built, but not here. There were players with broad muscular chests and abs like you wouldn't believe. Their biceps were huge! I was fit and built for my age, but I was no match for most of the older boys. I was going to have to work hard on the field and the weight room to catch up with them. I was truly thankful I was fit or I would have felt downright inferior.

I was at home on the field. The coaches ran us around and around the track. Even near the end, I didn't huff and puff like many of the other guys. Running seemed easier now than in middle school and I wondered if that was because I had quit smoking. Maybe what they said about smoking was true. Running faster and longer was something I could use to encourage myself to resist my craving for a cig.

I hoped the coaches would teach us some plays, but instead I was paired off with an older player to work on various skills. I didn't mind because I was assigned to Biff and he was hot. He had wavy blond hair halfway down his neck and he was one of the guys with broad shoulders, a muscular chest, and big biceps. I was sure he could lift me with one arm. I caught glimpses of his abs as he worked with me. I wanted to lick them. Biff we seriously hot. He even had the same brown eyes as Blaze.

I noticed boys more now than I had before. I had been attracted to guys for a long time, but it was as if my attraction had been dialed up from four to ten. I was having more trouble down below too. Sometimes, it would not go soft. I had been through puberty nearly two years ago so I wasn't sure what was going on. Maybe it was just that I hadn't done anything sexual in a long time except whack it.

"Pay attention!"

I met Biff's eyes. His stern look eased, but I could tell he meant business. I did not want to piss him off and I was serious about football. I had to keep my mind from wandering.

I did my best to focus despite my attraction to Biff. He seemed satisfied and even impressed now and then with my skills. He found my weak spots, criticized me without holding back, and then helped me improve. I felt like I could depend on him to guide me. He was a leader.

Practice passed without us actually playing, which sucked, but it was okay because I got to spend so much time with Biff. I liked passing, receiving, blocking, and all the rest too. It's just that it was more fun to actually play.

I had a very rough time in the locker room after practice and an even rougher time in the showers. It wasn't that anyone gave me trouble, but I had never been around older guys naked before. Well, I guess I had been in middle school, but even the older guys there weren't all that developed. Here, I was in the locker room and showers with boys as old as eighteen and... wow, it was a constant struggle to keep myself from getting completely hard. I wondered if maybe I should whack off before practice to decrease my chances of popping a boner.

I lost the battle to control my dick when I caught sight of Biff wet and naked. His body was incredible. His muscular chest drove me insane with desire and his abs were so sexy. What he had between his legs inspired immediate fantasies. My dick immediately stiffened. I did the only thing I could do. I turned toward the showerhead and blasted myself with cold water. That did the trick, but my balls still ached with need and longing.

It wasn't much safer looking at my other teammates. While some weren't all that special, most were a gay boy's dream. Part of me was thrilled with the sights that met my eyes, but unfortunately my dick was the most thrilled of all. It kept getting hard even as I fought to control and hide it. I rushed my shower as much as I could because I couldn't stand the torment of the hot boys around me. Blasting myself repeatedly with cold water wasn't much fun either.

I felt safer once I pulled on my boxer briefs and shorts. Now, I merely had a bulge and not a stiff penis sticking straight out from my body. No one had seemed to take much notice in the shower, but I sure didn't want to get stuck with a nickname like boner. I wasn't afraid of the guys knowing I was gay, but it's one thing to be gay and another to get hard in the showers.

My 'nads ached so much that as soon as I dressed, I slipped into the restroom, locked myself in a stall, and stroked until I relieved the pressure. I felt much better once I had. When I departed, I only had a pleasant instead of painful ache down there. Being a guy isn't easy sometimes.

I left the school and headed for home. Many of the players had their own cars, but I walked along with several of them who were heading for the bus stop on the corner. None of them mentioned me getting hard in the showers so either they hadn't noticed or were pretending they didn't. Guys got hard in the showers fairly frequently and I'd noticed guys usually didn't comment. That was probably because they didn't want to take any shit when they got hard. That didn't mean I was completely safe. There was always the risk of becoming the butt of a joke. Once that started, there was no end.

Several of my teammates bid me goodbye when we parted at the bus stop. I smiled. I was part of a team again and this time I was not going to screw it up.

Chapter Eleven
Casper

"Where's Scott?" Brendan asked as he stepped out into the backyard where I was planting black-eyed Susans.

"He's out running. Before that he was doing pushups and ab crunches in his room."

"I take it he made the team then."

"Yes."

"Wonderful. I think it will be good for him and he'll have less time to get into trouble."

"How was your day?"

"We practiced a new play I designed and it works beautifully. Of course, the way it works during practice and the way it works during a game will be different, but I'm confident."

"Oh, you have competition, Casper. One of my players has been flirting with me."

"Uh oh. Is he good looking?"

"He's gorgeous. He's extremely handsome, has a killer body and he's a freshman."

"I guess he has a thing for daddies."

"I would say so, but he will have to look elsewhere."

"Not ready to trade me in for a younger model?" I asked.

"Never." Brendan pulled me to him, hugged me, and kissed me.

"Just checking."

"It is nice to know I've still got it," Brendan said.

"I often tell you how attractive you are."

"Yes, but you are biased. Your opinion cannot be trusted. Having a young boy think I'm hot is validation."

"Like you care anyway."

"True, but it is nice to be considered a DILF."

"I know what you mean. There was a college boy checking me out on campus a couple of days ago."

"So it's your chance to trade up."

"There is no trading up. I have the best. I do wonder about these young guys who are into older guys like us. I don't think there are that many, but they are out there. They're surrounded by hot college boys and yet they like us much older guys."

"Sexual attraction is a bizarre thing. Everyone has their own likes and dislikes."

"I suppose. I thought he was checking out someone behind me, but when I looked there was no one there. He even winked at me!"

"I guess we both still have it."

"I almost told him he needed to look for a guy his age. I mean, I'm sure I'm older than his father."

"I'm glad you didn't. That boy should be free to pursue who he wants."

"True, it's just hard to imagine a boy that age being interested in me."

"Look in the mirror, Casper."

"When I do, I see an old man."

"You see a handsome, distinguished, wonderful man," Brendan said and kissed me again. "You're planting more flowers?"

"Yes, and I'm going to plant more and more until there is nothing left to mow. This backyard will someday be a cottage garden with only paths between all the flowering bushes, flowers, and herbs."

"Tired of mowing, huh? You know you can leave that for me."

"I have more time to mow that you do. I am thinking ahead to someday when we're too old to mow, but since I no longer have a farm to maintain, this is my project. Besides, I love flowers."

"I do too. I just don't like the work of planting and maintaining them."

"Planting them is a lot of work, but once they are established, there won't be that much work in keeping them going."

Brendan stayed with me until I finished up and then we went inside. I cleaned up at the sink.

"What's that scent?" Brendan asked.

"Baked beans and cocktail wienies. They have been cooking all day in the crockpot. I knew I wouldn't have time to cook supper. I cooked apples to go with them."

"You could have called and told me to bring something home. I deliver," Brendan said.

"I know you do."

"That's not what I meant, but that too. Behave yourself."

"Hey, Scott isn't around. I can do as I please."

We heard the front door open and close. Scott entered. He was shirtless and soaked with sweat.

"Do I have time for a shower before supper?" he asked.

"Yes. I'll put some breadsticks in the oven. Don't be too long."

"I won't!"

Scott disappeared. Brendan noticed me smiling.

"What?" he asked.

"He reminds me of you when you were a teen."

"Maybe I've been reincarnated."

"I think you have to die first, Brendan."

"Okay, maybe not."

A few minutes later we were all seated at the kitchen table. Scott was fully dressed and no longer sweaty.

"Oh, I love these little weenies. Why do the beans taste so good?" Scott asked.

"Probably because I add barbeque sauce, brown sugar, and onions," Casper said.

"You're a great cook."

"You should try my cooking," Brendan said.

"Uh... no thanks. I've heard stories." We laughed.

"How was practice?" Brendan asked.

"Amazing. We didn't get to scrimmage, but it was fun. One of the older players, Biff, worked with me. He's incredible. I learned some stuff. Soon, we get to work out in the weight room. I can't wait. Some of the older players are ripped. I wanna look like them."

I looked at Brendan. Scott definitely reminded me of him.

"Let me know what kind of workout your coach has you doing. I may be able to add something to it. You can go with me to the SRSC and use the equipment there," Brendan said.

"SRSC?"

"Student Recreational Sports Center. It's the main gym on campus. I could take you to the weight room at the stadium, but you're not ready for that yet."

Scott nodded. He had toured the stadium and seen the student athlete weight room and the huge weight plates used there.

"That will be awesome!"

"I can give you a lot of pointers too."

"I never quite escape from sports," I said.

"Why would you want to?" Scott asked, making me laugh. "It's such a relief to make the team. I'll admit, after seeing how big some of the guys were at tryouts I wasn't so confident. My backup plan was to try out for soccer, but it's a weak sport compared to football."

"Don't let Brandon or Jon hear you say that. On second thought, do," Brendan said.

We kept talking while we ate. It reminded me of when Clint, Cameron, and Conner were young. It was rare they were all at the table at the same time, but the old memories still resurfaced.

"Can I go to the skate park? My homework is done. I did most of it in study hall and finished up before I went running. The teachers were more merciful today."

"Sure, why not?" I said.

"Thanks!"

Scott disappeared with his board, pads, and helmet. Brendan helped me clean up the kitchen. He was always good about that. He even washed out the crockpot. He was a good husband, although we had never officially married. A ceremony didn't appeal to either of us.

An hour and a half later, I heard the front door open again. I caught a glimpse of Scott as he made his way to his room, but he didn't greet me. Brendan came into the kitchen from his office to warm up his mug of London Cuppa tea in the microwave.

"Uh, hi." Scott stood in the doorway, looking both frightened and ashamed.

"Are you okay?" Brendan asked.

"I... uh... did something really bad. It was stupid and I know better, but... I'm sorry."

"What did you do?" Brendan asked.

"I... smoked part of a cigarette. I didn't smoke it all. I stopped after only a couple of minutes, but... I did it. I'm sorry. Please don't make me go away. I'm so ashamed and I feel so weak. Why am I so stupid?"

Scott's lower lip trembled and tears spilled out of his eyes.

"Have a seat," Brendan said. Scott did as he was told and stared down at the table, crying. "We're not going to make you go away." Scott looked up and wiped his eyes. "What I want to know is why you broke your promise."

"I don't know. Quitting has been really hard. I want a cigarette all the time. There were a couple of boys at the skate park I've been trying to avoid. We used to smoke and do worse things. They offered me one. I said no at first, but... they talked me into it. It... uh... wasn't real hard for them to do. I'm really sorry and I'm really pissed off at myself."

"We are disappointed," I said. Scott paled. He looked so ashamed of himself I wanted to hug him.

"I know. I'm sorry. I won't break my promise again. I'm going to avoid those guys. If I see them at the skate park again, I'll turn around and come home. That is, if I'm still allowed to go."

Brendan and I looked at each other. He nodded slightly. We were in agreement.

"You can still go, but I think avoiding those boys is wise."

"So, what's my punishment?"

"There isn't any this time, but I want you to think about this and remember that you can't be a successful athlete and smoke or do drugs. Either you're serious about football or you're not. You can't have it both ways. If you go back to smoking, you can't be on the team."

Scott paled again and swallowed hard. Brendan wasn't exactly letting him off the hook.

"So if I smoke, you won't let me play."

"No. I won't. If you have that little respect for your body you have no business being an athlete. If I find out you've smoked again, you will have to quit football."

Scott nodded. "I won't smoke again. No matter how much I want it, I won't do it. I won't let anyone pressure me into it either."

"Good. We know it's hard to quit, Scott. We're very proud of you for doing as well as you have. This was a slipup, but you have to be very careful because one slipup can easily lead to another and another and then you've failed. You have to be very strong to beat this, Scott. We know you can do it."

Scott nodded again. When we all stood up, Scott hugged us both, then walked to his room like a dog with his tail between his legs. He was very ashamed of himself.

"What do you think?" Brendan asked.

"He's sincere, but it's hard for even adults to quit."

"We'll help him all we can, but most of it is up to him. I'm not entirely sure what to do. Kids really should come with manuals."

"I know. I wished for one often in the past. Did you notice he came and told us instead of trying to hide it?"

"Yes. I'm proud of him for that and I should tell him. We would have smelled it on him, but he probably doesn't know that."

"He's basically a good kid," I said.

"Yes, he is. I guess we should expect some backsliding. I just hope it doesn't involve drugs."

"He is trying to stay away from the friends he did drugs with."

"Yes, but that can be hard. It's easy to get pulled into things and he is only fourteen. A boy that age doesn't think the way adults do. It would be difficult enough for an adult. It will be doubly hard for him."

"So what do we do?"

"Guide him as well as can, hope for the best, and be there for him when he needs us. We've made our position clear. Saying more would be preaching and you know how that goes over with boys his age."

"I can see his eyes rolling now."

Brendan smiled. "Don't worry too much. This is a difficult time of life for any boy and for Scott especially, but he has something most boys don't—us."

***

My workload increased with Scott in the house. I had forgotten how much dirty laundry and how many messes teen boys generated. An additional person in the house meant that much more dirt tracked in and that many more dirty dishes. I cooked more frequently too. Brendan and I didn't eat as much as we did when we were younger, but Scott was voracious. Having him live with us was like having a swarm of locusts in the kitchen. Leftovers disappeared and loaves of bread and jars of peanut butter emptied. It was almost as if all the food in the house had begun to evaporate. I made a trip to Kroger two and sometimes three times a week. I was glad a Kroger was so close to our home.

I smiled. I loved it. With the boys grown up and no farm work, I had begun to feel as if I no longer had a purpose in life. I could easily keep myself busy, but I didn't feel as if I was doing anything meaningful—and then Scott came into my life. Everything I did for him was very meaningful. Scott needed me. Brendan did his part, but I was the one who was here when Scott came home from school. I was the one who made sure he had lunch money. I was the one who cooked for him to keep him from consuming his weight in junk food. Parenting was perhaps the most important job in the world. I was actually responsible for helping to form a living being. What I did could make the difference between Scott living a fulfilling, meaningful life or dying young in an alley from a drug overdose.

I kept busy throughout the entire week. On top of everything else, we were having weekend guests. Clint and Amanda were traveling to Madison for Amanda's class reunion and were dropping off the twins on the way. The boys would be with us from Friday evening until Sunday evening.

I was excited to see the boys again. It hadn't been that long, but I never got to see our grandsons enough. That was just as true back in Verona as it was here. They were so busy with their various activities that moving to Bloomington hadn't actually diminished the number of times we saw them.

I returned from Kroger on Friday evening as Scott was returning from football practice. Clint and his family were due to arrive soon.

"Want to help me carry in the groceries?" I asked when he entered the garage.

"It's what I live for."

"Okay, funny man, grab some bags."

"Whoa! Did you buy out the store?"

"No, but the twins eat like you do. I suspect all three of you might be part piranha."

"Uh oh. You sure you have enough?" Scott grinned.

"If not, I'll make another trip."

"What are we having for supper? I'm starving."

"Brendan is going to grill hamburgers as soon as everyone is here."

"I hope that's soon. I'll waste away!"

"Clint and his family could arrive any time now and so could Brendan."

"Good. Listen, I was thinking. If you need my room for the twins, I can sleep on the floor in the living room. They are your grandsons. I don't mind."

"That's kind of you to offer, but we wouldn't think of pushing you out of your room. That's your space and this is your home. The boys are just visiting. They're bringing air mattresses and sleeping bags. They'll probably sleep in the office, unless they prefer the living room." Scott smiled and I could tell he was holding his emotions in check. What I had just said touched him.

"You said they play football, right?"

"Yes. They are both on the football team, swim team, and baseball team at Plymouth. I'm sure you guys will have plenty in common."

Scott seemed both excited and anxious about Dax and Drew's visit. He likely feared he'd be pushed aside while they were here, but Brendan and I would make sure that didn't happen. The boys were a year older than Scott, but I didn't think that would make a difference.

Brendan pulled in. Before he could even get out of the car Clint's sport utility vehicle pulled into the drive as well.

"Let's go out and greet them," I said, leaving the remainder of the grocery bags sitting on the table.

Scott and I walked outside. Clint gave me a hug. Amanda did next and then the boys.

"We would like you all to meet Scott, our foster son. He's also quite the football player," Brendan said.

Scott smiled. If he was uneasy he didn't show it. He stepped forward confidently and shook Clint's hand. He smiled at Amanda, who surprised him by hugging him. Scott, Dax, and Drew all exchanged a "Sup?"

"Whoa! Are you guys moving in permanently?" Brendan asked as the twins began to unload their stuff.

"Shh! They don't know we aren't coming back for them," Clint said.

"Yeah, right Dad," Dax said.

"He tries to be funny," Drew said to Scott apologetically. It made Scott smile.

Scott grabbed a bag and helped the boys carry their stuff in. The rest of us had to help too.

"I thought you could take over Brendan's office. It's the room next to the bathroom. You can sleep there or in the living room if you prefer," I said.

"This is nice, but completely different from the old house," Clint said.

"Yeah, it was built a hundred years later than the farmhouse. It's much easier to take care of this place," I said.

"Yes, and you don't have an entire farm outside to worry about."

"It's Cameron's problem now," I said.

"I think he's turning the backyard into a farm. He's always planting something," Brendan said.

Brendan and I gave Clint and Amanda a tour of the house. Scott and the boys hurried out the back door with a football. So far they were getting along well. I was confident that would continue.

The grand tour didn't take long, and then Brendan disappeared to take care of the grill. Our house was a three-bedroom home, with the smallest bedroom converted into an office for Brendan. I found the house just the right size, not too small and not too big.

"I couldn't picture you living in a house built in 1960, but with your antiques it works," Clint said.

"Hey, Brendan and I were built in the '60's too. We're a perfect match with the house."

"I never thought of that. We could see the stadium as we turned off the highway. Brendan doesn't have much of a commute," Clint said as I worked on putting away groceries.

"We can drive downtown in six minutes. Brendan can be at the stadium in less than five."

"We want to bring the boys down for a game sometime this fall," Clint said.

"Let us know and Brendan will get you tickets. You can all stay here. Hotels are expensive in Bloomington on game weekends."

"That would be rather crowded."

"We can manage."

"Can I do anything Casper?" Amanda asked.

"You can fill glasses with ice. The glasses are in that cabinet," I said, pointing to one to the right of the sink. "I had planned to be back from Kroger sooner, but you know how it is."

"I certainly do," Amanda said.

"Grocery shopping is such a chore. I take much longer than Amanda does when she sends me with the list. She knows where everything is. I don't," Clint said.

"I guess I'll have to send you more often so you can learn the layout of the store," Amanda said.

"There's no need for that! I don't mind having to search!" Clint said.

"He thinks pretending incompetence will get him out of things. I'm onto him," Amanda said.

I laughed. "She has your number, Clint."

I finished putting away the groceries. Brendan returned to pat out hamburger patties and then disappeared again. I could see the boys passing the football in the backyard. Amanda and I worked together to set the table and gather everything we needed.

"How is Scott working out?" Clint asked.

"He's a lot like Cameron was when he was a teen."

"Uh oh."

"Actually, he's easier to handle. He doesn't have the attitude Cameron did."

"Good, Cameron was such a little shit."

"He was a handful."

"I figured he'd end up as a drifter. I think he would have without you and Brendan being there for him."

"He was a challenge, but he was a good kid."

"Ha! He's a good adult. He was a jerk as a kid."

"He did have his moments. Scott has been involved with drugs in the past, but he's remained clean since he's been with us. His main difficulty is staying away from cigarettes. He used to smoke quite a bit."

"Life in foster homes can be rough," Clint said. "It's an uncertain and unhappy life."

I knew Clint was referring to the time he spent in a foster home, between the death of his mother and the day Brendan and I took custody of Clint, Cameron, and Conner.

"Scott seems both happy and thankful to be here. That helps him deal with his drug and cigarette problems."

"He should be happy and thankful. The kid has hit the jackpot, just as Cameron, Conner, and I did."

"He appreciates being here. He was rather shocked at the amount of clothes and other things we purchased for him. He remarked that he had never had new clothing before. What was truly sad was that he asked if he could keep them when he departed for his next foster home. He assumed he wouldn't get to stay with us for long."

"That's heartbreaking," Amanda said.

"Yeah. I assured him that whatever we bought for him was his permanently and that this home was not temporary. I think most foster parents do their best, but most have very limited time and funds. Brendan and I are lucky. I have plenty of time to care for Scott and we have plenty of money."

"Yes and even more love to give. You saved Cameron, Conner, and me. After Mom died things were rough, especially when they split us up. I know Dad would have taken care of us if he could have, but it wasn't possible. That's why you and Brendan are as much our dads as Dad."

"Thanks. You know, for two guys who really had no plans for having kids, we sure ended up with a lot of them."

"This weekend you get two more," Amanda said.

"Just make sure you come back for them. We love them, but we're too old to deal with three teen boys at once. It was hard enough when we were younger."

"Sometimes I feel like I'm too old to deal with two of them," Clint said, grinning.

"What about me? Clint is a big kid, so I have three!" Amanda said. I laughed.

"Kids are a pain in the ass. They'll suck the life right out of you, but you can't help but love them," Clint said.

"That is true," Amanda said, giving Clint a quick one-arm hug.

A few minutes later, the seven of us sat around the kitchen table. Jack had built the table and benches for us years ago. With a chair at each end, we had plenty of room.

"Scott can really throw, Dad. If he lived in Plymouth, you would want him on the team," Dax said.

"Sorry, he's taken and I have plans for him to play for IU," Brendan said.

Scott beamed, but also looked a bit bewildered. I think he was trying to figure out if Brendan was serious or not.

"Brendan's burgers are even better than yours, Dad," Derek said.

"He is the grill master. I'm merely his apprentice. I can out cook him in the kitchen."

"Everyone can," Brendan laughed.

"Amanda has taught me a lot. I tried not to learn, but it seeped in anyway."

"He's great with French toast," Amanda said.

Our conversation continued while we ate our burgers, potato salad, barbeque chips, and brownies. The moment they finished eating, the boys disappeared into the yard again.

"The twins certainly like Scott," Clint said.

"They have sports in common. Scott loves all sports, he skates, and he runs," Brendan said.

"All three of them remind me a lot of Brendan in high school," I said.

"I'm outnumbered at home. The talk at the kitchen table is almost always about sports," Amanda said.

"We should get going soon. We have quite a way to go yet," Clint said.

"Let me help clean up first," Amanda said.

"Don't bother with that. Brendan will do it," I said mischievously.

"I have to do *everything*," Brendan said. "Casper does nothing but lie around all day and watch TV."

"Why don't I believe that?" Clint asked.

Clint and Amanda went outside to bid the twins goodbye and then returned.

"We'll be back on Sunday. Call us if you need us," Clint said.

"Don't worry about a thing. Just go have fun," Brendan said.

Clint hugged us both and then he and Amanda departed.

Brendan helped me clean up and then went outside and tossed the football around with the boys. I knew how Amanda felt. In many ways Brendan was a big kid. I had four boys to watch over this weekend.

I took a glass of iced tea out to the patio and sat and watched the boys. Brendan joined me after about half an hour, but the younger boys kept at it until they couldn't see the ball. They were all hot and sweaty when we went inside.

"I need a shower," Drew said.

"Me too," Dax said.

"I'll show you where the towels and washcloths are. Hey, can the twins sleep in my room?" Scott asked.

"You guys can sleep wherever you want," Brendan said.

"Cool!"

"That's going to be one crowded room," I said.

"They're boys. They won't care."

"True, but will we be able to sleep tonight?"

"I'll threaten them with a beating if they don't keep it down."

"Yeah, like they'll believe that."

The boys took over the TV after they all showered. Tomorrow was Saturday, so after Brendan told them to stay inside and keep the noise level down, we went to bed. I could hear them from time to time and it reminded me of the old days when Brendan and I were younger and had three boys to care for around the clock. We had lived a good life.

Chapter Twelve
Scott

On Saturday morning, Casper made us blueberry pancakes. He asked if we wanted to go to the farmer's market with him and Brendan, but who wants to look at vegetables when they can play football and do other fun stuff? We convinced him to let us hang out at home instead.

Drew and Dax were awesome. They were a little older than me, but no more than a year. They liked all the same stuff I did and I found myself wishing they lived here with us. At least I had this weekend and maybe they'd come back to visit again.

We went outside after breakfast and threw the football around again. It was already getting warm and the twins pulled off their shirts. They had great bodies and the fact that they were identical twins made them even hotter. I stole looks at their chests and abs and tried to control what was going on in my shorts. Fantasies of making out with them and doing more formed in my head, but I pushed them away because I didn't want the front of my shorts tented.

We moved inside when Brendan and Casper departed for the farmer's market and began to wrestle around on the living room rug. I'm strong, but they were stronger. I did pretty well against each of them, but I lost.

I watched as Drew and Dax wrestled each other. The sight was too much for me. I had to sit so that the bulge in my shorts wasn't too obvious. I was completely stiff. I should have gone to the bathroom and stroked out a quick one to get my dick under control, but I was afraid they'd noticed my bulge if I did. I was trapped.

I loved watching the twins wrestle shirtless. Either of them alone was hot, but together they were freaking magnificent! Drew finally pinned Dax and that put an end to the match. I was both relieved and sorry.

"Wanna wrestle again, Scott?" Drew asked.

"Uh... not right now."

Drew looked at my tented shorts. Even seated it was fairly obvious I had a boner.

"Are you gay?" he asked. I froze. His sudden and blunt question took me by surprise. I was scared and I mean really scared. It wasn't that I thought the twins would beat me up, Drew's tone wasn't belligerent in the least, but I really liked Dax and Drew and I didn't want them pissed off at me because I was perving on them. I didn't want to lose them as friends. I had no idea what to do. I was not ready to be asked such a personal question without warning. "It's cool if you are. I'm sure you know our granddads are a couple. Two of our uncles are gay too."

"Yeah, I am," I said, relieved at Drew's words, but still frightened.

"Thought so. If your dick gets any harder it's going to rip through your shorts," Drew said, then laughed.

"I was trying to hide that."

"There is no hiding that thing. It must be big."

"How about you guys?" I asked.

"We are freaking huge!" Dax said, grabbing his crotch, which made my dick flex in my shorts.

"That's not what I meant!" I said grinning. "Are you into guys, girls, or both?"

"We like girls," Dax said.

"But we're totally cool with gay dudes. I mean, what does it matter?" Drew asked.

"I think most people are okay with it. No one gives me any trouble when they find out I like boys."

"Do you have a boyfriend?"

"No. You have girlfriends?"

"I do. Drew got dumped," Dax said.

"Hey, we agreed to break up."

"Yeah, after she told you she wanted to break up."

"Details. Details. She's dating Horse now."

"Horse?" I asked.

"That's his nickname. He has a huge dick. I mean it's freakishly huge. It's a wonder he doesn't fall over when he gets hard. He's on our football team and he makes everyone else look small."

"Tell me more..." I said, grinning.

The twins laughed. "He's so big I don't think you'd want him. If he came at you with that thing, you'd run away screaming."

"Oh no. I'd run toward him!"

The twins laughed again. "Have you done stuff with guys?" Dax asked.

"Yeah, but mostly with one guy. Have you guys done stuff with girls?"

"I've made out with a few girls and felt up a couple. Three have given me head, but Dax has me beat," Drew said.

"You went all the way?" I asked.

"Yeah, recently and she's a junior!"

"Wow. Do your parents know?"

"Oh god no! You know how parents are. Oh, sorry."

"It's okay. Did you wear a condom?"

"Yeah. If I had a kid I'd really be in trouble. Dad gave us both a box of condoms. He said he wasn't encouraging us to have sex, but he remembered what being our age was like. He said he'd buy us more any time we wanted, no questions asked. I may have to ask for another box. I sure hope so! If I do I'm sure Dad will know I've been doing it," Dax said.

"I bet he won't tell Mom," Drew said.

"I hope not. She still thinks we're little kids. If Dad told her I had sex she might have a heart attack. Have you ever done anything with a girl, Scott?"

I wrinkled my nose and the twins laughed.

"So you're only into guys, got it."

"Yeah, girls have never done anything for me."

"That's how I feel about guys," Dax said.

"Me too. I mean, I know when a guy is hot, but I don't want to have sex with one. I did let Aaron Benchley suck my dick," Drew said.

"You did? Why didn't you tell me?" Dax asked.

"You never asked."

"Was he good?" Dax asked.

"Yes, and he swallowed."

"Oh man, it's so hard to get girls to swallow. Do you swallow, Scott?"

"Uh, yeah."

"I want to find a girl who swallows," Dax said.

"Hit up Aaron for head. He'll blow you and swallow," Drew said.

"Eh, I don't know if I could get into head from a dude."

"I closed my eyes and pretended he was Tara Smitha."

"Ha! The only way she'll suck your dick is in your fantasies. Tara is the hottest girl in school," Dax said.

"If Brendan and Casper were here, we could not talk about this," I said.

"Yeah, adults and sex don't mix. I'm sure Mom thinks were total virgins," Drew said.

"I don't know. She probably isn't that naïve," Dax said.

"Dad knows better. He used to be a guy," Drew said.

"He used to be a guy? What is he now?" I asked, laughing.

"I mean, he used to be our age. He knows what it's like."

"He also gave us the sex talk. That was a blast," Dax said, rolling his eyes.

"Talking to parents about sex is never fun," Drew said.

"I've never experienced that," I said.

"Oh, sorry. I didn't mean..." Drew began.

"It's fine. I think I had it easier than you. I learned all about sex from older foster brothers."

Dax raised his eyebrow.

"I didn't mean it like that!" I said, laughing.

We kept talking about sex and I was so turned on that my shorts remained tented. I wasn't worried about that anymore. Drew and Dax didn't care. I wanted to ask the twins if they'd let me blow them, especially since Drew had already let a guy suck him, but I didn't have the balls. I didn't want to make things awkward between us. While blowing twins would have been freaking hot, I liked what we already had and didn't want to screw it up.

The front of the twin's shorts bulged as we talked about sex. I almost couldn't believe it when Dax began rubbing his. I began rubbing it too—my own I mean. Fantasies of the three of us jerking together entered my mind, but Brendan and Casper pulled in the drive and that was the end of that.

Our shorts were severely tented when we stood up. Dax began laughing and it was contagious. Our laughter helped us to calm down so that when Brendan and Casper entered through the door from the garage there were no longer bulges in our shorts.

"What's so funny?" Casper asked suspiciously.

"You really do not want to know," Drew said.

"I'll take your word for it. What about fried squash and eggplant for lunch? Casper asked as he pulled yellow squash and a beautiful purple eggplant out of a bag. He and Brendan had also purchased a bouquet of zinnias and a dozen eggs at the farmer's market.

"I love fried squash," Dax said.

"I've never had it. Please tell me it's better than grilled squash," I said.

"Grilled? Eww! It has to be better! The taste is hard to describe, but it's good and eggplant tastes very similar," Drew said.

"What have you boys been up to... or do I want to know?" Brendan asked.

"Wrestling mostly," Drew said.

It was true, but he didn't mention talking about sex. I wondered what would have happened if Brendan and Casper hadn't come home when they did; probably not much, but then again, who knows? I had the feeling I might go crazy wondering.

"What is there fun to do around here?" Drew asked.

"We could go to the skate park, but we'd have to share my board," I said.

"We brought roller-blades," Dax said. "Can we go?"

"Did you bring your pads and helmets?" Brendan asked.

"Yes," Dax said.

"Okay then. Just try not to break anything. Your parents will not forgive us if we return you broken," Brendan said.

"Come on, let's get our stuff," I said.

The three us hurried to my room, where Drew and Dax had stored all their things. They pulled their skates, pads, and helmets out while I grabbed my stuff. I couldn't wait to get to the skate park. Was this what it felt like to have brothers?

"I'll text you when it's time to come home for lunch," Casper said. "That's something we need to get you, Scott, a phone."

147

My eyes widened. My own phone? I'd never had one. I guess I shouldn't have been so surprised considering everything else Casper and Brendan had given me, but I was surprised and also a little scared. What would happen if I screwed everything up?

Dax, Drew, and I departed and began walking toward the skate park.

"Are you okay?" Drew asked.

"Yeah, it's just that all this seems too good to be true."

"What do you mean?"

"Brendan and Casper taking me in as their foster son. You wouldn't believe how much stuff they've bought me. They buy me anything I need."

"What's so unusual about that? Our parents buy us everything we need," Dax said.

"Yeah, but Brendan and Casper aren't my parents. I wish they were, but they haven't even known me all that long. I've never had..." I had to pause because I was about to get emotional. Guys like Drew and Dax couldn't possibly understand. They had probably always had everything. "I'm just afraid that they'll get tired of me. I've lived in a lot of foster homes. I've never been in one for long. I've never had anyone be so nice to me. I don't want to leave. I feel like everything is going too well, you know?"

"Yeah, I know that feeling. It's like... you keep waiting on something bad to happen because things are going so well," Dax said.

"Exactly."

"Let me tell you about our grandfathers, they took in our dad and his brothers when Dad was about your age. They never sent them away. Casper is our grandfather's brother, but we consider Brendan and Casper our grandfathers because Dad considers them his dads just as much as Grandpa Jason," Dax said.

"Yeah, but your dad and his brothers were family. I'm not."

"I don't think that will make any difference," Drew said. "Dad told us that Brendan and Casper took in a homeless boy when they were in college. They helped him get his act together and now he's a professor at IU. They still keep in touch with him. They're like that. They help people," Drew said.

"They care about you too. I can tell," Dax said.

"I feel like they do but that seems too good to be true."

"It's not. You want to know what I think will happen? I think they'll adopt you," Drew said.

"That would be too much to hope for."

"Not with our grandfathers," Dax said.

"I want to believe you, but I'm so scared it's all going to go away. They're so good to me and I'm even playing football again. I got kicked off the team in the 8th grade. I've been in a lot of trouble too. I've been in Juvie."

"Really? What's it like?" Drew asked.

"It's not fun. It's very strict and the bigger guys pick on the smaller ones. Some bad stuff happened to me in there I don't want to talk about."

"Damn, I'm sorry. Listen, I know I can't make you believe this for sure, but trust me; our grandfathers will not give up on you or send you away. Our Uncle Cameron was a real bad ass when he was young. Our dad has told us stories about what he was like. He got in all kinds of trouble, but they didn't give up on him or send him away. Now, he runs the family Christmas tree farm."

"I want to believe you."

"You'll see we're right."

"I sure hope so."

"Wow, nice skate park," Drew said as it came into view.

"Yeah, it's pretty cool and it's close."

"I can't wait!" Dax said.

We hurried to a bench where the twins put on their roller-blades and I finished putting on my pads. In less than two minutes, we were skating. We had the place to ourselves for the moment and the twins were talented skaters.

It wasn't long before we were hot and sweaty. The twins pulled off their shirts so I did too. They were so sexy shirtless. I truly wished at least one of them was gay. I wished I could make out with them and do even more.

I needed to control myself. Sex was part of my old life. I couldn't help but want it, just as I wanted a cigarette even now, but I needed to resist. Sex is what pulled me into drugs and that is what had landed me in real trouble. The twins didn't seem like guys who were into drugs. I doubted they had even smoked pot.

Maybe wanting them wasn't so bad. It didn't matter anyway since they weren't into guys. Yeah, Drew let a boy blow him, but that didn't mean he was attracted to him. It was a pity and yet part of me didn't want to mess around with them. I had another fantasy playing in my head—one where they were my brothers. That would be even better than sex.

I admired the twin's bodies. They had muscular chests, big biceps, and defined abs. I wasn't quite as fit as they were, but I came very close and I was younger. I wasn't the least bit self-conscious about my body.

I tensed when my old skating and smoking buddies, Blaze, Felix, and Ace showed up. Dax noticed me looking at them warily. I looked at him and mouthed "later." He nodded.

The three eyed the twins and me, but didn't approach and began skating. They were probably wondering about Dax and Drew. I was glad I wasn't alone. It's not that I thought they'd hassle me. I was afraid one of them would pull out a cigarette or joint and lure me into smoking. Blaze was particularly dangerous in that regard. He was handsome, sexy, and oh so seductive. He was truly a bad ass and that made him all the more appealing. I don't know why, but it did. It was Blaze who had seduced me into trying a lot of things I shouldn't have.

Skating wasn't as fun with my former friends near, but I still enjoyed myself. The twins were every bit as good as me on their blades and that's saying something.

We skated for another hour and then Drew's phone quacked like a duck.

"Is that a duck in your pocket or are you happy to see me?" I asked.

"Ha!" Drew checked his phone and sent a quick text.

"That was Casper. We have to head back," he said.

We exited the skate park and began walking home. Blaze and the others watched us depart.

"Who were those guys?" Dax asked.

"Former friends I'm trying to avoid. Well, they weren't exactly friends. We skated together sometimes and smoked together more often. I, uh, lost my virginity to Blaze, the one with the spiked hair."

I didn't know why I told the twins that last bit. Maybe I needed to tell someone. I sure couldn't tell Brendan or Casper, just as I couldn't tell my earlier foster parents.

"You mean you took it up the butt?" Drew asked. There was no condemnation in his tone, only curiosity.

"Yeah."

"That's got to hurt," Dax said.

"It did, but I was pretty high the few times it happened. It was always the same. Blaze got me alone, we shared a joint or some pills and then we'd mess around. I was into most of it, but didn't really want him to top me."

"He forced you?" Drew asked, suddenly very concerned. He looked as if he might turn around, run back, and beat the shit out of Blaze.

"No. He just sort of did it. I let him. I guess I resisted a little, but not much. I was high and it was kind of like a dream. I never told him to stop."

"That's still wrong."

"If you were out of it, that was very wrong," Dax said.

"Looking back, yeah, but I didn't think about it much then. I was doing a lot of screwed up stuff then. I should never have messed with drugs."

"I do not want to think what our parents would do if we did drugs," Dax said.

"Me either, but we're not going to do drugs. You can't be a serious athlete and screw up your body like that," Drew said.

"Yeah, I guess you guys think I'm pretty stupid."

"We all make mistakes. You aren't doing anything like that now are you?" Drew asked.

"No. Brendan and Casper said that if I lived with them I couldn't smoke or do drugs. I'm also on probation. If I'm caught with drugs, I go straight back to Juvie. I messed up once and smoked part of a cigarette, but I won't do that again. I felt so bad about it I couldn't stand it. I told Brendan and Casper I did it. I don't think they would have ever known, but I felt like I'd betrayed them. We had a talk and they were cool about it. That makes me more determined not to smoke or do drugs, although I want a cig so bad sometimes I can't stand it."

"You're cool then. You must be very strong to be able to resist what you crave," Drew said.

"Thanks." I don't know why, but the opinion of Drew and Dax meant a lot to me. "Don't tell anyone what I told you about Blaze and me."

"We won't. Thank you for trusting us enough to tell us. It takes balls to open yourself up like that. Drew and I tell each other things like that, but we're twin brothers. You haven't even known us long," Dax said.

"You're lucky to have a brother."

"That's what I keep telling him!" Drew said. Dax punched him. "Seriously, I know what you mean. I can't imagine not having Dax."

"I'm not complaining. I feel so lucky now. Since Brendan and Casper took me in it's like every day is Christmas. I'm not talking about the stuff they buy me, although that's freaking awesome. This is the first foster home I've lived in where my foster parents pay a lot of attention to me. I've lived in places where I felt like a piece of furniture for all the notice anyone took of me. My last home, with the lesbian couple, was pretty good, but there were so many kids that they didn't have time to pay much attention to me. We all knew I was temporary too, so I was more like a visitor. It's so different here."

"Damn you, Scott! You're making me grateful for my home and parents," Dax said.

"Yeah, screw you, Scott!" Drew said, then grinned.

I laughed.

"Sorry. We probably shouldn't joke about that," Dax said.

"It's fine, but you guys are lucky to have parents who want you. Mine abandoned me when I was eight."

"They were fucking idiots then. You're awesome," Drew said.

"Yeah, I am, aren't I?" I grinned. Dax and Drew pretended to pummel me. Drew's words made me feel very good inside. He meant them.

We entered the house and walked into the kitchen.

"Oh, you're all sweaty. Grab some washcloths, clean up, and I'll start frying squash and eggplant," Casper said.

It was true, some of the sweat had evaporated on the walk home, but we were still quite sweaty from all the skating. We grabbed washcloths from the linen closet in the hallway and then crowded into the bathroom to clean our faces and chests. I wickedly wished I could wipe off Dax and Drew's bodies, but I was beginning to think of them almost as family.

A few minutes later, we were reasonably cleaned up, dressed, and sitting at the kitchen table. The aroma in the air was new to me, but wonderful.

I tried the squash. It was delicious. It was ever so slightly sour, like a lemon and sort of buttery too.

"This is really good," I said.

"Try the pork and beans. I cooked them myself," Brendan said.

"You opened the can all by yourself huh?" Drew asked mischievously.

"Yes, I even found the can opener in the drawer by myself."

"You're a gourmet chef now," Dax said.

"Hey, I even heated the rolls in the microwave."

"It's like having my own sous chef," Casper said.

I grinned. I liked how everyone teased each other here without being the least bit mean.

"I love fried squash, but mom grows so much squash at home that I rapidly grow tired of it. Mom hates to waste any," Drew said.

"Yeah, she fries it a lot, but we haven't had much yet this year. Thankfully, she didn't plant so much," Dax said.

"We planted none. We were far too busy moving in and transplanting a few things from the farm to even think about a garden. This year, our garden is limited to a tomato plant, a sage plant, and a chocolate mint plant, all in pots," Casper said.

"Mom and Dad plant too much. I hate weeding," Dax said.

I mostly listened as we ate. The conversation was so different from what I'd heard before. This was a conversation between family who had known each other all their lives. They had history and shared experiences. Was it ever like that with Mom and Dad? I couldn't remember or even imagine it. I had grown up in an entirely different world, even before Mom and Dad decided they didn't want me.

I felt separate, like an outsider as I sat there and yet I wasn't. I was not a member of this family and yet I kind of was in a way.

I hoped I got to stay here as long as possible. Despite what Drew and Dax said about Brendan and Casper adopting me, I knew that sooner or later this would come to an end. Before that happened, I wanted to enjoy it and store up all the memories I could to help me get through whatever came next. Most of life was unpleasant, but holding onto what was good helped me get through the rough times. I wanted to hold onto this as tightly as I could.

I put away bad thoughts and lived in the moment. I almost felt like Brendan and Casper were my dads and Drew and Dax my brothers. We had fun talking, laughing, and eating. There was even a birthday cake for dessert! It wasn't anyone's birthday, but the cake was a big, flat one that people got for birthdays. I'd had one for my birthday once, sort of. About three foster homes ago the three of us foster kids got a cake for our combined birthday celebration. Our names were even on it. That was a good day. I wondered where those kids were now.

"I am so sleepy," Dax announced after we'd finished our cake and ice cream. He yawned, which made me yawn, and then Drew.

"Me too. I need a nap," Drew said.

The three of us went to my room. Instead of lying on my bed, I grabbed my pillow and lay on the floor with the twins. I was between them where it felt safe and comfy. Soon, I fell asleep.

I don't know how long I slept, but I awakened to a fright. I opened my eyes and cried out, "Ack!, then jerked up, knocking my forehead against Drew's.

"Oww!" we both said. Dax laughed.

"You scared the crap out of me, Drew! I opened my eyes and all I saw was your face."

"Are you saying I'm ugly?"

"You are when you're grimacing and baring your teeth three inches from my face!"

Dax was still laughing, but Drew and I were still rubbing our heads. "That was hilarious," he said.

"Yeah, well you didn't smash your forehead into Scott's," Drew said.

"It's your own fault. The only innocent one here is Scott."

"Yeah, which is why I get all the leftover cake."

"Hey! Not all of it. You can have Drew's share," Dax said.

"You're being awfully generous with *my* cake," Drew said.

"I'm a generous guy."

"Yeah, with my cake!"

The twins began wrestling. I joined in. Dax and I ganged up on Drew and pinned him.

"Hmm, what should we do with him?" Dax asked as we held his brother down.

"Tie him up and make him watch us eat cake."

"No, not that! It's too cruel! Beat me instead! Tie me on an ant hill and cover me with honey, but don't make me watch you eat cake!"

"He's very dramatic, isn't he?" I asked.

"Yeah, he should probably join the drama department."

"I know, wedgie!" I said and immediately began to wrestle Drew onto his stomach. He struggled, but it was two on one. I reached for the band of his underwear but instead my hand slid over his bare ass. "Hey, you're not wearing underwear!"

Drew began laughing. "You just wanted to feel my butt."

"No one wants to feel your butt," Dax said.

"Eww! It was sweaty."

Drew laughed as I got up and hurried to the bathroom to wash my hand. His butt was sweaty, but there was a little part of me that enjoyed touching it.

When I returned, the twins were sitting up.

"I'm sorry you had to experience that. We'll gang up on him again later," Dax said.

"Yeah, it was foul. I'll have nightmares."

"Yep, Drew's butt, where absolutely no one wants to go."

Drew crossed his arms and glared, but I knew he wasn't angry.

"What are you guys talking about?" Brendan asked as he paused outside our door.

"Drew's butt," Dax said.

"I'm sorry I asked," Brendan said, but smiled. He continued toward the kitchen.

The three of us went outside into the backyard, threw the football around, climbed the walnut tree at the corner of the yard, wrestled on the grass, and played blind man's bluff. When I was it and had the blindfold on, I accidently grabbed Drew's stuff. I did not mean to do it. Really! It was truly an accident, but I must admit I liked it.

"You just can't keep your hands off me," Drew teased as I took off the blindfold and passed it to him.

"Sorry about that. I didn't know what I was grabbing."

"Sure you didn't," Drew said.

"Grr!"

"You didn't grab much," Dax said.

"We're identical twins, remember? What I've got, you've got."

"I mean... what a handful!"

I shook my head. I liked these guys. They were crazy.

We messed around until supper. Brendan and Casper ordered from Aver's Pizza. Brendan went to get them, so he claimed to have made them. I liked Brendan. He could be stern, but he was funny.

The day went by too fast. The twins were leaving tomorrow. I wished they could stay forever.

That night, I slept on the floor with the twins, right between them as I did during our afternoon nap. I liked hearing the sound of their breathing and feeling them close. I slept better that night than I had in a while.

The next morning, Drew, Dax, and I were all in the bathroom at the same time, taking turns in the shower and getting ready. I was able to see them both naked. Oddly, the sight of them naked inspired more of an appreciation for their beauty than lust. I also appreciated the twin's trust in me. They knew I was gay and yet they didn't mind being naked with me in close quarters. It made me feel accepted. That was far more valuable that seeing them naked, which was worth plenty!

We had slept in late, so Casper made us all brunch. He prepared French toast, biscuits & gravy, and scrambled eggs with melted cheese, and bacon.

"You guys have to come visit more often if we get to eat like this," Brendan said.

"You mean Casper doesn't fix a breakfast like this every morning?" Dax asked.

"Usually, he sets the butter on the table, tosses us a slice of bread, and tells us it's a toast kit. Isn't that right, Scott?"

"Don't involve me in this! I like to eat!"

"From now on, I'll cook breakfast for you, Scott, and give Brendan the toast kit he just invented," Casper said.

"Uh oh. I'll starve to death," Brendan said.

"This is a special occasion since you guys are here and it's breakfast and lunch combined," Casper said.

We stuffed ourselves and when lunchtime came around later I wasn't the least bit hungry. I wondered if I'd ever be hungry again.

After brunch, Drew, Dax, and I were feeling lazy so we sat in front of the TV and Dax flipped through the possibilities on Amazon Prime. It took a while, but we finally agreed on a movie.

"What are you guys going to watch?" Brendan asked.

"A classic film. We've never seen it, but Scott recommends it—*Back to the Future*," Drew said.

"I know I'm old if *Back to the Future* is considered a classic. We saw that at the theatre, didn't we Casper?"

"Yes we did and the sequels," Casper said from the kitchen.

"They had movie projectors back in those days?" Drew asked, mischievously.

"I'm going to smack you," Brendan said, but he grinned.

"Seeing it on a big screen must have been so cool! I love movies from the '80's. That was the golden age of film and music," I said.

"Hmm, if I knew I was living in the golden age back then, I would have paid more attention," Brendan said.

We started the movie. I almost could not believe the twins hadn't seen it. I'd watched it a few times and I always loved it.

Brendan and Casper watched bits and pieces as they came and went, but the twins and I stared at the screen. Watching it with guys who had never seen it was like seeing it for the first time myself. One thing I loved about movies and TV shows is that they were a part of life I could experience over and over again. Every time I watched a movie, it was exactly the same as it had always been. Movies like *Back to the Future* were the only stable part of my life. They were all that I could count on—at least before I met Casper.

"That was awesome!" Dax said when the film ended.

"Yeah, we have to watch the sequels," Drew said.

"They are really good too. Sequels usually aren't as good, but the *Back to the Future* sequels are cool," I said.

"So, you're into 1980's stuff?" Drew asked.

"Yeah. I wish I could have lived in the '80's. They had cool cars, sweet clothes, incredible music, and the best movies. The summer of 1982 is considered the best summer movie season ever—*E.T.*, *Poltergeist*, and *Star Trek II* all came out that summer. Can you imagine being our age back then and having all those in the theatre! If I ever get a chance to travel back in time, I'm going to the 1980's."

"Be sure to say hello if you do," Casper said from where he was seated at the other end of the living room.

"How old were you then?" I asked.

"Let's see. I was seventeen and Brendan was nineteen."

"I am so jealous."

"Don't get too dreamy about the past. We had our problems then too. There was never a golden age. The past wasn't better, only different."

"I don't know. The '80's were pretty sweet," I said.

"We didn't have cell phones back then or streaming video. There were no social media sites and since there were no cell phones, no apps. Video games were extremely primitive compared to today. There were no flash drives or mp3s and no email. We didn't even have DVDs. We had VHS tapes and huge video disks."

"How did you communicate?" Drew asked. I wondered the same thing.

"Smoke signals."

"Come on, really."

"We had phones, but they were connected to the wall with a cord. We wrote letters and sent postcards. Mostly we spoke face-to-face."

"That seems so primitive," I said.

"I suppose it was compared to today."

"How did you stand it?" Dax asked.

"We didn't know what we were missing. Only extremely rich people had portable phones. They were huge, incredibly expensive to buy and to use. Normal people didn't even think about them. The closest thing we saw to cell phones were the communicators on Star Trek. I think email might have been used by the late '80s. I'm not really sure, but at first it was extremely primitive. The Internet was in its infancy. I don't think it was until the '90s that it got going and even then it was very slow. We used something called dial up where we connected to the Internet through the phone lines."

"We do that now," Dax said.

"Yes, but these were the old phone lines, not fiber optic lines. Downloading a photo could take over an hour and a short video clip could take over a day. Steaming a movie would have been impossible."

"You had it rough," Drew said.

Casper laughed. "We did okay and we experienced the excitement of suddenly possessing new technologies. Think about what it was like for us. Anytime we wanted to make a phone call, we were tethered to a wall or we had to seek out a pay phone. If someone was going to call us, we had to make sure we were home. We spent a lot of time waiting around for phone calls. Suddenly, we had a phone we could carry with us. It was like being on *Star Trek*."

"That would seem really cool. I was excited about my first phone," Dax said.

"Exactly. We had to go to the theatre to watch a movie or catch one on TV. Before videotape came along, we didn't have access to most movies. Films were in the theatres for a few days or weeks and then they were gone. Videotape made lots of movies accessible that weren't before. DVDs increased the number and now with streaming video, it's possible to watch just about any film or TV show you want, any time you want."

"I guess the olden days weren't all fun," I said.

"Olden days?" Brendan asked as he entered and sat down.

"The '80's," Casper explained.

"Ah yes, that's when we walked to school..."

"In the snow, five miles there, ten miles back, and uphill both ways," the twins said together, which made me laugh.

"I think you've heard that before," Brendan said.

"Yeah, from Dad."

"We often did walk to school, but it was no further than Scott walks. There was a time when kids walked miles to reach school, but that was close to a hundred years ago and if you ask me what life was like back then I will beat you!" Brendan said. The twins laughed

"Would we do that?" Dax asked.

"Yes, you are too much like your dad."

My time with Drew and Dax was fast slipping away. We tossed the football around in the backyard with Brendan again, who was way better at it than any of us; we wrestled in my room, and messed around. Long before it seemed time, the twin's parents arrived.

I watched as Dax and Drew's Mom and even Dad hugged them. I could tell they were a little embarrassed by it, but they were lucky. I wasn't sure my parents had ever hugged me.

I gazed at Brendan and Casper as they talked with Clint and his wife. I was so lucky to be here. Brendan and Casper cared about me more than any foster parent had before.

We ate supper; fried chicken, mashed potatoes, biscuits, gravy, and green beans followed by chocolate cake for dessert. I liked sitting at the table with so many people and so much talking going on. I felt more like I belonged than I had the first time we all sat down to eat.

Eating supper with the twins and their family was fun, but after dessert it was time for them to go. Dax, Drew, and I went to my room where they packed up their stuff.

"Here are our emails and also our phone numbers for when you get a phone. Maybe you can come up and stay with us. We'll all get together at the family farm sometime too," Drew said.

"I'd like to see the farm."

"You will. You are part of the family now."

"I think that's a little premature," I said.

"I don't," Dax said, then gazed at me. "Let's see, *when* Brendan and Casper adopt you, our grandfathers will be your dads so that makes you... our uncle!"

"I'm younger than you," I laughed.

"You are still our uncle. When you meet our friends, we'll introduce you as Uncle Scott."

"You're crazy, Dax."

"You just noticed that?" Drew asked.

"Boys! We need to go!" called the twin's mom.

Drew and Dax looked at me.

"Everything is going to be fine, you'll see," Dax said and then hugged me. I hugged him back tightly.

"Yep, you're part of our family now. I just hope you're weird enough to fit in," Drew said. He hugged me too.

I felt like I was going to tear up, but I fought it off and smiled instead.

"I'll email you soon."

"Yeah, be glad this isn't the '80's or you'd have to write instead," Dax said.

I smiled and then helped the twins with their backpacks and bags.

I walked out with Brendan and Casper to the van, then watched as Drew, Dax, and their parents drove away. I felt very alone as they disappeared, but then Brendan put his hand on my shoulder and squeezed.

"You want to go to the gym?" he asked.

"Yes!"

"Want to join us, Casper?"

"No thanks. I'll do my workout here."

Brendan hugged Casper and gave him a quick kiss. I hoped I could find someone special like that someday.

"Come on, Scott, the weights are calling to us."

Chapter Thirteen
Casper

Scott, Brandon, Jon, Marc, Alessio and I took our seats just above the north end zone. IU was playing Purdue today and the stadium was packed.

"I can't believe all these people. I've never seen so many people in one place," Scott said.

"IU and Purdue have a long-standing rivalry. Any IU-Purdue football game is usually sold out," I said.

"I thought there were lots of people outside the stadium! I can't believe that big party across the street!" Scott said.

"A football game is more than a football game. There are parties everywhere."

I had attended many football games during my college years. I never missed a home game when Brendan was playing. We had come down to watch a few after we moved back to Verona too. Now, I would likely watch every home game again since Brendan was the head coach.

Scott watched with interest as the Marching Hundred performed, but was mesmerized by the players when they took the field. He was so into the game as it unfolded that he screamed, jumped up, and shouted throughout.

"I'm beginning to suspect that you might like football," Marc said after Scott had jumped up once more and cheered so loudly it hurt my ears.

"I love it!" Scott said. "Throw the ball!" he shouted at the quarterback on the field. Marc looked at me and laughed.

It was a tough game. There was a fair amount of scoring, but no sooner did IU score than Purdue came back with a touchdown. Close games were always more exciting. I thought Scott might grow hoarse with shouting.

I saw Scott gazing at Brendan on the sidelines now and then with what could best be described as hero worship in his eyes. I could understand Scott's feelings. Thousands of people were watching the game in the stadium and thousands and thousands more were watching on TV and there was Brendan, leading the IU team. That had to be impressive to a young boy. It was impressive to me. Brendan had always been extraordinary.

The game came down to the last minute and half when Brendan ran a play that kept me, and obviously Purdue, completely confused. I scanned the field, trying to figure out who had the ball. The quarterback didn't have it. He hadn't passed it so he'd obviously handed it off to someone, but when and how? I thought one receiver had the ball for a moment, but then realized my error and thought another had the ball. I was mistaken. Where was the ball? Had Purdue intercepted?

Everyone else was just as confused. Scott was going crazy trying to figure it out. Someone had to have the ball, but it was as if it had disappeared. I had watched a lot of football games, but I had never seen anything like it.

"There!" Scott said pointing. I followed his finger just in time to see a receiver cross into the end zone. The stands roared with cheers. "How did they do that?" Scott shouted. I shrugged.

Purdue did its best to come back with a touchdown, but the clock ran out. IU won. Scott jumped up and down and cheered like a crazy boy.

"I'm not coming to another game with you if you don't start showing a little enthusiasm," Brandon said to Scott, who grinned showing all his teeth.

"Did you see that? Brendan is so awesome!" Scott said.

"He wasn't even playing," Jon said, clearly intent on starting an argument.

"It was his play! He is the best football coach ever!"

"Brendan paid you to say that, didn't he?" Jon asked.

"No!"

"Yes he did. Admit it!" Jon tickled Scott, who laughed, but refused to agree.

"That was something," Alessio said.

"I'm totally confused," Marc said.

"Join the club," I said.

"So, we're all meeting at Marc and Alessio's place to mooch... I mean for a tailgate party?" Brandon said.

"Yes. We'll regroup there," Marc said.

"We'll be there as soon as we can. Come on, Scott. It will take a while for the parking lot to clear out. Let's go find Brendan," I said.

"Yes!"

We walked up to the top of the seating area and entered the Hall of Champions. There were a lot of people heading for the stairs, but the crowd here was nothing compared to most of the stadium. Our seats were some of the best available. Being the family of the head coach had its perks.

We stopped to use the restroom, which was crowded, but I knew we had time to kill. Brendan was no doubt meeting with the team so we'd have to wait on him.

We soon passed beyond the point where fans were allowed to go. Those guarding the hallway merely nodded as I passed. Most of the staff already knew me. I led Scott down stairs and through hallways until we reached the locker room.

I led Scott inside. The locker room was empty for the moment, but would soon be crowded.

"Where is everyone?"

"There is usually a team meeting after the game. We'll wait for Brendan in his office."

We entered Brendan's large office. The walls were covered with VHS football memorabilia, IU football posters, and a large dry erase board with a schedule for practices and games. On Brendan's desk was a cracked IU football helmet.

"I wonder who was wearing this," Scott said as he picked it up and looked at it.

"Hmm, I have no idea. Those helmets are practically indestructible."

It was several minutes before we spotted players entering the locker room. The noise level steadily increased. The team was obviously excited about their win over Purdue. It was some minutes later before Brendan finally appeared, carrying an antique oaken bucket.

"That was amazing!" Scott said as Brendan entered his office and spotted us.

"I'm still confused," I said.

"That's the idea," Brendan said.

"What' with the bucket?" Scott asked.

"This is a trophy that has been going back and forth between IU and Purdue since 1925," Brendan said.

"It doesn't look like a trophy, it looks like an old bucket."

Brendan laughed. "It is an old bucket, but believe me, winning this is a big deal. It will soon be on display for everyone to see."

"Wow, that's the quarterback from today's game," Scott said as a tall and especially athletic young man entered the locker room and began undressing.

"He's our main quarterback."

"Can I meet him?"

"Yes, but let's wait until he's showered and dressed."

"Hey, who was wearing this helmet when it cracked?" Scott asked, picking up the damaged helmet again.

"Thankfully, no one. A truck backed over it."

"I couldn't imagine what caused it to crack," I said.

"Yeah, these things are tough. They saved my head more than once," Brendan said.

Scott was quite in awe. I noticed he kept stealing glimpses of the players in the locker room. I wondered if he was interested in them because they were college football players, because he was physically attracted to them, or both. I had noticed Scott checking out guys before, especially older, built guys. That could be nothing more than hero worship, but I had a feeling he was gay or bi. Time would tell.

"Can I get some autographs?" Scott asked Brendan.

"Yes, but wait until the players are dressed before asking."

"I'm not going to walk up to them while they're naked!" Scott said.

"Good. Here, you can have them autograph this," Brendan said, handing him the white helmet with crimson IU insignias on the sides.

"Seriously?"

"Yes. It's unusable, so it's no good for anything except display."

"Wow! Thanks!"

Brendan found a marker and Scott walked into the locker room with the helmet. He was not shy about approaching the players, even though they were more than twice his size.

"I see Scott is having a good day," Brendan said.

"He's in Heaven."

"I am too. Beating Purdue is huge. I am so proud of my guys."

"It was a tough game and an exciting one for fans. Scott was going crazy."

"He does love football."

"If you had a biological son, I think he would have been Scott."

"You may be right about that."

I remained in the office while Scott accosted players for their autograph and Brendan attended to business. It was half an hour before we could depart.

"We can't all fit in the Corvette. Why don't you ride with me, Scott?" Brendan asked.

"Yes! I love your car, not that I'm insulting your Prius, Casper. It's cool too."

"Don't worry. Brendan's Corvette is a much cooler car than my Prius. It just isn't practical. I'll meet you guys there."

Scott entrusted me with his helmet, which was now covered with signatures. There was certainly no room for it in the Corvette. I walked to the Prius alone and headed for Marc and Alessio's apartment on Kirkwood Avenue near IU. It was located above Marc's bike shop.

I arrived at the same time as Brendan and Scott, which surprised me because Brendan had a great parking spot right behind the stadium.

We entered Marc and Alessio's apartment together. It was empty, except for Alessio, who was working in the kitchen.

"Everyone is on the roof. I'll be up with this last tray in just a moment," Alessio said.

We continued up to the rooftop garden. It was an amazing space on the top of a two-story building, two of them actually because Marc and Alessio owned the building next to the bike shop and had expanded their apartment to cover the second floor of both buildings.

Large containers held plants and even trees. Raised beds were overflowing with fresh vegetables. There was a grill area and plenty of space to sit, hang out and relax. The weather was perfect, sunny and bright, but not too hot.

"I see you had to make an entrance. You always did love attention," Brandon said when he spotted Brendan.

"That was a great game. Everyone is talking about that last play," Marc said.

"They can talk, as long as they don't figure it out," Brendan said.

"What do you think, Scott? Do you think Brendan did okay coaching?" Jon asked.

"He's incredible!"

"Okay, that's it. I'm not asking your opinion again," Jon teased Scott.

"I got the autographs of a lot of the players on a helmet," Scott said.

"Well I hope you don't ruin it by having Brendan sign it," Brandon said.

"Hey, yeah! You have to sign it when we get home," Scott said.

"You're hopeless, kid, absolutely hopeless," Brandon said, making Scott smile.

Alessio appeared carrying a tray. "Let's eat," he said.

"Now you're talking," Brandon said.

We grabbed plates and got in line. Scott was right in front of me.

"I don't recognize some of this," he said.

"Alessio is from Italy. These are different types of salamis and cheeses. The olives are likely different from those you've seen before. You should try a little of everything. I guarantee it will all be good."

Alessio was the best cook in Bloomington, better even than the best chefs. Today was his version of cold cuts, cheese and vegetable platters, but that description does not do justice to the incredible food spread that was set out before us.

We sat down in comfortable chairs around the central patio area and ate.

"I hate to tell you this, Brendan, but this is a hundred times better than your cookouts with hog dogs," Jon said.

"I have to agree," Brendan said.

"I can't believe how many players I met today," Scott said.

"Knowing the head coach does have perks," Marc said. "Thanks for the tickets, Brendan."

"No problem."

"Did you ever play football?" Scott asked Marc and Alessio.

"No, we were bike racers," Marc said.

"Marc is a legendary Alpha Little 500 bike racer," Alessio said.

"What's Alpha?"

"Our college fraternity."

"It's a home for those who get bad grades," Brandon said.

"Ha! No one gets into Alpha without at least a 3.5," Marc said.

"Yeah. Yeah. Like bike racing matters. It's not important like soccer," Brandon said.

"Don't make me come over there, Hanson!"

Scott laughed. He loved it when the older guys acted like kids.

"This is a nice place. I've always loved your rooftop garden. You have the perfect location," Brendan said.

"Before we created this rooftop area I felt too closed in and I had nowhere to grow fresh vegetables, but I'm very happy here now," Alessio said. "This garden has been here a long time, so we even have fruit trees bearing fruit."

"I couldn't stand not having an outdoor area," I said.

"Not me! I'm thinking of paving our yard so I don't have to mow," Brandon said.

"I do most of the mowing anyway," Jon said.

"You big liar!"

"Your place also has the advantage of *not* being next door to Brandon and Jon," I said.

"Hey!" Jon said.

"You know, Scott, I think you might be the most mature guy here," Marc said.

Scott nodded.

"Hey, I have an idea. Scott can mow our lawn," Brandon said.

"I'll do it, but it will cost you."

169

"What? I was going to ask you to pay me for the privilege of mowing our yard."

"No thanks. I've seen the film *Tom Sawyer*."

"That's what's wrong with kids today. They aren't gullible enough."

"I hope you don't mind me mentioning this, Scott, but when Scott met Brandon and Jon he thought they were a gay couple," I said.

Marc began laughing.

"I'm still not convinced they aren't. They sound like an old married couple," Scott said.

"Old?" Brandon said.

"Yes, OLD!" Scott said.

"How would you like to try to fly off the top of this building, kid?"

Scott laughed.

"Can you believe he called us old?" Brandon asked Jon.

"Well, we are over sixty. What do you call that?"

"Mature."

"No one has every called you mature, Brandon," I said.

"Just wait until you're our age, Scott, then some young punk will come along and call you old. I'll have the last laugh then."

"Well..." Scott said.

"Well what?"

"When I'm your age, you'll be way over a hundred."

"In other words, dead," Jon said.

"Oh no! I am sticking around until I can say, 'How do you like it, Scott?'"

"He'll try. Brandon is like that," Marc said.

"I don't care if I have to stick around until I'm a hundred and fifty, I will get the last laugh," Brandon said.

"Sure you will," Jon said.

"You might as well know, Brandon is a little deluded," Brendan said.

"A little? In high school, he actually thought he was hot," Jon said.

"I was hot! I was hotter than all of you. I had to buy a new shirt every day because girls were so desperate for my bod they ripped it off me."

"Brandon, we've discussed this before. There is fantasy and then there is reality. We know better. Except for Alessio and Scott, we were all there," Jon said.

"Your memory is going, Deerfield. I was the hottest guy ever at VHS. Just how many girls did Brendan get, huh? How many did Casper or Marc get?"

"They're gay, Brandon."

"Don't bother me with details. They got none because I was hotter. I still am."

Scott looked between Brendan and Brandon and shook his head when Brandon wasn't looking. Everyone laughed.

We had a wonderful time talking and hanging out and the food was incredible. I missed Verona, but I was happy to be back in Bloomington.

Chapter Fourteen
Scott

I stopped in my tracks for a moment in the hallway, but quickly continued on as kids began to go around me on both sides. I had just spotted *him* again.

Today, Mohawk Boy was wearing a pale blue dress shirt, tight jeans, and sneakers. I noticed others gaze at him as he passed and why not? He was handsome, sexy, and quite unique. I think I was in love. Okay, probably not since I hadn't so much as spoken to him and didn't know his name or anything about him, but I yearned for him to be my boyfriend and just plain yearned for him. Merely gazing at him made my pants dance.

Mohawk Boy was one more reason I liked school better now. While some of my old teammates kept their distance, no doubt because of my past, the new ones were cool with me. I was especially tight with Noah and Ethan. I had proven myself on the field and I was accepted. I ate with the team at lunch, my teammates were in my classes and I spotted them in the hallways throughout the day. It was like belonging to a fraternity, as Marc had described it.

I had to meet the kid with the Mohawk and it wasn't going to be easy. He wasn't in any of my classes. I never saw him in the cafeteria. I wasn't even sure he was in my grade, but somehow I had to arrange to meet him. He likely had zero interest in guys and might not be into me even if he was gay, but I had to find out.

The day passed quickly. I was better prepared for my classes than I had ever been in middle school. Brendan and Casper had made it clear that my job was school. They didn't make me mow the lawn, take out the trash, or do any of the chores I had to do in other foster homes, but they expected me to study and do as well as I could. My foster dads were kind and yet they weren't pushovers. When either of them said something, he meant it. They had done so much for me and I wanted to stay with them so badly I wasn't about to screw it up by getting in trouble and certainly not by failing to do my homework. I had also discovered something about being prepared for class. It eliminated the anxiety I'd felt before; the dread of being called upon to answer a question I couldn't answer and the anxiety of quizzes and tests. I actually knew the answers now—most of the time.

If I keep this up, I'll turn into a nerd. I laughed out loud. A kid walking past looked at me strangely, but I didn't care.

I liked school better now, but the best part of the day by far was football practice. I couldn't help but smile as I entered the locker room after school, opened my locker, and began to strip.

I noticed Fred, one of my teammates from middle school eying me as I changed into my practice uniform. I don't mean he was checking me out. I wouldn't have minded that. He looked at me as if I was something nasty he'd stepped in and wanted off the bottom of his shoe. Fred had played both football and baseball at Tri-North. It was my former baseball teammates who had it in for me. To them, I was a quitter and deserter. What had happened last baseball season was beyond my control and yet I was entirely to blame.

I had received similar looks from my other old baseball teammates who now played football at North. They didn't want me here, but thankfully they were extremely few in number. When I sat with the team at lunch they sat at the other end of the football tables and ignored me. I knew why and it was entirely my fault.

I had truly let my middle-school teammates down. When I was busted for drugs, kicked off the team, and out of school, I hurt not only myself but them. I was a good player; one of the best on the team and the team went to hell after I was kicked off. I had single-handedly ruined their 8th grade baseball season. I was thankful it didn't happen during football season because there were even more guys from my old team playing at North.

I realized more and more how stupid I'd been and how I'd thought only of myself. That didn't make me feel very good, but it helped me to resist returning to my old ways. I needed all the help I could get. Staying off drugs wasn't so bad, but I swear I craved a cig fifty times a day!

Keeping my distance from Blaze, Felix, and Ace helped too. I missed skating with them and hanging with them, but we always ended up smoking a joint or popping whatever pills we had been able to obtain. I had never meant to get into drugs. I was curious, sure, but I never thought I'd get out of control. Yeah, I was a stupid kid.

Staying away from the guys wasn't particularly easy. Avoiding Blaze was the hardest. A part of me was very much drawn to Blaze and I feared what would happen if we were alone. He was dangerously seductive. Blaze had taught me what two guys could do with each other naked. Some of it, I didn't like so much. That's where Blaze's seductive qualities came in. No matter how much I protested, he could always get me to do what he wanted. That's why I had to avoid him. If I spent time with him, he'd get me into drugs again. He was dangerous.

I closed my locker door and headed out to the field. I didn't have to worry about Blaze here. He would have nothing to do with organized sports. He'd constantly put me down because I played football and baseball in middle school. I tolerated it because... well, I guess because he was Blaze.

Blaze was just like cigarettes. He was something I craved, but couldn't have. Whenever I wanted him, I had to think of something else. Mohawk Boy. I'd think about him.

I worked harder during football practice than I did during the school day. I loved football, so work on the field wasn't actually work. I liked to run before practice, even though the coach pushed us to run further each day and all of us were out of breath by the time we stopped. There was a rumor he was trying to see how long we could run before we collapsed and died, but I think it was just a joke.

Practice today was extra cool because Coach put the older guys in charge of teaching us freshmen standard plays. I had a good head for plays, but executing them was a challenge, especially when some of my teammates screwed them up.

I took my place on the line and looked into the chest of the guy across from me. I had to look up to meet his eyes. He was big! He was also quite handsome, not that it mattered at the moment. I loved his ebony skin. It was about the opposite of mine. I was a pale blond, slightly tanned from the summer sun, but not much. I never tanned well.

We ran the play. The dude across from me plowed into me and knocked me on my ass. That was no surprise. He was not only big, but built. I'd seen him in the locker room and showers and he was ripped.

"I'm Darrell," he said, as he offered me a hand up.

"Hey. I'm Scott."

"You're not bad for a freshman."

175

"Thanks."

"That's why I took it easy on you."

I gulped. That was taking it easy? I pitied whoever had to try to hold him back during a game.

I repeated "Darrell" in my mind a few times so I could remember his name. It shouldn't be too hard. Darrell made quite an impression.

Practice continued. Luckily, I was moved around a lot so I didn't have to face Darrell each time. Almost all the older guys were bigger, except our place-kicker, but then he didn't do much besides kick. That would be boring in a way and yet a game could come down to whether he kicked the ball through the uprights or not.

After an hour of practice, we took a break and everyone headed for the water coolers. I swear I sweat at least a gallon during practice. My jersey was soaked and sweat ran off me in streams.

"Hey, Scott, I'd like you to meet my twin brother, Darrell," said Darrell.

The Darrell who had knocked me on my butt draped his arm over the shoulders of a blond linebacker who was shorter and flabbier.

"Uh... okay." Darrell and Darrell could not have been more different. I mean—one of them was black and the other nearly as blond and white as me!

"What's wrong, Scott?" Biff asked. "Oh, I know. You can't tell them apart. Can you? None of us can. They're identical twins."

Noah and Ethan grinned at me as they sipped water from their cups.

"Yeah, we sometimes go to each other's classes and our teachers never catch on. Even our parents can't tell us apart," Darrell said, the blond one that is.

"So, you're identical twins and you're both named Darrell?"

"That's right and they are my brothers," Biff said. "Let me officially introduce you. This is my brother Darrell and my other brother Darrell." He grinned.

"That sounds vaguely familiar," I said.

"Newhart," Ethan said.

"Newhart?"

"It's an old show. There were three brothers on it; Larry, Darrell, and Darrell."

"It's an amazing coincidence," Darrell, the ebony one, said.

I wasn't quite sure what to do. Biff, Darrell, and Darrell acted as if they were completely serious.

"I'd love to meet your parents," I said at last.

The guys burst out laughing.

"Dudes, quit fucking with the freshman," said another player. "Hey. I'm Luke."

"I'm Scott."

"Come on. I'll get you away from the freaks," he said, putting his arm over my shoulder and leading me away.

"Luke is just sore because he can never tell us apart!" Darrell called out.

Luke smiled and shook his head. "It's on ongoing gag."

"They seemed so serious!"

"That's how they fuck with you."

"It's actually pretty funny, but I didn't know what the hell to do."

"Yeah, I noticed the deer caught in the headlights look. I've seen it often. They're great guys, really!"

"Are both their names really Darrell?"

"Yes, that part is true. That's how the whole thing got started back in middle school."

"So am I their only victim on the team?"

"No, they do it all the time. They'll hit every freshman they can."

"I feel accepted now," I said, holding my head high.

I liked Luke. He was as kind as he was handsome. He was very pale, but he was a ginger and gingers, like blonds, didn't tan easily. His muscles pushed against his jersey and I breathed a little harder. High school boys were so much hotter than middle school boys.

Practice continued. I added Darrell, Darrell, and Luke to the growing list of teammate's names I had memorized. There was no way I was going to forget Darrell and Darrell now. I had to tell Brendan and Casper about them.

After practice, I departed from the locker room with Noah and Ethan. Most guys drove to school, but Noah and Ethan were freshmen like me and couldn't drive yet.

"You could have warned me about Darrell and Darrell," I said as we walked toward the bus stop.

"We didn't want to deny you the experience," Ethan said.

"I assure you, I would have been okay with that."

"Are you as wiped out as I am?" Noah asked.

"Nah, I'm thinking of running home," I said.

"Me too!" Ethan said.

"That would be one long run," Noah said. I lived close enough to school to walk, but Ethan and Noah did not.

"I feel like throwing myself on my bed and sleeping the moment I get home, but I have homework," I said.

"Welcome to my sad and pathetic world," Ethan said.

Noah and I laughed. Ethan was both funny and friendly. He wasn't hard to look at either. I loved his brown hair and eyes. He had a nice body too. He wasn't as muscular as me, but he sure looked good naked.

"See you tomorrow guys," I said as we reached the bus stop.

"Yeah, see ya!"

I continued on alone. My life was coming together. I lived in the nicest home and neighborhood I ever had in my life and had the best foster parents I ever had too. Brendan was even the head football coach at IU! How can you beat that?

I was doing well in school and during football practices. I hadn't touched any drugs and I hadn't smoked a cigarette since that one I told Brendan and Casper about. Even my hard ass probation officer was pleased with me and he wasn't easy to please. I had also passed a random drug test. That was fun!

I was more than half the way home when I turned toward the sound of a push mower. I quickly did a double take. It was Mohawk Boy! He was wearing the same boots I'd seen him wear before, North High School shorts, and he was shirtless! He had a hot, hot body. He was both muscular and defined. The sun glistened off his sweaty torso.

He turned and caught me looking at him, so I waved casually. He nodded to me and then continued with his work. I walked on with a painful and yet pleasant bulge in my shorts. Did he live only a few blocks from me or did he have a lawn mowing business? I sure hoped he lived close. If he did, it might give me a way to meet him.

I thought about Mohawk Boy the rest of the way home. The image of his sweaty, muscular chest and abs were burned into my mind. I wanted to lick him.

"Scott? Come into the kitchen," Casper called out as I entered the front door a very few minutes later.

I walked into the kitchen. "Did I do something wrong?"

"I don't know. Did you?" Casper asked with a slight smile.

"Not that I know about."

"Something came in the mail for you today." Casper held out a smart phone.

"My own phone? Really?"

"Yes, we told you we were getting you one."

"Thank you!" I said and hugged him tightly.

"It has unlimited everything."

"I've never had my own phone before."

"There are two rules that go with it. One—finish your homework before you become lost in your phone. Two—answer quickly if Brendan or I call or text you. We won't call or text unless we really need to, but we expect you to respond if we do."

"Certainly! Here, I'm going to do my homework right now and then I'll come back for my phone," I said, handing it to Casper. "Thanks!" I hugged him again. Casper hugged me back. I didn't say so, but the hug meant even more than the phone.

I hurried to my room, dropped my backpack on my bed and started right in on my homework.

When I finished, an hour and a half later, I walked back into the kitchen. Casper pointed to the counter where my phone was sitting.

"Supper will be ready very soon. Brendan texted that he is heading home," Casper said as he stood at the stove frying fish.

"Great. I'm starving."

"I activated the phone, but I left the setup for you. I figure you can do it faster than me anyway."

"Done."

"You're done?"

"Yeah. This is like the tablets I've used at school. It's easy."

"I know who to call on if I have trouble with anything electronic."

"Hey, you do great. There isn't one piece of electronics in the house with the time flashing."

Casper laughed. We heard the garage door open, then close. Brendan entered the kitchen from the door that led into the garage moments later.

"Look what I got!" I said, holding out my phone. Brendan took it and examined it.

"Hey, this is better than my phone."

"It's my first phone. Thanks!" I hugged Brendan and he hugged me back. My foster dads always returned my hugs. I was so happy right then I almost felt like crying, which was a strange sensation. I don't think I'd ever edged toward tears because I was happy before.

"Want to trade?" Brendan asked.

"I don't think so! I mean, I would, but that would make me seem very ungrateful and we don't want that, do we?"

"We certainly don't."

In minutes, we sat down to a supper of fried catfish and homemade French fries.

"You're such a good cook. When we had fish at my last foster home it was the frozen kind out of a box."

"I have more time than your foster moms did and I only cook for two kids."

"Two?"

"You and Brendan."

"Ha! Brendan's not a kid."

"What did he do all day? He played around with a football. He sounds like a kid to me."

"Yes, and I will never grow up," Brendan said.

"Yes, Peter Pan."

"You do have a sweet life. You do exactly what you want to do," I said to Brendan.

"I actually do a lot of things I don't want to do, but you're right. I have been able to pursue football my entire life. I have

Casper to thank for that. He's always been supportive. He even gave up the farm we both loved so I could come to Bloomington to coach."

"Hey, I just wanted to take it easy," Casper said and grinned.

"What do you want to do, Scott?" Brendan asked.

"I don't know. I'm not really good at anything. Well, I'm good at sports but that's about it."

"You're a talented artist," Casper said.

"Yeah, but what can I do with that; sell paintings on the sidewalk?"

"You could be a commercial artist. We have a friend from high school who makes a living by creating architectural art. His partner restores old buildings and homes."

"Partner? You mean like boyfriend?"

"Yes."

"You know a lot of gay guys, don't you?"

"Yes we do. I know you think our high school days are ancient history, but we met quite a few gay boys then, such as Marc, who you met. We've kept in touch with most of them," Casper said.

"When I coached high school football and taught, I was approached by a lot of gay students and players over the years for advice and guidance. So I know several that way," Brendan said.

I paused for a moment, looking back and forth between Brendan and Casper. I had been thinking about something for quite a while, and as I sat with them in the kitchen I quickly made up my mind.

"There's something I want to tell you... I'm gay," I said.

Casper nodded and Brendan smiled. "I'm glad you told us."

"You don't seem surprised," I said to Casper.

"I've picked up on a few things. I thought you might be gay, but I wasn't sure. I haven't thought about it much because whether you're gay, straight, or bi, I love you the same."

"I am and I'm not bi either. I'm only attracted to guys."

"If you want to talk or need advice, you know we're here," Casper said.

"Yes, we have extensive experience with being gay," Brendan said and grinned.

"There is a topic we should broach. Condoms," Casper said.

"Uh..."

"You know you should use them, right?"

I nodded. I could feel my face getting hot and hoped I wasn't turning too red.

"I'll buy you a box. I'm not encouraging you to use them, but I want you to have them in case you need them. If you need more, I'll get them for you, no questions asked. I know talking about sex with someone older can be uncomfortable and even embarrassing, but it's important that you ask us questions if you have any," Casper said.

"Thanks," I said, not knowing what else to say.

"We are glad you shared this with us, Scott. It helps us to know you a little better," Brendan said. I nodded.

"Now, back to our earlier topic—art. There are a lot of options you can consider. You could be a graphics artist. You could even design graphics for games."

"I'd never thought of that," I said. I was as intrigued by that idea as I was relieved that we were no longer talking about sex.

"You don't have to make any decisions now, but it's something to think about."

Brendan and Casper were not like any adults I'd ever had in my life before. They didn't treat me like a kid. They treated me as if I was mature and responsible and yet they didn't go ballistic when I screwed up, like with the cigarette. I didn't know adults like them actually existed.

After supper, I linked my phone to all my online stuff. For a moment, I thought I didn't have anyone to call or text, but then I remembered that Drew and Dax had given me their numbers. It took me a bit to remember where I'd stashed them, but when I did, I quickly put them into my phone and sent a text.

"This is your Uncle Scott. I got a phone!" was my very first text ever.

"LOL, sweet!" Dax texted back.

"Great, this will be better than email," Drew texted.

"Oh yeah! I also told B&C I'm gay."

"They were totally cool about it, right?" Dax asked.

"Yes, but they did talk to me about sex."

182

"Ouch! Embarrassing!" Drew texted.

"Very!"

We texted back and forth for a while. It was as if Dax and Drew were right there with me. I wish they were. I had missed them since their visit. We had kept in touch by email, but it wasn't the same. I loved texting!

I spent the rest of the night putting apps on my phone and getting it just like I wanted. I couldn't believe I had such a great phone. I knew Casper said he'd get me one, but I expected something very basic. This was way better!

The phone almost overshadowed the fact that I'd told Brendan and Casper I was gay. I was glad I had done it. It seemed like the right time. At first, I didn't tell them because I wasn't sure it was safe to do so. I thought Casper was a nice guy and Brendan seemed cool, but it wasn't safe to be too trusting too soon. They were older gay guys and if they knew I was gay, they might have taken advantage. I didn't think they were like that, but I needed to be sure before I told them. I had been sure for a while and more certain every day. My foster dads were just what they seemed. They had no hidden dark side. I felt safer here with them than I ever had before.

***

I had the skate park to myself. I liked being around other skaters, but sometimes it was cool to do my own thing. I practiced some of the moves I didn't have down, such as the heel flip, which was hella difficult. There were far more difficult tricks, but I wasn't ready for those. There were a few that could even be fatal if performed wrong. I didn't even think about attempting those. I was brave, but I wasn't crazy.

I stiffened when I spotted Blaze approaching with his board. He was alone. I wasn't sure if that was a good thing or bad, but I was uneasy.

He didn't do more than nod to me when he entered the fence. He began skating, doing tricks that were far beyond my abilities. I had always admired his skills on a board. That's what had originally drawn me to him. I had asked him to show me how to do a trick. At first, I thought he was going to tell me to get lost, but then he'd become sort of a skating mentor. I wish things could have stayed like that, but Blaze had other ideas. All that seemed so far in the past now.

Blaze skated up to me. Flipped his board in the air and caught it in one hand.

"Why have you been avoiding me?" he asked.

"I've been busy. I'm on the football team."

"You're wasting time with *that* again?"

"I like to play."

"You're being used. Do you know how much money the school makes off football games?"

"I love football."

"Whatever. At least you're still skating and haven't turned into a total loser."

"I should get home." I knew I needed to get out of there. Every moment I spent with Blaze was a risk.

"No. Stay a while. I've missed you and I have some good stuff."

"I don't do that anymore."

"Yeah, right. I know you."

"I'm not doing that anymore, Blaze," I said firmly. I almost couldn't believe I had the balls to say it, but I did.

"What the fuck has happened to you? You used to be cool."

"I ended up in Juvie because of drugs. I got kicked off the baseball team and out of school. My old teammates hate me."

"So? Who cares about those losers? Are you gonna let other people control you your entire life?"

"I'm not being controlled."

"Sure you are."

"I'm not. I just don't want to do that anymore. I have a new foster home now and my foster dads are great."

"Dads?"

"Yeah."

"Ah, I see. That explains the clothes and the new skateboard. What do you do for them to get all that stuff, Scott?"

"It's not like that!"

"Hey, dude. It's okay. I know how it is. If you want to keep that shit on the down low I understand."

"There is nothing to keep on the down low."

"Right." Blaze winked, making it obvious he was insincere. I wanted to punch him, but didn't dare. He'd murder me. "Come on, let's share a joint. Show me you're still cool."

"No."

"Come on, man. You know you want to. I really have missed you. I've missed what we do when we get fucked up."

"You miss using me," I said and knew immediately I'd gone too far.

"What did you say to me, you little shit? I've never used you. You wanted it and you know it."

"I'm leaving," I said. I reached for the gate, but Blaze slammed it shut.

"No, you're not. You're not going anywhere until you smoke with me."

I was angry, afraid, and unsure of what to do. Blaze was bigger and stronger than me. He could make me do anything he wanted. I was determined to resist, but I knew I was screwed.

Luckily, as these thoughts went through my head and I considered punching Blaze in the gut and trying to run for it, a car pulled in and a dad and two boys got out. The boys were carrying boards. Blaze took his hand off the gate. I opened it as the family approached and made my escape.

I walked quickly away. I left the park and headed north. My heart pounded in my chest and the bulge in my shorts was so big I feared people in cars driving by would notice it. I experienced a mix of terror, lust, longing, and pride as I walked toward home.

I calmed down as I walked and began to sort things out. The truth was that part of me wanted to go with Blaze and do the things we'd done before. I knew I couldn't do that. It would ruin everything. I had a good home, at least for now. I was on the football team and I was doing well in school. I wasn't going to mess all that up. Blaze scared me. I'm not sure what would have happened if that guy and his kids hadn't pulled in, but it wouldn't have been good. Blaze would probably have beaten me up at the least and I didn't even want to think about his worst. Blaze was dangerous. I could never go back to the skate park alone. It wasn't safe.

Part of me was proud. I had feared the temptation of Blaze. I had been very much afraid I'd cave to him, but I didn't. I stood up and told him "no." Even when he pressured me, I wouldn't give in. I truly didn't think I had that in me. I think I was prouder of myself just now than I could ever remember being before.

I was proud, but still scared. I even trembled a little. I wasn't sure what Blaze would do now. I had to avoid him and be careful not to take the least chance of him getting me alone. I knew how to take care of myself, but he was bigger and meaner.

When I arrived home, Casper was in the living room. He took one look at me and asked, "Are you okay?"

I bit my lip. I had planned to keep this to myself, but Casper was onto me and I didn't want to lie to him.

"I ran into a boy at the skate park who used to get me into trouble. He tried to get me to do drugs with him." Casper looked alarmed. "I didn't. I told him 'no,' but when I tried to leave he wouldn't let me."

Casper stood up, walked to me, and hugged me.

"Did he hurt you?"

I shook my head against his chest, but didn't speak for several moments because I was about to get choked up.

"A dad and his sons arrived, so I was able to get away from him. I... I can't go back to the skate park alone anymore," I said when I more or less had my voice under control.

"Brendan or I will take you."

Casper released me. I looked up at him and smiled.

"There is one good thing about seeing him again. I was afraid I couldn't say 'no' to him, but I did. He has always been able to talk me into doing things I shouldn't do, but not today."

"I'm very proud of you. Sometimes, it takes a lot of strength to say 'no.'"

"It did today."

Casper hugged me again. Nothing felt quite so good as his arms holding me tight. At that moment, I felt like he was really my dad.

***

I sent Casper a quick text after football practice. He replied in less than a minute. I looked up and smiled at the guys.

"I can go."

"Great, I'm starving," Ethan said.

The two of us waited until Noah tied his shoes and then the three of us departed from the locker room.

"I'm going to order a sandwich with extra everything," Ethan said.

"Maybe you can order one of those party-size subs meant to serve twelve," I said.

"I'm not that hungry."

"Scott, what was up with you and Jaxon before practice? I thought you were going to punch him in the face," Noah asked.

"Yeah, I heard him mouthing off," Ethan said. "He said something like, 'You won't be on the team long. You'll do something stupid and get kicked off.'"

"He was referring to last year at Tri-North. I did something stupid, got kicked off the baseball team and out of school. I was about to punch him in the face, but then I realized that would only prove him right. Attacking him would have been stupid and would probably have got me kicked off the team."

"True."

"What did you do that got you kicked out of school?" Noah asked. Ethan and Noah were sophomores so they were a grade ahead of me and missed the Tri-North drama last year.

"Drugs."

"Seriously?" Ethan said.

"Yeah, I don't do that shit anymore. Jaxon was right. It was stupid. I was stupid."

"I wouldn't touch that shit. I had a cousin who was a druggie. He's dead now," Noah said.

"I got in with the wrong crowd. You know how that is," I said.

"Yes, but you're with us now. We're the right crowd," Ethan said, draping his arm over my shoulder for a moment.

"Mind you, we're not exactly choir boys," Noah said.

"We mostly stay out of trouble. The key word is mostly," Ethan said.

"There was that time we held up a liquor store," Noah said.

"Don't forget the gas station robbery."

"Yeah, I almost forgot about that. You know I still have gas?"

"You guys are weird," I said.

"Everyone knows that," Noah said.

"We're weird, but we do mostly stay out of trouble."

"Me too, now. The hardest part for me is resisting the urge to smoke a cigarette."

"You smoked too?" Noah asked.

"Yeah. It's not so hard to keep away from the drugs, but sometimes I want a cig so bad I can hardly stand it. Whatever you do, don't start smoking. It's SO hard to quit."

"I didn't know you were such a bad boy," Ethan said, grinning.

"Hey, I'm a perfect angel now."

"Sure you are," Ethan said, patting me so hard on the back I stumbled forward.

"Did you drink too?" Noah asked.

"Yeah, I was putting down as many as six Cokes a day there for a while."

"I mean alcohol, dufus!"

"I tried vodka once and only once. It's nasty and I barfed all over the place."

"You really know how to have a good time," Ethan said.

"Yeah, right. That was not a good time. I, uh... ended up in Juvie."

"We're hanging out with someone with a prison record, Noah," Ethan said.

"Yeah, we better watch what we say or Scott will cut us."

"Ha. Ha. You guys are okay with all that, right? I don't do any of that shit anymore."

"We all make mistakes. When I was a kid, I tried smoking oregano," Ethan said.

"Wow, what an idiot," Noah said.

"Oh, like you never did anything stupid."

"Well, I did eat a whole bunch of peanut butter and gummy bear sandwiches once. You don't want to know the details, but it involved multiple trips to the bathroom."

"Peanut butter and gummy bears? You sicko," I said.

"Hey, they're good, but whatever you do, don't eat too many of them at once."

"I can safely say I will never do that," Ethan said.

"Thanks for telling us about what happened. I'm glad you trust us enough to tell us," Noah said.

"It's not exactly a secret and I don't go around announcing it, but since you asked why Jaxon and I got into it, I thought you should know."

"So, if we need anyone bumped off, can you hook us up?" Ethan said with a grin.

"Keep it up and I'm going to bump you off."

Ethan grabbed Noah and shoved him between us as a shield. "Over Noah's dead body!"

"Hey, don't volunteer me for anything, especially that!" Noah said.

"You guys are very strange," I said.

"We're weird and strange. Wait, isn't that the same thing? Anyway, I figure that's why you like us," Noah said.

Ethan and Noah were cool. Not that many sophomores would hang out with a lowly freshman. I had hesitated only slightly before telling them about my past. I wasn't certain about their reaction, but I figured they would be okay with it. I definitely didn't want to lie to teammates and guys I considered my friends.

I checked out the skate park as we walked past. There were five guys skating, but I couldn't tell if any of them were Blaze and his buddies. Part of me yearned to skate, but I wasn't going alone again. It was too dangerous.

We soon arrived at the Subway, which was one of two places to eat within walking distance of the house. The other was Aver's Pizza, which was located in the same small strip mall out in front of Kroger.

"There's where I'll be playing soon," Noah said, pointing to the IU stadium in the near distance. I smiled to myself. I had not yet told anyone at school that one of my foster dads was the head coach and that I'd met the team.

"Sure, you will," Ethan said with great insincerity. "You believe him, don't you, Scott?"

"Oh yeah! Absolutely. Then, he'll play pro!"

"Screw you guys!"

We laughed and then the three of us entered.

We began to browse the menu and then suddenly I froze. Mohawk Boy was behind the counter working. I was mesmerized for a few moments, but then remembered I was supposed to be figuring out what to order, not gawking at Mohawk Boy like an idiot. Luckily, my companions were ahead of me and didn't notice.

Ethan and Noah ordered first and then it was my turn. I stammered out my order for a six-inch spicy Italian on Italian bread. I did better picking out the toppings but actually speaking to Mohawk Boy, Jonathan that is, overwhelmed me. I finally discovered his name—on his nametag.

Ethan, Noah, and I filled our drinks and sat down with our sandwiches. I tried not to look toward Jonathan, but I couldn't resist stealing a few glances. I loved his Mohawk and he was so handsome. Jonathan—I loved that name.

"I think we're going to have an even better team than last year," Ethan said as he bit into his sub.

"Because I'm on the team now, right?" I teased.

"Yeah, sure. That's what I meant," Ethan said in a tone that meant he didn't.

"Jerk."

"Actually, you are good. You're the best freshman we have. Of course, you're nothing compared to us sophomores."

"Didn't he fumble the ball during practice?" I asked Noah.

"Yes, I believe he did."

"Oh, I did that on purpose so as not to appear too talented. Jealousy isn't good for a team."

"You're selfless, truly selfless," I said.

"I like to think so."

"I'd tell you what I think, but we're friends," Noah said.

Ethan growled.

My attention was continually drawn toward Jonathan as we talked and ate. Later, I almost tripped over my own feet as I went to refill my drink. When I returned to the table, both Noah and Ethan gazed at me knowingly.

"Why don't you just ask him out?" Ethan said.

My face paled and my alarm was no doubt obvious. I thought about asking Ethan what he meant, but I had obviously been nailed.

"Because I'm afraid to?" I asked instead.

"You're into him?" Noah asked.

"Yeah."

"I thought so. You can't keep your eyes off him. So, do you swing both ways or..."

"I'm just into guys." I waited expectantly. Ethan and Noah seemed okay with my interest in Jonathan...so far.

"I would never have guessed you are gay, but then I never guessed my uncle was gay either," Ethan said.

"I am and now that we're on the topic, what about you guys?"

"I'm one of those perverts who likes girls," Noah said.

"You disgust me," Ethan said, clearly without meaning it.

"Hey, you like girls too."

"Yes, but I also like guys. I'm a hybrid."

"That just means he's a slut," Noah said.

"Oh, how I wish that was true!"

We all laughed.

"This is interesting—straight, bi, gay," I said pointing to Noah, Ethan, and myself.

"We need a trans guy to complete the set," Noah said.

"And a hermaphrodite," Ethan said.

"There are a couple of trans kids at school, but I don't know any hermaphrodites," Noah said.

"Maybe when you hook up with a girl, she'll have a surprise for you," Ethan said.

"I wouldn't know what to do with it. I mean, I know what to do with *mine*," Noah said.

"That's not what the girls say," Ethan said.

"Oh shut up."

"So, that's your type?" Ethan asked, nodding toward Jonathan.

I nodded. Ethan smiled.

"You should ask him out."

"Chances are, he likes girls."

"It's true, us perverts are everywhere," Noah said.

"So what if he does like girls? He's not going to get pissed if you ask him out. It's no big deal. No one cares anymore except for a few fake religious assholes and Neo-Nazis and who cares about them? He is hot. You should grab him before someone else does."

"Yeah, someone like Ethan," Noah said.

"Nope. Scott is into him so he's off limits for me."

"What's your type?" I asked.

"Skinny boys."

"Really?"

"Yes, I don't know if you've noticed, but skinny boys usually have huge dicks."

"You know, now that you mention it..."

"That's the trouble with you gay and bi guys, you're obsessed with dick," Noah said.

"Yeah, well you're obsessed with certain girl parts."

"Mmm, yes."

"I'll give you twenty bucks if you go ask him out," Ethan said. "If he turns you down, Noah will suck your dick."

"No, Noah won't," Noah said.

"You're not being a team player, Noah."

"Sorry, the only dick I like is mine."

"You can do that?"

"Huh? No! That's not what I meant!"

"Hmm, you say you can't do it. That means you've tried."

"I have not!"

Ethan laughed. "Noah and his dick are very close. They've been dating for a long time. Okay, no blow job from Noah, but I will give you twenty bucks if you ask him."

"I can't."

"Are you scared?"

"Yes!"

"Come on, get it over with. You won't have to worry anymore. Just ask him out."

Ethan did make sense. If I did it now, I wouldn't have to agonize over it. Before I lost my nerve, I stood up and walked toward the counter. No one else was around. Jonathan smiled at me as I approached.

"Can I get you something else?"

"No, uh... I was wondering. Would you like to... um... go to a football game with me, at IU? I, uh... like you," I said. How awkward could I be?

"What's your name?"

"Oh, uh... Scott."

"Give me your phone."

"Okay," I said, slightly confused.

I handed my cell phone over the counter. Jonathan messed with it a few moments while I waited expectantly. My heart was racing. I heard a cricket chirp and then Jonathan handed back my phone, took his out, and typed on it. My phone chimed.

"Look at your phone."

I did so. I read the text that had appeared. "I would love to go with you."

"Really? Awesome! I'll... uh... text you later."

"I'll look forward to that."

I turned and walked back to the booth, grinning like an idiot.

"That was sad. I could hardly bear to watch," Ethan said.

"Shut up and give me my twenty bucks."

Ethan pulled out his wallet and handed over the cash.

"I want to hear all the details of your date. If it wasn't for me, you wouldn't be going out with your dream boy," Ethan said.

"Ethan is a pervert. Next, he'll want to watch while you have sex."

"What's wrong with being a pervert?"

"It depends on what kind of pervert."

"Oh, like you and your sister, that's disgusting," Ethan said.

"Ha. Ha."

"Actually, Noah's sister is hot."

"You sicko. She's eight."

"Not your little sister, dumb ass, your big sister."

"First of all, she's way out of your league. Second, there will be no dating my sisters."

"Why not?"

"Because I know too much about you."

"Hmm. I see your point. Oh my god! Will you stop grinning, Scott?"

"Not so loud," I said, looking toward Jonathan.

"Oh, he didn't hear. He's taking an order. You're smiling so much you look like a Disney character."

"Probably one of the dwarfs—Horny," Noah said.

"That is not one of the seven dwarfs."

"Maybe there was an eighth one that Disney didn't dare to talk about."

"You are definitely weird."

"That's why we get along so well."

"Hmm, you have something there. So, where are you taking dream boy?" Ethan asked.

"A football game, at IU."

"That will be expensive."

"Oh, I can get us tickets for free. I'm pretty sure I can anyway."

"How?"

"One of my foster dads is the head coach."

"Are you *serious*? Why didn't you tell us this before?"

"You didn't ask."

"Wait. Dads?" Noah asked.

"Yeah, they are a gay couple."

"I didn't know you were in a foster home," Ethan said.

"You didn't ask about that either."

"Grr. You drive me crazy!"

"What else have you not told us because we didn't ask?" Noah said.

"Hmm, well that's it for all the big stuff, but there are thousands of little things, such as I hate sushi, I am the world's greatest skater, and I'm probably destined to be a pro football or baseball player."

"Hmm, I believe the first one. The last two seem unlikely," Ethan said.

"Okay, I'm not the world's greatest skater, but I'm pretty good. As for my pro career, who knows?"

"This is true," Noah said.

"Wow, you are so much more interesting than I thought, not that I thought you were boring," Ethan said.

"Yeah, and now you and Jonathan can have a torrid love affair and be the talk of the school," Noah said.

"Another gay couple—boring! They'll only be the talk of the school if they blow each other in the hallway between classes," Ethan said.

"Well, don't hold your breath for that," I said.

"Come on, that will be nothing to a bad ass like you," Ethan said.

"Yeah, right. I don't think so, but you can keep on calling me a bad ass if you want."

"Eh, the mood has passed," Ethan said.

"Yeah, if you aren't going to blow your boyfriend in the hallway at school, you're not a bad ass," Noah said.

"I just asked him out, so he's hardly my boyfriend. I'm not even sure he's into guys yet. Even if he becomes my boyfriend, I am not blowing him in public."

"How are we going to start a scandal if you won't do anything scandalous?" Ethan asked.

"I did plenty last year, believe me, and I am not doing that again. There are plenty of guys who still think I'm a loser, like Jaxon."

"He's certainly not very friendly with you," Noah said.

"Not at all."

"I suppose notoriety has its costs. I was planning to run through the hallways at school naked, but now I guess I won't," Ethan said.

"Yeah right!"

"I would have way too many girls and guys after me if I did that. I can only handle so many."

"Ethan lives in his own little fantasy world," Noah said.

"Hey, I look great naked. You know I do."

"Eh-eh," Noah said.

"Be honest. I'm aware you're into girls, but you know I'm hot."

"Since we're friends, I'll admit it. You're hot, but Scott is hotter."

"Hey, no one asked about Scott!"

"It's okay, Ethan. You're almost as hot as me," I said.

"I need better friends."

"You're lucky to have friends as awesome as us. Believe me, I do not go around telling guys they are hot. You should feel special," Noah said.

"Okay, then."

I kept looking at Jonathan as we ate and talked. He looked in my direction a few times and smiled. When he did, my heart beat faster and I felt giddy and happy.

I gave Jonathan one last glance as I departed. He caught my eyes and grinned at me again. I sighed as we walked outside.

"I think he's in love," Ethan said.

"Maybe it's just lust," Noah said.

"Jonathan is hot, but I think this is far more serious than lust. Don't worry, buddy, we'll help you through it," Ethan said, draping his arm over my shoulder.

"I do like him a lot. I felt like I loved him the first time I saw him, but I know that's ridiculous."

"I've felt that way about girls. I know what you mean," Noah said.

"I've felt that way about guys and girls."

"I've never felt this way before."

"Well, you're lucky. You approached Jonathan and didn't get shot down," Ethan said.

"Have you been shot down?" I asked.

"This is only between the three of us, but yes."

"Me too," Noah said.

"I mostly like to play the field," Ethan said.

"That means he gives free blow jobs in the end zone after practice," Noah said.

"Hmm, there's an idea," Ethan said, pretending to think it over.

"Maybe you could charge a fee," I said.

"Hey, I could become a prostitute and become the talk of the school," Ethan said.

"I don't think that's the kind of fame you want," Noah said.

"True and I like to keep my sexual encounters discreet."

"That's for sure. He won't even tell me about them," Noah said.

"Do you really want to hear?"

"Only about your encounters with girls."

"That's too bad. I'm only willing to tell you about my hookups with guys."

We kept talking, but I was only half aware of what was said. My mind continually returned to Jonathan.

Chapter Fifteen
Casper

Brendan and I jumped up with the rest of the crowd and cheered as the North receiver ran into the end zone, scoring the winning goal of the game. It had been a close one.

"I miss high school football," Brendan said.

"I'm glad to see you kept yourself from coaching from the stands."

Brendan laughed. "I would never do that. I had far too many problems with fathers coaching from the sidelines at VHS."

"Scott did really well today, didn't he?" I asked.

"I may be biased, but he has a lot of talent. I'm very proud of him," Brendan said.

He meant it. I could tell. He was as proud of Scott as he had been of Clint when he played. Brendan was always proud of Cameron and Conner for their achievements as well. Sports were his thing, but he wasn't narrowly focused on them.

Quite a few spectators approached Brendan while we waited on Scott after the game. As the head football coach of IU, he was a celebrity. Even back in Verona he was well known, but in Bloomington we couldn't go anywhere without someone wanting to talk to him or asking for an autograph. A lot of people were crazy about sports.

Brendan was still talking to three football fans when Scott returned to the field from the locker room and met us on the sideline.

"Hey, Scott," I said. "Are you ready to go eat?"

"I'm starving!"

"Is this your son?" one of the guys talking to Brendan asked.

"Yes, he is."

Scott looked momentarily surprised but then grinned.

"Are you going to play football for your dad at IU?"

"I hope so," Scott said, grinning even more.

"We need to get going. It was nice to meet you," Brendan said, shaking hands all around.

The three of us walked toward the parking lot. I noticed Scott eying Brendan and me. We were nearly to the Prius before he spoke.

"You told that guy I was your son," Scott said, his voice catching in his throat.

"I know I'm not your biological father, but that's how I feel about you," Brendan said.

Scott was obviously fighting back tears. He hugged Brendan tightly and released him. I noticed him wiping his eyes as he turned from us and opened the back door. I smiled at Brendan over the top of the car.

"What do you feel like eating?" I asked as I turned on the car.

"Mexican," Scott said.

"Sounds good to me," Brendan said.

"Let's go to La Charreada," I said.

I pulled out of the parking lot. Soon, we passed our home and a minute later reached the stoplight at the bypass. I turned left, then right at the light on College Avenue, and drove around Miller-Showers Park to the restaurant.

We were soon seated in a booth, munching on chips & salsa as we browsed the menus. When the waiter returned with our drink orders, Scott ordered a Chimichanga, Brendan ordered steak fajitas, and I ordered a burrito. We all ordered rice and refried beans.

"You did an excellent job today," Brendan said.

"I was just a lineman."

"I was a quarterback in high school and college and believe me, without my teammates keeping the other team off me, I couldn't have done anything. Each member of a football team truly is valuable. That's not merely something coaches say to make everyone feel good. It is the truth."

"I thought that one was going to plow right through me."

"I noticed him. He was huge. You did an amazing job against him. He had skills," Brendan said. Scott smiled.

"He looked too old to be in high school," I said.

"Some high school boys do. Some physically mature earlier than others."

"Sometimes I feel like a shrimp out there," Scott said.

"You're no shrimp, but I know what you mean. That will change as you get older," Brendan said.

"I was a shrimp when I was your age," I said. "My nickname was Casper The Friendly Runt," I said.

Scott laughed, but then quickly stopped. "Sorry."

"It's okay. It's funny now. It wasn't then."

"Were you really that small?"

"Yes, I was skinny and not very tall."

"You sure changed."

"You will too. By the time you're a junior, you'll be one of the big guys," I said.

"When you reach that point, don't forget what being one of the smaller guys felt like," Brendan said. Scott nodded.

Our food soon arrived. The service at La Charreada was quick.

"This is so much better than Taco Bell, and I like Taco Bell," Scott said.

"This is real Mexican food. Taco Bell is an Americanized cheap copy, although I like it too," I said.

"Can you get me a couple of tickets to an IU game soon?" Scott asked Brendan.

"Sure."

"Can you give us a ride there? I, uh... sort of have a date," Scott said, looking at me.

"A date, huh? Yes, I can. So you've found someone you like?"

"Yeah, his name is Jonathan. He has a Mohawk, but don't worry. He's not anyone who might get me in trouble. He goes to North and works at Subway and he's wonderful."

I was a little concerned when Scott told us Jonathan had a Mohawk, but I had learned long ago not to judge by appearance. I refused to prejudge him.

"So I take it I'm not invited," I said mischievously.

"No, but you get to drive us there and maybe take us somewhere to eat later?"

"That sounds like a great deal, Casper," Brendan said, grinning.

"Yeah, I can't pass that up. Brendan and I can eat somewhere separately after the game."

"I'll get you seats well away from Casper's too," Brendan said.

"Although I may take my field glasses so I can spy on you," I said.

Scott cocked his head and gave me his "yeah right" look. "You two are the best."

"We should be recording this," Brendan said.

"So what can you tell us about Jonathan?" I asked.

"He dresses really nice, not at all like you'd think a boy with a Mohawk would dress. He's very handsome. I don't really know a whole lot about him, but I really like him."

"Will this be your first date? I don't mean with Jonathan, I mean your first date ever?" I asked.

Scott nodded. "I'm nervous, but excited. I couldn't believe he said "yes" when I asked him out or that I had the courage to ask him out. I'm not totally sure he's into guys, but I think he is."

"Even if he's not, it never hurts to have another friend," Brendan said.

"Yeah, but I hope he is," Scott said a bit dreamily. I looked away to hide my smile.

I was excited for Scott, because he was obviously excited. This was a big event for him. I hoped it worked out well and that he didn't get his heart broken. Heartbreak was inevitable at some point for nearly everyone, but I couldn't help but hope Scott would be spared that pain. He had experienced enough pain in his life.

After we ate, we made a trip to College Mall to pick up a few things at Target. Strolling through the mall with Scott brought back memories of our days with Clint, Cameron, and Conner. Who would have guessed that after all these years we would have a boy in our care again?

Scott texted his friend Ethan while we were browsing in the mall and Ethan was waiting on him by the time we returned home. The pair departed immediately for the skate park, which gave Brendan and me some rare time alone.

"Think I should have another sex talk with him?" Brendan asked as we carried in shopping bags.

"I think we covered it already."

"Yeah, but you know what teen boys are like. You know he's raring to have sex. At his age, his body demands it constantly. He obviously likes this..."

"Jonathan," I said.

"Yeah, Jonathan and if he returns Scott's interest it probably won't be long before something happens between them."

"I don't think that much will happen on his first date and we bought him condoms."

"I'm just worried about him."

I smiled. "Me too, but we don't want to nag him. We didn't hassle Clint, Cameron, and Conner about sex and they turned out more than okay."

"I'd forgotten how much I worried when they were young."

"It's part of being a parent. I'm sure you noticed Scott's reaction when you said he was your son," I said.

"Yeah."

"What do you think about taking the next step and adopting him, Brendan?"

"That's a big step, but I've been thinking about it too. He already feels like our son."

"He hasn't turned out to be as difficult to handle as we thought. We knew going into this that drugs might be a problem, but Scott has stayed away from them. There could be problems yet, but he's made it this far so I think we should give adopting him serious consideration. We're going to keep him as a foster son and adopting him will give him an even greater sense of stability. It will confirm what we've been telling him about being there for him."

"I agree. Let's keep thinking about it and at the same time start to lay the groundwork. I don't have to remind you there is quite a bit involved, and it may be more difficult this time."

"Do we need to keep thinking about it? I know this is a huge commitment, but we've both been considering it since the moment Scott moved in."

"I have been considering it since the beginning, since I met Scott, in fact, but I want to make sure we're doing the right thing and not taking on more than we can handle," Brendan said. "I feared we might be too old to take on such a responsibility, but we're doing okay so far. Truly, it's more up to you. I'm working on campus so much that most of raising Scott will fall on you. I'll do as much as I can, but I am out of the house for several hours a day. You're the one who is home when he returns from school. It is you who bears the brunt of making on-the-spot decisions. I don't have to tell you about the time involved in raising kids and we're a good deal older now than when Clint, Cameron, and Conner were young."

"We're talking about one boy instead of three this time and I have much more time than I did back then. I became Scott's Big Brother partially because I had too much time on my hands and I didn't feel needed anymore."

"I need you."

I smiled. "I know, but I felt... sort of like a housewife. I stay home, I cook, I clean, and I do the shopping. I like doing all that, but it's not enough. Since Scott has been in our lives, I've felt needed and useful again."

"You're always needed and useful, but I understand what you mean. I have my team and my job. I know you feel that you're in the background. I couldn't do what I do without you to support me, but I also understand you need more. Scott definitely needs you."

"He needs us. No one has ever loved that boy and been there for him. I love him."

"I do too."

"Then do we really need to think about it?"

"No. I guess we only need to ask Scott."

I smiled. I knew Brendan would understand and I knew he loved Scott as much as I did. "Congratulations, it's a fourteen-year-old boy."

"Hmm, it seems as if we've been through this before," Brendan said.

"Yeah, and wasn't it great last time?"

"It was horrible! You do remember the teen Cameron, right?"

I laughed. "He's why I have gray hairs, but look at him now."

"Let's not wait. Let's ask Scott when he gets home," Brendan said.

"Hmm, and you were the one who wanted to think about it more."

"I've thought about it and my conclusion is we've thought about it long enough."

"Five minutes was all it took, huh?"

I hugged Brendan tightly. I was so lucky to have him in my life.

Brendan went into his office to get some work done. I began to make brownies, mostly out of a need to keep busy. I wasn't sure why I felt so nervous. Was I having second thoughts?

I gave that idea some thought as I pulled out the brownie mix, eggs, olive oil, and the dark chocolate I always melted and added to the mix to improve it. No. I wasn't having second thoughts. In the back of my mind, adopting Scott had been the plan all along. Taking him in as a foster son was the trial period to see if we could handle him and help him or if he'd turn out to be too much for us. I had feared great difficulties considering Scott's past, but I'd discovered he was a good kid who had made some mistakes and bad choices. If someone had been there for him, maybe none of that would have happened. He was certainly making every effort now to keep from repeating past mistakes and he was honest.

The brownies were finished and Brendan had already snatched a couple "to make sure they were okay" before Scott returned home. As soon as he'd put his board, pads, and helmet away we called him into the living room.

"Uh, did I do something wrong? You look serious," Scott said

"You didn't do anything wrong, Scott," Brendan said.

Scott looked uncertain, uncomfortable, and even a little afraid. "Are you going to send me away?" he asked as tears welled up in his eyes.

"On the contrary. We have something to ask you," Brendan said, then nodded to me.

"Scott, how would you feel if Brendan and I adopted you?" I asked.

Scott completely lost it and began bawling. He ran to us and hugged us both while he cried. It wasn't the reaction I'd expected, but then I guess I didn't know what to expect. Brendan and I both held him close.

"There is nothing I'd like more," he said when he finally stopped crying and stepped back.

"Let's sit," Brendan said.

"It's a long process," I said as we all sat down. "It will likely take months."

"I don't care how long it takes. Do you really mean it? You really want to adopt me?"

"Yes, we do," Brendan said.

Scott grinned. "Drew and Dax said you would, but I didn't believe them."

"They know us too well," Brendan said, looking at me.

"We want you to be a part of our family. We want you to be our son," I said.

Scott hid his face in his hands. "I'm going to wake up and find this is a dream. If it is a dream, I don't want to wake up."

I laughed. "It's not a dream."

Scott took his hands away from his face. "It's just that this is what I've dreamed about for so long. I don't know why my parents didn't want me. I thought something must be wrong with me. I've dreamed about having a real family again, one that wouldn't decide they didn't want me anymore. I've been so scared you'd get tired of me. I didn't think about it much because I wanted to enjoy being here with you while I could, but I figured eventually even you wouldn't want me anymore."

"You can stop worrying about that, Scott. Casper and I love you. We never abandon someone we love. Never."

"I can't wait to tell Drew and Dax. They already call me Uncle Scott, even though I'm younger than them."

"Let's hold off on telling them for a little while. I'd like to tell the rest of the family in person. What do you think about a road trip to Verona next weekend?" Brendan asked.

"That sounds great! I can't wait to see Drew and Dax again."

"You can meet everyone and we'll give them our news."

We stood. Scott hugged us both again and then went to his room. Brendan and I gazed at each other and smiled. We knew we'd made the right choice.

Chapter Sixteen
Scott

The last few days had almost been overwhelming. Brendan and Casper were going to adopt me. They were going to be my dads, not my foster dads, but my dads. It didn't seem real, but it wasn't a dream. I kept expecting to wake up, but the only waking up I did was in the mornings to get ready for school. When I did awaken, it was to the reality of knowing that I was going to have a real family again.

I checked myself out in the mirror. I was wearing a red IU Football tee-shirt. Was it too causal? No. I was going to a football game. IU was playing Ohio State. I had the tickets in my pocket. Jonathan and I were about to have our first date. I was so nervous I thought I might hurl.

"Scott? Are you ready? We need to get going," Casper called out.

"Yeah, I'm ready. I'll be right there."

I gazed at myself in the mirror again. I guess I was as ready as I'd ever be.

Casper and I climbed in the Prius and departed. Jonathan lived near. It was his yard he was mowing that day after football practice that now seemed so long ago, so it took only a minute to arrive. Casper honked the horn and I moved to the back seat to sit with Jonathan.

"Hey, Jonathan. This is my dad," I said. It felt so good to utter those words.

"You can call me Casper. It's nice to meet you, Jonathan."

"It's great to meet you."

Casper knew just what to say and even more importantly, what not to say. He didn't tell Jonathan that I'd talked a lot about him or anything else embarrassing like that. I appreciated it. I was nervous enough!

Casper pulled out and we were on our way. We were soon in the pre-game traffic heading for the stadium and it took quite a while to get into the parking lots, but once there it didn't take long to reach our spot. Casper had dropped Brendan off much earlier so that he could park in Brendan's spot behind the stadium.

"Wow. How did you get this parking spot?" Jonathan asked.

"My other dad is the head football coach," I said proudly.

"Other dad?" Jonathan asked, but with only surprise in his voice and not a hint of disapproval.

"My husband, although we're not actually married," Casper said.

"That is so cool," Jonathan said. I smiled and we all climbed out of the car.

"You have your phone? I'll text you after the game when we're ready to depart. You'll have at least half an hour to kill, maybe an hour," Casper said.

"Yeah, I have it," I said.

"Okay, I'll see you two after the game."

"Thanks," I said and gave Casper a quick hug. I think I surprised him.

"Let's check out the tailgate parties and see what free stuff we can get first," I said.

"Sounds good to me."

We walked toward the east side of the stadium and soon passed tents erected by various organizations. The scent of hamburgers and hot dogs was in the air. Of more interest was the huge Coke truck that was giving away free drinks. Jonathan and I both grabbed a paper cup and filled it with Coke and ice.

"This is amazing. You know I've never been to a football game here?" Jonathan asked.

"I had never been to one until Casper brought me. He was my Big Brother then, through Big Brothers & Big Sisters."

"Oh okay."

"Right now, Brendan and Casper are my foster dads, but they're working to adopt me. Oh, that's supposed to be a secret so don't tell anyone."

"I won't. It must be really cool to have a family that actually chose you. I love my parents and they're great, but they didn't know what they were getting with me. Your dads know you and they picked you."

"I can barely believe it. I have to admit, I'm very excited and happy they are adopting me. It's my dream come true."

"Having two dads must be different."

"I guess, but my own parents gave me up when I was eight. I don't really remember much about them. I've been in foster homes since then."

"That must have been rough."

"Yes, but everything is great now."

"I'm glad." Jonathan smiled at me. He meant it.

"I might as well go for broke here. I'm gay and I really like you. I hope this is a date, but if you're not into guys..."

"I am. You told me you liked me when you asked me out, so I figured this was a date."

"There is liking and *liking* and I *like* you. I am so glad you're into guys. Things have been going so well lately I feared it was too much to ask of the universe. Are you gay or bi?"

"That's hard to say. I'm attracted to girls a little, but I'm far more attracted to guys so I guess I'm bi, but I'm almost completely gay, if that makes sense. Who needs labels anyway?"

"I guess you're right about that."

"I thought you were cute when you came into Subway, but I didn't know you were so interesting. If I'd known I would have asked *you* out," Jonathan said.

"I was into you the moment I spotted you at school. I gotta admit the Mohawk did it for me."

Jonathan laughed. "You're in luck. I let guys feel it on a first date, my Mohawk that is!"

"I also thought you were very handsome and wanted to get to know you."

"I'm afraid I'm not as interesting as you. I come from a boring average home, I don't have gay dads, and my dad is not the head football coach at IU."

"I'm sure I'll find you interesting. Do you have brothers or sisters?"

"Two brothers, one older and one younger. One younger sister."

"You're lucky."

"I don't think so! They are all yours if you want them."

"I'll take them!"

"You would be very, very sorry."

"Maybe I can take them on a trial basis."

"Nope, no returns."

"I don't think Brendan and Casper would go for that anyway."

"Yeah, and I'd probably miss them eventually, like in a year or so."

"I still think you're lucky."

We soon found the tent where IU gave away stuff. We picked up football posters, IU magnets, and boxes of popcorn to go with our Cokes.

"This is awesome and the football game hasn't even started," Jonathan said.

I grinned at Jonathan. I knew I was doing that far too often, but I couldn't help it. I had never spent time with another guy like this. I had spent time with other guys. Recently, I'd hung out with Ethan and Noah quite a bit. Last year, I was with Blaze, Felix, and Ace, but I didn't even want to think about them now. I'd had other friends and teammates too, but none of them were like Jonathan. There was an added dimension to our relationship that was present with none of the others.

I wanted so badly to kiss Jonathan, but it was too soon. This was the beginning of our first date. While part of me, mostly the part down between my legs, wanted to jump straight to sex, the vast majority of me wasn't thinking about sex at all. I just wanted to be with Jonathan, have fun with him, and get to know him.

"This is kind of like a fair, without rides," Jonathan said.

"Yeah, I guess it is."

"There are thousands and thousands of people here. I wonder how many?"

"Let's count them. One, two, three... Oh no. They moved. I'll start again..."

Jonathan laughed. "Have you noticed how many hot college guys are here?"

"This is a college football game."

"Yeah, but I mean, most of these guys are hot."

"I might have noticed that."

"Might have. Ha!"

"Oh, did I tell you I've been in the locker room, *while* the team was changing?"

"Oh man. Did you see anything interesting?"

"Yes." I grinned mischievously. "I was actually in my dad's office most of the time, but I could see in the locker room and... all I can say is wow."

"I would say you have the perfect life, but you've told me enough already I know that's not true."

"My life feels almost perfect right now. I'm a little scared because it's almost too good to be true. I couldn't believe it when Brendan and Casper took me in as their foster son. I didn't really trust my luck, you know? I was afraid there was a catch, but there wasn't. Then, just a few days ago they asked me if I'd like them to adopt me. I felt as if I was dreaming. There is also you. I'd seen you at school and then again when I was walking home and you were mowing. I don't know if you remember, but I waved. Now, here we are—together."

"I remember. I thought *Who is that hottie?*"

I blushed. "I was drawn to you the first time I spotted you at school. I was determined to meet you, but when I saw you in Subway, I was too scared to approach you. My friends pushed me into it. One of them offered to give me $20 if I asked you out."

Jonathan laughed. "Did he pay you?"

"Yes. If you're interested in going out with me again, we can go eat somewhere and I'll pay. It will be on Ethan."

"You don't have to pay. You already got me a ticket for the football game."

"Yeah, but that didn't cost me anything. Besides, I look at that $20 as our money. I can tell Ethan what a good time we had on his cash."

"Okay then, but after I want to take you out and then we'll each pay our own way."

I nodded. I was so excited I couldn't stand still, so I began walking again. We toured the endless groups tailgating and checked out sexy college boys together.

When time for the game to begin drew close, we headed for our gate. Our seats were above the north end zone, where I had sat before. When we drew near Jonathan's eyes widened in amazement.

"Wow! These seats are incredible!"

I looked around for Casper, but didn't see him anywhere. I knew he was watching the game, but he was nowhere in sight. I was glad. I would have been uncomfortable with my dad watching us. I smiled. Every time I thought "my dad" it made me smile.

Jonathan and I watched the Marching Hundred perform, which was reason enough to come to a game. They were awesome and truly athletes themselves.

"That's my dad," I said pointing over to the sideline when the game was just beginning.

"He looks fit. I thought all football coaches were overweight."

"Not Brendan. He's built. He's got abs and everything. I didn't know older guys could have muscles like that. He used to play for IU and he was a quarterback."

"Wow."

I was very proud of my dads. I was in a continual state of disbelief that they had chosen me.

Jonathan wasn't the football fanatic that I was, but he was into the game. We cheered together when IU made a great play or scored and suffered together when something went wrong. Everyone around us rooted for IU and the band was directly on our left. The weather was perfect too—sunny and bright without being hot.

This game wasn't as exciting as the IU-Purdue game. IU got an early lead and held onto it. There was none of the nail-biting apprehension of the earlier game, but it was still a thrill to watch it live.

The biggest thrill of the game came when Jonathan grabbed my knee in excitement. I'm not even sure he knew he did it, but it made me want to hug him. So far, we were having a great time together. I hoped that continued. I wanted to spend a lot more time with Jonathan.

After the game, we went back outside the stadium and watched the mass exodus as thousands of people departed at once. There was a steady line of cars on 17th and Dunn Streets. Not everyone departed. Several tail-gaters remained, but the stadium parking lots quickly cleared out.

"I've had a great time today. Thank you so much for asking me," Jonathan said.

"Thank you for accepting. I was so afraid you wouldn't. If Ethan and Noah hadn't been there to push me, I don't know if I would have had the courage. I didn't even tell them I was into you, but I guess I was pretty obvious."

"I did see you looking at me a few times. I thought you might be interested in me, but I wasn't sure. I remembered seeing you that day I was mowing so I figured you went to North. I was actually thinking about tracking you down at school."

"Really?"

"Yeah. I couldn't ask you out while I was working, but I figured I could find you."

I grinned—yet again.

We kept talking until Casper texted. I thought it was way too quick but then I noticed an hour had passed.

"It's time to head to the car."

We were on the far side of the stadium, so we set out. By the time we arrived Brendan and Casper were waiting on us.

"Dad," I said, getting a thrill out of saying it, "this is Jonathan."

They shook hands. "You can call me Brendan."

"It's very nice to meet you. Thanks for getting us tickets."

"You're welcome."

We all climbed in the car. Casper was driving and Brendan took the passenger seat. Jonathan mouthed, "Your dad is hot" over the top of the car before we got in.

"Where would you boys like to eat?" Casper asked. "We are paying, no arguments."

"There's a good Chinese buffet called Great Taste Buffet on West 3rd Street," Jonathan said.

"I love Chinese, but are you sure you don't want to go somewhere better?" Brendan asked.

"I'll be happy with anywhere, but I love that place."

"Let's try it out then. I used to eat at the China Buffet near College Mall on East 3rd Street, but it closed down many years ago," Brendan said.

"The game was great," Jonathan said.

"We did well. Ohio State wasn't quite as tough as we suspected. I think they were having an off day. Are you into football, Jonathan?"

"I don't play or anything, but I like it. I don't do any team sports, but I'm into martial arts and skate boarding."

I quickly looked at Jonathan. He was a skater! Yes!

The Great Taste Buffet was over by KFC, Taco Bell, and Burger King on the west side. It was located in a strip mall with Big Lots and The Dollar General Store.

The buffet wasn't large, but when we sat down with our plates and tried the food it was very good.

"This is much smaller than the old China Buffet, but it's great," Brendan said.

"We can add this to the list of restaurants we frequent," Casper said.

"I like anywhere there is food," I said.

"What are your other interests, Jonathan?" Casper asked.

"I like art a lot. I mostly paint, but I do some sculpture as well."

He was a skater and an artist? How perfect could he get?

"Scott is quite a good artist," Casper said.

"Yeah?" Jonathan asked.

"I mostly draw and paint."

"I paint all kinds of different things—portraits, landscapes, and still life," Jonathan said.

"That's what I do. I even sold one of my drawings at the Farmer's Market several weeks ago. I was drawing one of the stands and the lady running it came over and looked at my drawing and offered me $10 for it."

"You're tied with Van Gogh then. He only sold one painting during his entire life."

"Yeah, but he's a little better known than me."

"So far."

"I was never any good at art. I think it would be great to be able to paint and draw," Brendan said.

"I wasn't much good at that either. I'm more of a gardener," Casper said.

"Gardening is like painting with plants," Jonathan said.

"I never thought of it like that, but I do plan out complementary colors and textures."

We kept talking and eating, but mostly eating. I was pleased Jonathan got on well with my dads and that they obviously liked him. I knew they might have been concerned when I told them he had a Mohawk, but I was sure they weren't now.

After we ate, we dropped Jonathan off at his house. It wasn't quite the way I wanted our date to end, but I planned to text Jonathan as soon as I was home.

I had barely stepped into my room when I received a text from Jonathan.

"Today was a blast. Let's get together again soon. XOXO."

My heart beat faster, especially when I read the last part. I quickly texted back, "Very soon! XOXO."

I lay back on my bed and thought about Jonathan. He was a skater and an artist. I almost couldn't believe it. I didn't know a thing about martial arts, but it was already obvious that we had plenty in common.

Chapter Seventeen
Casper

"This place looks familiar. Hey, did they film that old TV show here?" Scott asked.

"TV show?" Brendan asked.

"Yeah, that one with Aunt Bea and Opie you showed me."

"Oh, *The Andy Griffith Show*. No, that was not filmed here."

"This reminds me of that town. Is this *really* all there is to it? There's not a mall or something on the edge of town?" Scott asked, looking out the windows at Verona in all its autumn glory.

"What are you talking about? This is an exciting place. There are three restaurants right on main street and a library, antique store, and hardware store," I said. Scott looked at me as if I'd lost my mind.

"Main Street gets crazy on Friday nights. Back in high school, we always came here then because that's when the hardware store changes its window display," Brendan said.

Scott laughed. "I seriously hope you're kidding."

"I am."

"Whew! I was worried about you for a minute. Compared to this place, Bloomington is New York City!"

"Life moves slower here, but that's not always a bad thing," I said.

"There's a gay youth center?" Scott asked a short time later as we passed the Potter-Bailey Gay Youth Center.

"Yes, there is."

"It looks really big."

"It is big. The center has a major benefactor. Have you heard of the music group Phantom?" Brendan asked.

"Yeah, they were huge way back and I've heard them on the radio. I like their music."

"Phantom funds the gay youth center."

"Cool."

We drove out of town and soon passed the Selby farm, where Brendan and I had so many fond memories.

"Hey, scarecrows," Scott said, pointing as we passed a scarecrow wearing an older letterman's jacket.

"It looks like Cameron has been busy. He's... well, he's your brother, Scott. He runs the farm now. In the fall, dozens of scarecrows are set up on and near the farm," I said.

"That's cool, about the scarecrows and having a brother."

"Oh, you have three brothers," Brendan said.

A short time later we pulled into the drive of the Brewer-Westwood Christmas Tree Farm. Scott stared out the window at the rows and rows of trees, then turned his attention to the farmhouse.

"Wow, that is one big house."

"This is where we used to live," Brendan said.

"It's cool, but I wouldn't want to live here. There's nothing out here, well except for scarecrows. There are lots of them and they're cool!"

"There's more here than you think," I said.

I parked the Prius. We got out and grabbed our bags from the back. We walked up the long brick sidewalk to the old brick farmhouse. Brendan and I had spent a lot of great years here.

Before we could knock on the door, Cameron opened it.

"We heard this bed & breakfast has cheap rates," Brendan said.

"The cheapest, free. It's hard to beat. Come on in. We have your old bedroom ready and another for Scott. Leave your bags in the hall, we'll get them later." We dropped our bags and Cameron turned to look at Scott. "It's very nice to meet you. I'm your brother, Cameron."

Cameron hugged Scott, who hugged him back, smiling.

"It's nice to meet you, bro. I like your house."

"Thanks. My house is your house. Are you guys hungry? The cookout begins in about an hour, but there's plenty of food in the kitchen."

We shook our heads.

"Need any help with the grilling?" Brendan asked.

"I'm glad you asked. Let's go through the kitchen so you can say 'Hi' to Spencer."

We followed Cameron down the hallway to the kitchen, where his husband, Spencer, was busy cooking.

"Hey, dads," Spencer said and hugged us. "It's nice to meet you Scott." Spencer shook Scott's hand.

"It's nice to meet you too."

"We're heading out to the grills," Cameron said. He and Brendan departed.

"Need any help?" I asked.

"You can help me carry things out soon. Jason should be here in a few minutes and we invited Ethan and Nathan as you asked. Betsey isn't here yet, but we expect her soon."

"Great. Scott, why don't you go out and explore. You have your phone, right?" I asked.

"I have it."

"If you're not back by the time we're ready to eat, I'll text," I said.

"Just watch out for bears and wolves," Spencer said.

Scott looked at him. "You're kidding. Right?"

"Yeah, I'm kidding, although I did see a rather ferocious looking bunny yesterday. I think it's killed three people already. I tried to warn them, but..."

"I told you, but oh no, it's just a harmless little bunny!" Scott said, laughing.

"I see you're familiar with *Monty Python & The Holy Grail.*"

"Yeah, I love that movie."

"Well, keep your eye out for the vicious bunny then."

Scott headed outside.

"We miss you guys around here and all the work you did," Spencer said.

"We miss being here, but we love Bloomington."

"What do you do with yourself now you don't have a farm to run?"

"He just walked out the door."

"I was surprised when Cameron told me you had a foster son, but he wasn't surprised at all."

"Brendan and I have a habit of taking in strays."

"That's what Cameron said."

"We're thrilled to be back for a visit with the entire family. We keep in touch with everyone, but it's not the same as seeing them in person."

"True."

Brendan's mom Betsey arrived, followed soon by my brother Jason and then Clint and his family. Drew and Dax went out to find Scott right after they gave me a hug. Everyone else helped carry things out.

Ethan and Nathan arrived just before we were ready to eat. The last to appear were Conner and Colin.

"Wow! Who are those guys?" Scott asked.

"That's your other brother Conner and his husband, Colin," Dax said.

Scott couldn't stop looking at them. Conner and Colin were in their mid-thirties and both were extremely fit. Conner was a ballet dancer and Colin had the most impressive build I had ever seen. He was even fitter than Brendan was when he was younger, and that's saying something.

Cameron approached us. "The ribs and chicken are just about ready."

I nodded. Cameron knew Brendan and I had an announcement to make, but he didn't know what it was.

"If I can have everyone's attention," I said. Everyone grew quiet and drew in closer. "Brendan and I asked for this family gathering because we have important and wonderful news. Our family is going to get a little larger. Brendan and I are adopting Scott."

Everyone cheered or clapped. Scott didn't quite know what to do because he was suddenly on the receiving end of hugs from every direction.

"We told you!" Drew said.

"Finally, I'm not the youngest," Conner said.

"You know the youngest brother has to do the dishes," Clint told Scott.

"And wash my car," Cameron said.

"He's also required to clean my loft," Conner said.

"Don't believe anything they say," Betsey said. "I'm so glad to have another grandson." She hugged Scott and he grinned.

"Now you really are our Uncle," Dax said.

Everyone chatted until Cameron interrupted us, "The ribs are done. Let's eat."

Scott was quite overwhelmed, but Drew and Dax pulled him toward the table that held plates and silverware and insisted he be first in line as the newest member of the family. They were 2nd and 3rd, of course.

Brendan caught my eye and we smiled at each other. We were truly happy.

Scott sat between Dax and Drew. I sat between Brendan and Jason. It was wonderful to be with our entire family again. Even Colin was home from his most recent on-location film work. We were lucky Conner was home too. He was on tour performing as often as not.

The barbeque ribs and chicken were delicious as were the baked beans, potato salad, yeast rolls, and corn. Cameron and Spencer had wisely provided everyone with wet cloth napkins. Ribs could be messy.

Everyone talked and caught up as they ate. I overheard Drew and Dax explaining who was who to Scott. I was sure the family was quite confusing to Scott, but he'd get it.

For dessert, there was blackberry cobbler with homemade ice cream. Scott had never had either. He was a city boy. As soon as Scott, Dax, and Drew finished eating they took off. I wasn't concerned about them. Drew and Dax knew the farm well and the three would be safe together.

"Scott seems like a great kid," Ethan said. "How old is he?"

"He's fourteen," I said.

"You and Brendan are a magnet for kids. I bet you never thought you'd raise kids when we were all back in high school."

"A lot of stuff has happened that we never thought would happen," Brendan said.

"True, we can say the same. Can't we Nathan?"

"That's for certain. You'd think life would be more boring in the country!"

"Scott actually asked if *The Andy Griffith Show* was filmed in Verona and he was serious," I said.

That made Ethan, Nathan, and Jason laugh.

"He's lived his entire life in Bloomington. We have a big back yard and live across from the Cascades Golf Course. That is as close as he's ever been to living in the country," I said.

"Perhaps you'd better keep the chickens away from him. We might have another incident like we did with Dorian."

Everyone laughed. No one ever forgot the night Dorian freaked out at a wiener roast when a chicken sneaked up behind him and pecked him.

"Scott met Dorian. He couldn't believe we knew him."

"He is the most famous of our group from high school."

"I'm not surprised. He's a born actor," Nathan said. "Conner is nearly as famous."

"Yeah, at least in the world of ballet. It's amazing to see what kids become when they grow up. Our biggest surprise was Cameron."

"No kidding," Jason said. "I would never have dreamed he would take to farming."

"He's even helped us make *our* farm more profitable," Ethan said.

"We're proud of all our kids, aren't we Jason?" Brendan asked.

I smiled. There was a time I never dreamed Brendan and Jason would get along, but that was an old, old story now.

"Yes, we are."

"Did you ever think we'd get this old?" Nathan asked.

"Scott thinks we're ancient," I said.

"Well you are old enough to be his grandfathers," Ethan said.

"True. I sure wish Grandmother and Jack could have met him. I bet he would have loved Jack. Conner sure took right up with Jack when he first met him. Grandmother would have loved Scott too."

"I always loved Jack," Conner said.

"Yeah, we miss them. The farm isn't the same without them. I keep thinking I'm going to run into Jack in the barn. I miss his orneriness," Ethan said.

"Everyone remembers him for his gruff exterior and his heart of gold," Brendan said.

The afternoon wore on and soon turned into evening. The boys returned after nearly four hours shirtless and with wet hair.

"We went skinny dipping in the pond!" Scott said.

"Scott actually thought he had to wear a swim-suit," Drew said.

"They told me there were snapping turtles that would bite my... you know! I wouldn't get in until they convinced me they were kidding," Scott said.

"Welcome to the farm," I said.

"If you boys have been in that pond you need to shower," Amanda said.

"Ah, mom!" Dax said.

"Go shower."

"Okay." The boys grumbled, but did as they were told.

Cameron, Jason, and Brendan built a bonfire when it grew dark and we roasted marshmallows and made smores. It was another new experience for Scott, but Drew and Dax showed him how it was done.

Sitting on a hay bale by the fire reminded me of all the bonfires we'd experienced here while Clint, Cameron, and Conner were growing up and all the bonfires on the Selby Farm when Brendan and I lived there during high school. I was glad to introduce Scott to the tradition.

Our party didn't begin to break up until late. Ethan and Nathan departed first, followed by Conner and Colin and then Betsey.

"We should head out, boys," Clint said.

"Can we stay, please?" Drew asked.

"It's fine with us, you know we have plenty of room," Cameron said.

"Yeah, please. We want to spend time with Scott while he's here," Dax said.

Clint and Amanda looked at each other. "Okay, but stay out of trouble and do not be a nuisance."

"Us?" Drew asked.

"Yes, you."

"I'll beat them if they are," Cameron said.

"Feel free," Clint said.

Clint and Amanda departed. My brother, Jason, took off right after them. The rest of us carried what little there was to take inside. Most of the cleaning up had been accomplished earlier.

"You know your way around. Pick out whatever room you want," Cameron told the twins.

"We're going to stay in Scott's room," Dax said.

"Let's move a mattress in there then."

"I'll give them a hand," Brendan said.

"I'm warning you guys right now, if you wake me up tonight, I will make you work all day tomorrow," Cameron said.

"We won't! We promise!" Drew said.

Brendan and the boys departed, leaving only Cameron, Spencer, and me in the kitchen.

"I like the way you threaten kids," I said.

"Yeah, I was thinking of opening a day care center," Cameron said, making Spencer laugh. "The twins stayed overnight a couple of times during the summer. They helped us trim trees and they liked it."

"They sound like you when you were younger."

"Are you sure you want to take on the responsibility of a kid again? You do remember what I was like. Right?" Cameron asked.

"Some nights I wake up screaming," I said.

"Funny!"

"Brendan and I hadn't planned to raise a kid again, but then we didn't plan to take you and your brothers in. I started with spending an afternoon a week with Scott, but as I grew to know him, it became obvious that he truly needed someone in his life. That kid has been through a lot."

"How's he doing? Are drugs a problem?" Cameron, Clint, and Conner knew about Scott's past. I had informed them when we took Scott in as a foster son.

"Thankfully, no. He's having more trouble keeping away from cigarettes. It's very hard for him, but he's doing it. Scott is far less trouble that we thought he would be. He's responded well to Brendan and me. Even the best kid requires a tremendous effort, but Brendan and I love having Scott."

"I wouldn't mind to have kids, but Cameron isn't crazy about the idea," Spencer said.

"That's because I remember what I was like when I was a kid. The things I did..."

"You were never boring."

"Who was never boring?" Brendan asked as he returned to the kitchen.

"Cameron."

"That is certainly true and what a temper."

"Yeah, I remember that temper," Spencer said.

"I'm glad I'm not like that anymore. I used to get totally out of control."

"You turned out okay," Brendan said.

"I used to worry about Conner. I figured the guys at school would beat him up when they found out he was into ballet. He was so sensitive and quiet and now he's famous!" Cameron said.

"That's some boyfriend he's got too. Damn! Colin is the most gorgeous guy I have ever seen in my life, although I much prefer Cameron," Spencer said, hugging him.

"You have poor taste then," Cameron said, smiling.

"Not at all."

"We're just glad you're all happy," I said.

"I think we are. Clint has his football team. We have the farm. Conner has his ballet career. I know Dad is thrilled with his farm store."

"Now you all have a new little brother," I said.

"The twins sure like him," Cameron said.

"They started calling him Uncle Scott when they stayed with us this summer."

"That's right. I guess he is their uncle."

"I think Scott gets a kick out of having nephews that are older than him. I think he truly appreciates having a family," Brendan said.

"Yeah, his parents gave him up when he was eight," I said.

"Why would they do that?"

"From what we've found out, they simply decided they didn't want him. He didn't get into any trouble until after they abandoned him."

"They should have their asses kicked," Cameron said.

"Like I said, he's been through a lot. Knowing his parents didn't want him has done a lot of damage."

"I can imagine. There was a time when I thought Dad didn't want me and I didn't think Brendan and you did either when I first came here. I know the pain and the problems that caused me. The truth was that Dad did want me, but he couldn't take care of me. Brendan and you wanted me too. It took me too long to realize that."

"You went through a lot as a kid too. Your brothers did as well."

"Yeah, but everything started to be okay when we came here. I'm glad you were patient with me. I was such a little shit."

"You kept us entertained and we always loved you," Brendan said.

"I know. Scott's a very lucky boy. I hope he realizes that."

"He appreciates everything we do for him. He seems rather astounded by it. He takes very good care of his things. He had never owned new clothes before he came to live with us."

"You two do so much for so many," Spencer said.

"We're merely passing on what others did for us. When Jack took us in we were homeless and I was on the run from my parents," Brendan said.

"You guys make me feel guilty. I have great parents," Spencer said.

"There is no reason to feel guilty, but you should be thankful," I said.

"I am."

"Spencer is a better son than me. Do you know he calls his parents every other day?" Cameron asked.

"They worry," Spencer said.

"Hmm and Cameron calls us once every couple of weeks," Brendan said.

"I should never have mentioned that," Cameron said.

"It's fine. We know you're busy," I said.

"I do appreciate everything you've done for me. I know Clint and Conner appreciate everything you did for them too."

"We know and we are very lucky to have you all in our life. That includes you, Spencer," Brendan said. Spencer smiled.

***

Before we departed from Verona, we stopped in the florist and purchased two bouquets of flowers and then drove to the graveyard. This was where everyone from the past of Verona was buried.

"Some of these stones are really old," Scott said.

"Verona has been here a very long time," I said.

Soon, we came to tombstones bearing the name "Selby" and then reached our destination. Two tombstones side-by-side read, "Jack Selby – July 25, 1923 – July 27, 2023" and "Ardelene Selby – August 18, 1925 – August 31, 2025."

"They both almost died on their birthday," Scott said.

"Yes, their 100th."

We placed the flowers in the vases beside the tombstones.

"Ardelene is my grandmother," I said. "She's your great grandmother and she would have loved you. I wish she could have met you."

"Jack is the one who took us in when we weren't much older than you," Brendan said.

"Took you in?"

"We were homeless, wandering, and on the run from my parents. We'll tell you the whole story sometime. I don't know what would have become of us if it wasn't for Uncle Jack."

"How is Ardelene your grandmother and Jack your uncle?"

"Everyone called him Uncle Jack. Biologically, he was only Ethan's uncle, but he was an uncle to all of us. He's my grandfather by marriage, but I also called him Uncle Jack," I said.

"He must have been a great guy."

"He was. He could be very gruff, but he had a truly kind heart. His first wife and son died young. He was alone a lot of years, but then Ethan came into his life just as you have ours.

Jack helped so many people during his lifetime. If everyone could be like him, the world would have no problems."

"Why are there people who care for other people's kids and others who don't want theirs?"

"I don't know, Scott," I said. "My mother died when I was very young. My father acted as if he blamed me for it. He was not a good father until the very, very end. My brother, who is your Uncle Jason, was very cruel and abusive to me growing up, but later he became a truly good man. Everyone is different. Everyone has their own story and their own reasons for being who and what they are. What's important is to decide the kind of person you want to be."

"I wish I could have met Jack and Ardelene," Scott said.

"They would both have loved you, although Jack might have scared you at first; then, again, maybe not. Conner took right up with him when he was younger than you," Brendan said.

"I'm sorry I missed out on knowing them, but I was sure glad to meet everyone else. Conner is beautiful. I can't believe he's a famous ballet dancer or that his boyfriend works in movies. Did you know Colin knows actual movie stars?"

"So do you. You met Dorian," I said.

"Oh yeah, but he knows lots of them. This is sure an interesting family."

"Yes, and everyone is very glad you are now a part of it," I said.

"Well, I will be once I'm adopted."

"You are already," Brendan said. We both gave Scott a hug and then the three of us departed from the graveyard and headed for home.

Chapter Eighteen
Scott

"I am starving! Let's go," I said as I approached Casper and Jonathan where they sat on the bleachers by the football field.

"Hey, *we've* been waiting on *you*," Casper said. "That was a great game today, Scott. You did an excellent job. I shot some video so Brendan can see it when he returns."

"Yeah, you were magnificent," Jonathan said.

I grinned. We walked to the Prius. Jonathan and I climbed in the back for the very short ride to the house.

When we arrived, about two minutes later, we went straight into the kitchen.

"Bring on the food!" I said, sitting at the table.

"You are hungry," Casper said.

"Yes."

"Then set the table."

I hopped up and did so in a flash. Casper unplugged the crock-pot and ladled out baked beans with cocktail wienies. He pulled potato salad out of the refrigerator and warned up yeast rolls in the microwave.

"This is so good!" I said, as I began to devour everything.

"Slow down, Scott," Casper said.

"Sorry, I'm really hungry."

"I told you to eat more for breakfast."

"I've never had baked beans and wienies before. This is great," Jonathan said.

"Thanks. It's also easy to prepare. I put it in the crock-pot this morning."

"I need to get mom to make this."

"So what do you boys have planned for the rest of your Saturday?" Casper asked.

"We're going to the skate park," Jonathan said, since my mouth was full.

"After that we plan to be lazy," I said after I swallowed.

"Oh, I like that. I might do that too."

"Skate?" I asked.

"No, be lazy. Right after I mow the lawn. If you return and I'm asleep, try not to wake me."

"We'll be quiet. We may skate a long time."

"Just make sure you have your phone in case I need to reach you."

"Yes, Dad," I said just a touch sarcastically. I loved calling Casper, Dad.

"I bet I'm no worse than Jonathan's parents."

"You're better," Jonathan said.

"Don't tell him that!" I said. Casper laughed.

"Hey, you have to admit, I rarely text you," Dad said.

"True."

Our late lunch was wonderful. I ate and ate and then finished off with chocolate chip cookies. I ate so much I hoped I didn't spew while skating. That would be a sight, and not a good one.

"That was great and I'm no longer starving," I said when I finally stopped eating.

"Yes, thank you," Jonathan said.

"I think you ate enough for all of us, Scott," Casper said.

"Hey, it was a tough game."

I put my dirty dishes and Jonathan's in the dishwasher.

"We're going to grab our stuff and head out," I said.

"Have fun."

Jonathan and I walked down the hallway to my room and picked up our boards, pads, and helmets. Jonathan had dropped his stuff off this morning before my game. We headed out the front door and walked toward the skate park.

"Does your dad come to all your games?" Jonathan asked.

"Yes, and Brendan comes when he can. I wish he could have watched my game today, but IU is playing at the University of Virginia. He won't even be home until tomorrow."

"Yeah, he can't exactly skip his game to come to yours."

"This is true. I've never asked, are you into sports other than skating and martial arts?"

"I hate to disappoint you since I know you're into every sport that exists or has even been imagined, but no. I hate playing team sports and am not interested in anything physical other than skating and martial arts."

"I'm not disappointed. The world would be boring if everyone was the same. I'm thrilled you like to skate and are into art, but I like that you have different interests too. I know nothing about martial arts, but I think it's fascinating. Maybe you can teach me some stuff. So what are you, like, a ninja?"

"I'm afraid I haven't worked up to ninja yet. I mainly practice Muay Thai and Krav Maga."

"Okay, I have never heard of those."

"Krav Maga means 'contact fighting.' I practice it for self-defense. Muay Thai is the national sport of Thailand. It's like kick boxing, but blows below the belt, to the elbows, and knees are legal."

"Whoa!"

"We don't actually do any of those in class, but we practice how to do them. Muay Thai teaches that almost every body part can be used as a weapon."

"I didn't know I was dating a badass."

Jonathan laughed. "You aren't. I'm better described as an artist/skater. I just happen to also be a trained fighter."

"Remind me not to get into a fight with you."

"That seems unlikely."

There were only a couple of guys our age skating when we reached the park. I didn't recognize them, so they probably went to South or were from out of town. Then again, I didn't know everyone at North.

Jonathan and I began skating. He was beyond good. I have to admit I'd looked forward to showing off a bit, but I couldn't because he was better than me. I was unhappy about that for a few moments, but then realized I was being petty. Why would I wish for Jonathan to be less talented than me? That wasn't right at all.

Without a word, we began to skate in unison. It was almost as if we were performing a dance, but on skateboards. I wished someone was filming it so I could set it to music and put it on YouTube.com. Jonathan did some moves I couldn't match, but I did my best and played to my strengths. He grinned as we passed each other. This was a great date.

The other boys departed after nearly an hour and no one else had arrived so we had the place to ourselves. We skated all over the park. I had always loved to skate, but this was the best!

I watched Jonathan carefully when he performed a move that I had yet to master and tried to duplicate it. Without a word spoken, he began to teach me by doing the same move over and over so I could watch and figure it out. The more I tried, the better I became. There were advantages to having a boyfriend who was a better skater than me.

We stayed so long I feared I'd get a text from Casper telling me to come home, but my phone remained silent and we kept skating. Three different skaters arrived, skated, and departed and still we kept going.

"Uh oh," I said when I spotted Blaze, Felix, and Ace entering the park."

"You know those guys?"

"Yeah, I used to hang with them. They're part of my dark past and I got into a huge amount of trouble last year because of them. The one with the spiked blond hair is Blaze. He is a bad ass. Let's get out of here."

Jonathan looked at me. He could tell I was scared, which humiliated me to some extent, but I feared what Blaze and the others might do and didn't want Jonathan to get mixed up in my past.

"If that's what you want."

"Yeah, I think it's best."

"Okay then."

We didn't get far before Blaze blocked us. He stepped between the nearest gate and us.

"Hey, Scott. Who's your friend?"

"I'm Jonathan."

Blaze looked him up and down. "He the reason I haven't seen you much?"

"The reason you haven't seen me much is that I don't want to hang out with you anymore. I've changed."

Blaze grinned. "I doubt it. Do you do for him what you did for me?"

I could feel myself turn red. I was humiliated. Jonathan's expression hardened as he looked at me. I nearly began to cry.

232

"We're leaving," Jonathan said and moved to step past Blaze, but Blaze grabbed his forearm. "I'm going to give you one chance to take your hand off me and let us leave."

"Or what?" Blaze said and laughed.

That's when Jonathan took him out. He moved so fast it was difficult to tell exactly what he did, but Jonathan did something with his foot and leg that left Blaze on the ground. Felix and Ace immediately jumped us. I punched Ace in the face, but he slugged me in the stomach. I rushed him and took him down. Two swift punches to the face took him out. I turned to help Jonathan, but he was the only one standing. Blaze and Felix were both lying on the pavement.

"Let's go," Jonathan said. He opened the gate and we departed. Jonathan didn't say a word as we left the park and walked across North Kinser Pike.

"I'm sorry you got mixed up in that, but thanks."

"That's what boyfriends are for."

I looked quickly toward him. "You still want to date me?"

"Why wouldn't I?"

"You looked really angry when you looked at me back there."

"I wasn't angry with you. I was angry with Blaze."

"That's a relief, but I need to explain a few things. I was going to tell you later, but I should tell you now about my dark past."

"You don't have to do that. We all have a past, Scott."

"Yeah, but you should know. I promise, I was going to tell you, but it's not the sort of thing you bring up this early in a relationship."

"I understand. There's plenty I haven't told you. We haven't been together long enough to tell each other much."

"I got in some real trouble last year. I want you to know that I no longer do what I did then. In the 8th grade, I got kicked out of school and put in Juvie because of drugs." Jonathan nodded. "I used to smoke joints with Blaze, Felix, and Ace. Blaze got me into more serious drugs. I'm not trying to lay the blame on him. I'm the one who messed up and did stupid stuff. I haven't done any drugs since then. I'm on probation and I get randomly drug tested, but that's not the reason I don't do drugs. I know I made a mistake and I don't want to repeat it."

"Good."

"I also smoked, but I've quit. Well, I slipped up once a few weeks ago, but only once. Giving up cigarettes has been the hardest."

"I tried a cigarette once. It was nasty!"

"Yeah. I started smoking to be cool. I know; it was stupid. I've done some truly stupid things."

"We all have. I knocked myself out trying to throw a rock with a slingshot," Jonathan said, moving his fist in a circular motion. "It seemed like a good idea at the time. I didn't know what I was doing and didn't release it correctly, so it hit me in the back of the head. My mom found me lying in the back yard. I woke up in the emergency room. It wasn't one of my stellar moments."

"It's not as bad as what I did."

"It's not a contest."

"There's something else you should know. Blaze mentioned it, sort of—I'm, uh, not a virgin. Blaze and I… we used to do stuff or I guess I let him do stuff to me when I has messed up on drugs. I, uh... bent over for him, several times."

I bit my lip. I wanted to be honest and knew I should be, but my honesty was going to cost me a boyfriend.

"I'm not a virgin either."

"Really?"

"Why do you act so surprised?"

"You seem... too nice."

Jonathan laughed. "Nice boys have sex too."

"Yeah, I guess. My experiences have been... not so nice."

"I'm sorry. I did stuff with a friend's older brother."

"How much older?"

"I was thirteen and he was fifteen. I bent over for him, but only once. I didn't like it much. I almost told him to stop, but part of me was afraid he wouldn't and part of me felt like a loser for not being able to take it."

"But he didn't force you?"

"No."

"That's good. Did he want to do it again?"

234

"Yes, but I said "no" and he accepted that. He did try to talk me into a few times, but he never tried to make me. We did other things, but never that again. He wouldn't bend over for me."

"Did your friend ever find out?"

"No. They moved. He never knew."

"I liked a lot of what I did with Blaze. He kind of forced me, but not exactly. Well, I guess he did force me since he wouldn't stop if I told him to, but mostly not."

"I'm sorry."

"It was my fault. Well, I don't mean it was my fault, but I made the choice to do drugs with him. I knew what would happen when we did and were alone, but I met up with him anyway. Like I said, I've made some stupid mistakes. I hope you don't think I'm trashy now."

"I don't. You made mistakes. They were big ones, but nothing more than mistakes. I've spent enough time with you to know that's not you now. I'm glad you told me about the 8th grade Scott, but you aren't him anymore. I admire your courage in telling me and I appreciate your trust."

"Thanks. I don't want you to think badly of me. I like you *a lot*."

We were nearly to the house by then. Jonathan stopped, turned to me, and kissed me. I thought I might float right up off the sidewalk.

"There is your answer. I do not think badly of you in the least."

Jonathan accompanied me inside. Casper gazed at us from his chair as we entered the living room. He took in our mussed hair and rumpled clothing.

"Are you okay?" he asked.

"Yeah. Blaze, Felix, and Ace showed up and gave Jonathan and me some trouble, but my ninja boyfriend took them out," I said.

"It was a minor scuffle. We left them all lying on the pavement, but they aren't seriously hurt either," Jonathan said.

"I don't like you getting in fights, Scott, but it sounds like this one was unavoidable," Casper said.

"It was. We tried to leave and they wouldn't let us. When we tried to go around them they jumped us. You should have seen Jonathan. He knows martial arts. He's going to teach me some stuff," I said.

"That might be a good idea."

We continued on to my room.

"Your dad is cool. My mom would freak out if she knew I'd been in a fight," Jonathan said.

"Brendan and Casper aren't like other adults. I think they remember what it was like to be my age. They understand me. It's spooky."

"I wish my parents understood me. Mom didn't want me to study martial arts. She seemed to think I was joining an underground fight club. I don't even compete."

"I don't think most females understand guy stuff. I'm sure there are some who do, but most don't. They don't understand that most guys are okay with getting into a fight. I never go looking for a fight and I was scared earlier, but I also kind of liked it."

Jonathan laughed. "Yep, you're a guy. I know how you feel. I love Muay Tai sparring."

"That actually sounds like a fight club."

"When we spar, we don't perform the more dangerous moves. That's for serious competitions and actual self-defense. Today, I held back. I could have put those guys in the hospital. I'm not saying that to brag, but I could have seriously hurt them if I wanted."

"I'm glad you were there. I can take Felix or Ace without too much trouble, but Blaze could kick my ass all by himself."

"He's strong and tough, but untrained."

"Thank you for saving me. You're my hero."

Jonathan puffed up his chest and placed his hands on his hips in the Superman pose. It made me laugh. He definitely wasn't stuck on himself.

"Just don't make the mistake of thinking I can take anyone. I regularly get beat when I spar. I'm no match for those better trained and there are guys who seem to have a natural talent for martial arts that I lack."

"Well darn. I was all ready to be the sidekick to your superhero."

"I'd be one lame superhero. I have no special powers and I'm not especially strong. You're stronger than I am. Hey, maybe I can be your sidekick."

"No, I don't want to be a superhero. I'm not into wearing tights."

"Pity. I'd kind of like to see you in tights."

That's all it took to make the front of my shorts tighter. I wished we were alone in the house. If we were, I might do something daring. Instead, I leaned in and kissed Jonathan deeply. That was plenty nice and it would have to do... for now.

Chapter Nineteen
Casper

Amanda pulled into the drive and moments later Dax and Drew walked past the front window, which I could easily see from the kitchen. Scott let them in and hugged them both.

"Happy Birthday, Uncle Scott!"

"Thanks!"

"I want you guys to meet my nephews, Drew and Dax. These are my buds Ethan and Noah and *this* is my boyfriend, Jonathan."

"Need any help?" Amanda asked as she walked into the kitchen.

"I think I've about got it. Scott thankfully wanted pizza for his birthday so that made things easy. I had Kroger do the cake. What do you think?" I asked, uncovering it to reveal a very large sheet cake decorated with a boy on a skateboard and a football player wearing Scott's number. "Happy 15th Birthday, Scott!" was written in teal icing.

"He will love that. Clint sends his love. He wanted to be here, but you know how it is."

"Yes, I do, but maybe he just wanted to avoid a house full of boys."

"Hmm, now that you mention it..."

Brandon and Jon arrived from next-door bearing a large wrapped gift, which they handed to Scott.

"Thanks, but no one was supposed to bring presents," Scott said.

"Rules are for mere mortals, not us," Brandon said.

"Thanks for coming," I said as they entered the kitchen moments later.

"Hey, we're just here for free food," Jon said. "We're professional moochers."

Brendan arrived with a stack of pizzas. I already had two-litre bottles of assorted soft drinks, cobalt blue tumblers filled with ice, plates, and napkins set out on the counter. The table was cleared off for the pizzas.

"Okay boys, come and get it," I said.

There was a stampede of teen boys into the kitchen. The guys began to scoop up slices of pizzas and fill their glasses. Drew and Dax paused long enough to hug Brendan and me.

The boys returned to the living room, which was only partially separated from the kitchen where the adults remained. We grabbed pizza and sat down at the table.

"So what do you do now that football season is over? Sleep in your office?" Jon asked Brendan.

"I have plenty of work to do. Successful football teams do not create themselves. I have to go out and find exceptional players. There is a senior down at South Gibson I have my eye on."

"Why oh why did you start him in on talking about football? I swear, you are the stupidest person on the face of the earth, Jon," Brandon said.

"I can't be more than runner up because you hold that title."

"Are you still coming up to help Cameron with the Christmas rush at the farm?" Amanda asked.

"Yes, we'll be there the next two weekends. Scott is thrilled," I said.

"So are Drew and Dax. They love Scott."

"Too bad there isn't a game those weekends, we could rent out their house while they're gone," Brandon said to Jon.

"Pity."

We continued talking while we ate, interrupted only by boys coming in for more pizza and drinks. The younger crowd talked and laughed in the living room. They were obviously having a great time.

After everyone had finished with pizza, we cleared off the table for gifts, to be followed by cake. The guests were instructed not to bring gifts, but Brendan and I had presents for Scott and Brandon and Jon had ignored the rule.

Scott opened his first present to discover ice skates. He had recently expressed an interest, so Brendan went out and found him a good pair. Scott next tore into a gift wrapped with purple and gold striped paper to find a pair of headphones.

"Sweet! These are the ones I wanted!"

"They're actually a gift for us so we don't have to listen to your music," Brendan said.

"You might want to open the present from Brandon and Jon next. Stand back everyone. They are not to be trusted. There could be anything from a skunk to a glitter bomb in there," I said. The boys laughed.

"I'm hurt and we have never given anyone a skunk for their birthday. A ground hog, yes, but a skunk, no."

Scott hesitantly opened his present to find it filled with junk food.

"All right! Doritos! Snickers! Peanut M&Ms! There's all kinds of stuff in here."

"Yes, and you have to eat it all right before bed tonight," Brandon said.

"Uh no," Brendan said.

"Here is your last present," I said, handing Scott a large box wrapped in blue paper covered with images of skate boarders.

Scott opened the box. His eyes lit up and he pulled out the latest game console.

"That's the one we want for Christmas!" Dax said.

"There's also a gift card for games. We thought you'd want to pick out your own," Brendan said.

The boys were all over the game system. It was all we could do to keep them in the kitchen, so I figured Brendan and I had done well with picking out gifts. I looked at Brendan and he nodded to me.

"Before we cut the cake, there is one more thing Brendan and I want to give Scott. It's not a present, but we think you'll like it."

Brendan handed Scott a folder of documents. Scott opened it and read what was on the first page. He immediately set it down and hugged first Brendan and then me.

"What is it?" Jonathan asked.

Scott looked choked up, so I answered for him. "Those are the adoption papers for Scott. As of today, Scott is officially our son," I said.

"Now you are officially our uncle," Drew and Dax said and hugged Scott.

Everyone congratulated Scott. Brandon caught my eye and grinned. He knew this moment meant a lot to all of us.

"Okay, who wants cake?" Brendan asked.

"What a stupid question. Everyone wants cake!" Jon said.

I placed the cake on the table and unveiled it. Scott grinned. I quickly lit fifteen candles.

"I don't have to make a wish, because it already came true," Scott said and blew them out.

Made in the USA
San Bernardino, CA
10 November 2019

59715049R00149